A Dance Between Light and Darkness

M. C. Ryder

M.E.C. Publishing— Lebanon County, PA
ISBN: 979-8-9870746-2-6
eBook: 979-8-9870746-3-3
Library of Congress Control Number: 2023903830
Title: *A Dance Between Light and Darkness*
Author: M. C. Ryder
Digital distribution | 2023
Paperback | 2023

This is a work of fiction. The characters, names, incidents, places, and dialogue are products of the author's imagination, and are not to be construed as real.

Dedication

To the ones who think they don't have a voice, do not let the whispers of fear limit you from progression. Search deep within and find that inner fire to rise above…

The Dark series

The Darkest Side of the Moon
A Darker Demise (A Compilation of Dark Shorts)

Acknowledgements

I'd like to take a moment to express my wholehearted appreciation to the collaborating team at New Book Authors Publishing for helping me, a novice, achieve my longtime dream. I had the vision and the team helped me accomplish by making it into a product that can be read and enjoyed by everyone. Shout out to E. Hughes, who has been an immense help as I navigate the publishing world. I've always been a writer, now I can call myself an author! I value the honesty, hard work, and swift correspondence every step of the way. Affordable and worth every penny invested. Exactly the team I've been waiting for to start my journey as a published non-traditional author. And we're just getting started!

I'd also like to express my gratitude to my family and friends who have supported me through this new chapter in my life. Thank you for taking the time to read my compelling stories, even if they do go a little dark. I hope I inspired some enlightenment in your everyday lives. Shout out to my mom, who has always been my champion and for helping me catch many of those minor editorial details. We've shared many good laughs. If only my fingers typed as fast as my brain processes.

And lastly, I'd like to thank YOU, the readers. For taking a chance on me and continuing to turn each page. I dug deep and poured out my heart and soul to give each character their own voice and riveting narrative. My wholehearted passion has always been to write captivating stories that leaves a lasting impression. I hope you enjoy each unique journey. I know I did.

Content Warning

Some scenes may be difficult to read that deal with assault.

Prologue

There's hunger in his eyes. The way he inspected her up and down made her skin crawl. She watched all day and into the night as the men rounded up the cattle and began the process to collect the meat from their bones. As a group, they left. The opportunity she had been waiting for, so she could sneak in and collect the spilled blood. She thought they had all left.

She studies him as he studies her. She never saw him before. He must be a new hand. Something she had come to learn about the farm was new hands came and went like clockwork. To most, it was a job. A means to make a living. The life they took was expendable. It was a high demanding industry.

This one was different. He hung back to take pride in his handy work. To enjoy what it was like to take a life. To fulfil a primal evil that's inside himself. An animal that curbed his appetite, but it would never be satisfactory for the killing need inside.

She dodged behind a carcass before pushing with enough strength to knock it into the next one that knocked into the next one, like a domino effect, until the one next to the man hit its mark.

She took off in the opposite direction, her hair swished behind her, before slipping on the blood and crashing onto the hard cement ground. He hovered over top of her as he flipped her onto her back. She kneed him in the groin. His body tensed. Enough time for her to slip out from under him and start crawling away.

His hand grasped her right ankle. She kicked out with her left and missed. He pulled her back towards him. With anger, she bared her true facial features. He froze. Froze only a moment before he placed a hand upon her neck with an iron grip and pulled out a pocketknife from his back pocket.

She was powerless. Despite being a sinister monster herself, the decision she made weakened her. If she were at full strength, she would be able to overpower this wicked man. Only she was no stronger than who she was when she was a human.

He carved a line into the side of her face. She clenched her teeth, but refused to scream. If this was the way she was supposed to go out, so be it. Knowing he faced a true monster; he'd never be satisfied again with just an animal carcass or human being.

His weight shifted off of her with force before slamming into the carcass. She lifted her head in time to see him crumple onto the floor, unconscious.

She looked behind herself. A tall, large, hooded being stood dressed in all black. She could not see a face.

"My dear, why do you allow yourself to become so weak when you are meant to be powerful?" The voice was and masculine.

"Who are you?"

"I am your new master," he removed some sort of rock medallion.

Her eyes followed as it went back and forth and back and forth and back and forth.

"My dear, it is time to embrace what you are."

Part 1
The Light

Chapter 1
Vince

He stood at the perimeter fence, at the back of the correction facility, aligned with the courtyard facing the war armor she had worn to represent why they were all here. Every day the black one-piece suit, urumi, and sword were a constant reminder of their unity and driving force in reconditioning the ones with corrupt minds. Most were hopeless cases. Centuries of devilry was not an easy disposition. It was the only thing that kept him going another day without her. The girl he had fallen in love with. The girl who was destined to take down his father, Vladimir, the very first vampire in existence. A father he disapproved of for he was cruel and despicable. Relished the pain and misery from others breaking down their spirits. Tortured them. Enjoyed watching the light fade from their eyes until all that was left was darkness.

The only light in his life had been his mentor, Kumal. He wouldn't be who he was today if it had not been for him. He would have been swallowed whole by the darkness if he hadn't had one person who showed him kindness. Kumal was his safe haven. The one he hadn't had to pretend he was someone else around. The closest link he had to his mother, Immilla. He was young, barely five, when she left him for good, but her love for him lingered. The smell of wood reminded him of her every day. It was the essence of her. His time with her was spent mostly in her workshop crafting works of art from all kinds of wood.

He never knew the truth about her until Kumal gave him her journal. He read her story. A powerful witch of dark magic tricked into falling in love with a mortal, Vladimir, by her father to close herself off from magic so her father could siphon dark magic undetected. Only she discovered his deceit after he turned Vladimir into a soulless monster, breaking the spell cast upon her mind by her father. She left Vladimir, but not without giving him something to fear. Wrote a prophecy about him in her journal before she went to battle with her father. One she had no intention of winning. A trick she devised against her father. Her death snuffed out the use of magic for everyone. The one thing her father loved more than his own daughter.

Along with her journal, Kumal also had her wand. One she had crafted herself out of dragon tree wood. Faded resin visible at the tip. He wanted so badly to feel a connection when it came into his possession and touched it, but it had only been a stick in his hand.

Cold.

Powerless.

He had no idea what possessed Kumal to give both the journal and wand to him out of the blue. He had safeguarded them for such a long time. If only Kumal had been more careful. If only he had been more discrete going to his room. Someone had reported them to Vladimir. After bursting through the door, with rage, Vladimir took both the journal and the wand, tossing them into the fire. He finally had something of his mother's in his hands and it was gone just like that.

To make matters worse, Vladimir punished Kumal. He had to watch, while held back, as another vampire, Marc, cut out Kumal's eyes for all the vampires to witness in the center of the pit. A reprimand for lying and seeing something he shouldn't have.

At the time, he thought Kumal's crime was for having possession of the journal and the wand. Only he discovered later it was something more.

His own punishment was to be sent to a high school full of teenage drama in order to be out of Vladimir's sight. His mission, to locate anything associated with the Dragon's Eye from the prophecy. That was when he met her. Nadine Drexel. Bumped into her more like it. He had a sour attitude. Mouthed her off because he could. She was nothing to him. Only, he wasn't prepared for her to sass back. She had a fierceness in her beautiful hazel eyes. The green striking against the hue of brown. He had been memorized.

Annoying her turned into his side hobby. Her friend, Camille Epler, was all over him like the rest of the girls at the school. Nadine was the only one not interested in him. The guys at the school despised him. He threatened their hierarchy.

Unlike the rest of the student body, Nadine tended to notice things. He gradually backed off. Yet, he still wanted to know her. She was a loner. Lived with only her mother and an orange tabby cat, Leo. Worked at a bank after school and on the weekends. Camille was her only true friend. She didn't mingle with anyone else at school. She knew who she was and was content with it. She didn't need to go out every Friday night or the weekends to socialize. She was content being on her own.

He remembered the day he took up Camille's offer and sat with them at lunch, for the first time. He loved seeing the fire in Nadine's eyes. Only, he went too far. Deliberately called her by the wrong name, Nadia. Instead of fire, there was a fleeting moment of hurt. An expression Kumal had told him about, a short time a person allows a glimpse into their past without meaning to. He knew what pain looked like in a person's eyes. Had seen it over and over again. The look in her eyes was a different kind of pain. An agitation. Something he had caused to stir up. He didn't like how he felt about it and wanted to take it back.

After apologizing, he tried staying away, but she didn't make it easy. He felt protective of her. Seemed like everywhere she went trouble followed.

One snowy winter night, he had to reveal himself to her when she got caught up in a situation that she couldn't get herself out of. A defining moment that changed everything.

Erasing her mind was the last thing he wanted to do, but she gave him no choice. It was for her own safety, especially since she was on Jomar's radar, one of Vladimir's prodigies.

Compelling her turned out to be fruitless. Was unable to since she had asparagus in her system. A natural defense against compulsion. It wasn't long after when he found out the truth. She was the one foretold from the prophecy. A prophecy she had no interest in fulfilling.

He had been selfish. They had agreed to go their separate ways, yet he had wanted one more occasion with her. A dance at prom. To breathe in that vanilla fragrance of hers to commit to memory. The moment it all went south when Jomar crashed the party.

The last thing he wanted for her was to make her go on the run. Not only had that happened, but her friend Camille had got mixed up in it too. A friend that was supposed to have Nadine's back, but was also the friend who betrayed her and ended up snapping Nadine's neck.

He wanted to avenge her. Found a reason to stand up to his father when he never stood up to him before. It was the only thing that kept him living. If he died trying, it would be worth the effort. Someone had to stop him.

And then he found her, again. She died, but was reborn a vampire. Something she never wanted to become. Only, it suited her. She was lethal. She even scared him.

He had been naïve to think he had a second chance. Along her journey, she had fallen for the one vampire he could never forgive for taking Kumar's life, Marc. Somehow, she saw beyond his monstrous nature. Her love for Marc was a love she could never give him. She preferred death over a life with him when she defeated Vladimir, as the prophecy foretold.

Now all that remained of her was the clothing off her back after she turned to ash and dust. He wanted to go where she went, but he was afraid. He was a sinful creature by nature, which meant there was only one place for him in the afterlife. A place he wasn't valiant enough to succumb to.

The only thing that kept him going each and every day was trying his best to recondition Vladimir's vampires. Vampires that only knew how to take what they wanted by force. Vampires that lusted for blood. They didn't have to be monsters. They could be moral, but retraining their brains was a difficult task. Even if they wanted to live ethically, trusting them to do the right thing when they were not behind bars was another matter.

"Vince, are you there? Do you copy?" a voice screeched out from waist level.

"Copy. What is it, Parker?" he raised the radio.

"I got a hit. You might want to come look."

"On my way."

He followed the fence line to the gate in long strides where he was promptly left in by his guards and headed towards the back of the facility. He continued his way into the control room where Parker was located. The only vampire created by his father he trusted enough not to have locked behind bars. His addiction to technology outweighed his appetite for blood, plus he was bound to a wheelchair. He wouldn't get far.

"Where is she?" he demanded, eyeing the monitors.

"At a convenience store in a town called West Milford, here in West Virginia, about thirty minutes ago."

"How far is that?"

"Less than a hundred miles from here."

"What is she doing there?" Lamont's deep voice asked from the doorway.

"I don't know and I don't care," he spun away and grabbed a pair of keys from a hook on the far wall. "Send the coordinates to vehicle three."

"Done," Parker replied after a keystroke.

"You should let me drive," Lamont stood firmly just inside the doorway.

"Get out of my way."

"First, give me the keys," Lamont held out his hand.

"You're wasting time."

"If you get pulled over, you'll waste even more."

He grumbled before slapping the keys into Lamont's hand.

Chapter 2
Vince

T he wind was steady, rocking the black SUV as Lamont drove at a stable speed. He kept checking the odometer while shaking his leg, wanting to go faster. It was late, he should have taken off on foot. He would have gotten there faster.

"You think she's going to strike again, tonight?" Lamont asked in a casual manner.

"She's up to something."

"Do you think there is a reason why she is leaving the Dragon's Eye mark on the forehead of bodies left for officials to find?"

"I don't care what reason she has. All I care about is catching her."

"It's been over six months since," Lamont paused. "She's been under the radar until these last two. Why would she risk exposure by leaving evidence behind on those four bodies?"

"I don't know, Lamont," he griped between clenched teeth.

He was getting more agitated by the minute. Until a month ago, he had no idea Camille Epler had survived and was out in the world living on her own. He had Parker keep surveillance for any unusual activity. Some of Lamont's wolves had dispersed to start a life of their own, now that the threat, Vladimir, had been eliminated. Most stayed and helped patrol. The vampires he had created, an army of his own against his father, were all loyal to him. The wolves and vampires were each assigned a rival to recondition that kept them mainly busy.

He knew there was a potential that the vampires that Vladimir had kept imprisoned and tortured may have slipped away from the underground tunnel. He thought they found them all after they fed on the imprisoned humans, who had been released at the same time as a diversion. For months, nothing odd was reported until October. The first body to show up with the Dragon's Eye symbol. The same symbol that Nadine bore from the prophecy. He knew there was no way it was a coincidence.

The headlights flashed over a sign welcoming them to West Milford after Lamont bared left. He sailed the slight curve with ease. Traffic was light as midnight neared. They were nearly on top of the convenience store when the landscape became sparse. They drove by a cemetery when something caught his eye.

"Hold on," he leaned forward.

Lamont came to a halt in the middle of the road.

He narrowed his eyes and could make out some figures in the distance in the middle of the cemetery.

"That's Caden," Lamont jerked the SUV into the parking lot, parked it, and hopped out before shifting into his white wolf form.

A dark brown wolf, Caden, stood next to a hooded being completely covered from head to toe in black while the back of a long blonde-haired girl held onto Camille, her face buried into Camille's neck.

Caden broke from the hooded figure's side and headed straight towards Lamont before they clashed. They growled with spurring jaws on their hind legs.

He reacted without thinking. Closed the distance to the two girls and forcefully ripped the blonde girl from Camille. She had a chunk missing with a stream of crimson blood running down. Her brown eyes locked onto his and froze. He felt nothing except absolute fury just by the sight of her.

Out of the corner of his eye, he saw Lamont sprint and throw his weight up against the hooded figure. With strength, the hooded figure heaved Lamont to the side. Lamont was quick to get back up on his paws when Caden cut him off.

"Don't let him take her," Camille shouted with a hand pressed against her neck.

He looked down and frowned. What sort of game was she playing? Who was under the hood? Who was the blonde girl? Why would he want her?

He didn't stop to ask. He already knew something wasn't right with the whole situation. He raced over and grabbed onto the girl's left arm as the hooded figure pulled her along on her right.

The hooded figure released his hold abruptly while he tripped over his own feet, falling backwards. He watched as the hooded figure turned and hustled away. As he got back up onto his feet, he heard a scream.

9

He looked over and saw the blonde girl on top of Camille, again, sucking the blood from the side of her neck. He took half a second to debate what he wanted to do. He knew full well he needed questions answered and he was going to make Camille answer them, but she needed to be alive.

With a grumble he rushed over and snapped the blonde girl's neck and let her limp body fall to the ground. When he looked back over, he found the hooded figure was gone.

"What did you do?" he barked.

"You have to get her out of here," Camille whispered.

"I'd like nothing more than to let you die," he yanked her up onto her feet, "but that's not going to happen right now."

He marched through the grass, around some headstones, back towards the parking lot dragging her with him. She stumbled with every step, weak from the blood loss.

"Something's off with him," Lamont expressed with concern as he carried a growling, but wounded Caden still in wolf form.

"That's because he's hypnotized," Camille declared as Lamont set Caden down in the back of the SUV he opened for him.

"Why aren't you?" Vince demanded, gripping her arm tighter.

"I managed to break free."

"You expect me to believe a word you say?"

"I know you won't, but maybe he will," her eyes passed over to Lamont.

"Let's worry about what to believe later. Right now, we should get out of here," Lamont stated as he closed the hatchback.

"Watch her," he shoved Camille forward. "Don't let her out of your sight for even one second. And don't turn your back on her."

He strolled back through the cemetery to the blonde girl still lying on the ground unconscious. He kneeled beside her and gently pushed her onto her back. She wore a name tag on her black sweater, Amelia.

Her fine natural blonde hair was long down the length of her back. No skin was visible other than her hands and face. Her sweater covered the top portion while her long black skirt covered her lower portion. She wore black flats on her feet.

She had a pale complexion. She looked small. So fragile and yet, now she was vampire. Only not just any vampire. She wasn't one that fed on human blood. She was one that fed on vampire blood, just like Nadine did. Only this girl wasn't Nadine. He knew nothing about her.

He had no idea if he should let her live or end her life right here, right now.

Only he couldn't make that call. Not yet, at least. He needed more information. He hated the fact that only Camille could provide it. That was, if he decided to believe what she might have to say.

He scooped her off the ground and tensed at the discomfort she fit naturally in his arms. She was so light. So airy. What was her life like before she was robbed of it? Was she happy?

He paused halfway back to the vehicle when she stirred before opening her eyes. Slowly, she rotated her head until her eyes landed on his. In the soft moonlight, he could make out hues of green mixed in her brown eyes. The green was not as prominent as Nadine's eyes were yet, this girl's eyes still reflected them.

"Why are you sad?" she asked in a soft honey-sweet voice.

Chapter 3
Amelia

The moonlight glow appeared brighter. Enough light to illuminate the radiant, calm blue-sky eyes looking down at her. She recognized the same sentiment behind them. The one she often wore herself. Why this boy had looked at her with such sadness was beyond her. It haunted her mind.

She didn't know how she had ended up in his arms. A sense of safety washed over her. She couldn't help but to stare at his features. He had a bald head. It didn't seem to suit him. She wondered what he had looked like with hair. What his natural hair color was. Blonde or brown or black?

He gave her a vial of something red to drink claiming it would make her lethargic. She drank it willingly, sensing she could trust him. That he didn't mean her no harm. Only it didn't make her weak. She never felt so strong. A strength she had never known before. She had so many questions. Questions he promised to answer. Until he could, he asked her to practice breathing exercises through her mouth while he drove them away from the only home she had ever known.

Every time her mind had wandered, senses or emotions started to overwhelm her. He had been quick to remind her to just keep breathing. In and out. Inhale, exhale. Why her body wasn't naturally breathing on its own was beyond her comprehension.

She continued to practice them even now as she sat on the bench along the far wall in a holding cell. Why he had brought her to a prison was a bit unnerving. Bits of images flashed through her mind as her breathing slowed.

She had been walking through the cemetery after her shift at the food mart, like she usually did. Only something happened to her. The only ones normally at the cemetery, after eleven, were six feet under. The one place she didn't have to feel guarded.

The girl with brown hair pulled back in a high ponytail, who wore a dark jacket and skinny jeans that hugged her features, crossed her mind. She made her uneasy. Had never seen her in town before. She shouldn't be at the cemetery late at night.

She inhaled deeply before slowly releasing to bring her mind back to the present. Her eyes skimmed over the gray concrete walls and steel bars. She was the only one behind them. She should feel cold. Only she felt neutral. Not cold or cool. Not hot or warm. She touched her hand. Felt the bone under her skin, but no temperature from her body.

She hadn't had to tell her legs to run. They just did, instinctually. Took off from the single driving lane into the headstones, following an open path of grass between them. No one had to tell her she was in trouble. She just knew. When it came to fight or flight, her natural reflex was subsidiary.

She hadn't gotten far. Had to come to a dead stop when she saw a dark hooded figure standing in the middle of the cemetery with a dog. Or was it a wolf?

"My dear, do not be afraid," a deep masculine voice uttered from under the hood.

She shuttered and not because the wind was blowing against her even though it had a chill in it. His voice was fluent with command.

Remembering the girl, she tossed her head over her shoulder and saw she stood directly behind her. Her face hideous. Pupils blown. Lips slightly parted with her two upper teeth longer than normal. Something unreal that could only be out of a movie.

The memory dissolved as her mind snapped to attention at the sound of the latch on the door reverberated in her ear, as if it wasn't across the room from her. As if she was standing right on top of it.

She watched as the bald head and blue-eye guy entered the room with a chair in one hand and a cup in the other. He walked directly towards her cell and placed the chair on the ground before sitting.

A coppery aroma filled her nose, traveling down the length of her dry throat to her stomach. Everything around her dimmed out as her mind demanded to get a hold of the cup.

She sprung up from the bench and crashed into the bars, reaching out towards the cup just out of her reach. In a rage, she pulled at the bars that stood in her way.

"Breathe with me," he calmly spoke before inhaling deeply.

13

Her eyes darted from him to the cup back to him. She mimicked him once before her attention diverted back to the cup in his hand.

"Breathe."

Her eyes darted to his again before following his lead, in and out, in and out. The jitteriness her body rippled with slowly subsided. Her mind became aware of the situation.

"I'm so sorry, I don't know what came over me," she apologized before releasing the bars and taking a step back.

"It's a normal reaction, at first."

"What do you mean, normal reaction?"

"You're, oh, different now."

"Different?"

"What do you remember?"

Her eyes followed the cup as he exchanged it to his other hand. Part of her was slipping back into wanting what he had.

"At the cemetery?" he persisted.

She jerked as her eyes refocused onto his blue ones.

"I don't know. Everything happened so fast," she shook her head, trying to recall the memory.

An abrupt image flickered through her mind. One minute she was afraid of the girl behind her and the next she was drinking from her neck, greedily, as if her life depended on it.

"What did I do?" she backed away into the wall.

"Deep breath."

Her breaths were coming in fast and heavy. Her eyes locked onto his and gradually she got her breathing back under control. "I killed her," she covered her face with both hands and began to sob.

"No, you didn't."

"I didn't?" she lifted her head from her hands, pausing momentarily at the sight of a crimson staining her hands.

"I stopped you before you could."

She flicked her eyes to his as the image materialized. She had been ripped with force from the girl. Had been angry. Wasn't done with her. Tried rushing back and then nothing until she woke up in his arms.

"Why did I attack her?" her eyes narrowed.

"You were after her blood."

"Blood?"

"You're not, oh, human, anymore."

"I'm not?"

14

He extended his arm towards her with the cup in hand through the bars and nodded his head.

Part of her was reluctant to go, but the other part insisted. Despite the tug of war in her mind, she slowly stepped forward. A deep breath and willpower kept her from running towards it and snatching the cup from his hand.

Two of her fingers grazed his. There was a warmth that spread within. She looked away from him, with her head slightly angled, hoping her checks weren't flushed red.

Her eyes grasped the contents of the cup. Sticky red. Her mind took over as she tipped it back and swallowed the coppery liquid in two big gulps.

It made her feel even more alive. Her body vibrated with energy. Like she was high off of sugar. She wanted to run. Wanted to embrace this enlightenment.

"You're a vampire."

She narrowed her focus on him, but everything looked slightly different. Her mind spiraled with overloaded sights and sounds. She could see grains of dust clearly, as if she had her nose to the floor. The strains of green fabric from his shirt. Could hear footsteps, voices, and the clanging of metal. It all invaded her mind at once. It was starting to become overwhelming.

"Breathe."

She took a breath; the clanging stopped. She took another breath; the voices became mute. Another breath, before she stopped hearing footsteps. One breath more, her vision cleared enough for her to refocus back onto him.

"All of this intensity is because I'm a vampire?" she blinked.

"Yes."

"Will it always be like this?"

"That depends on you."

"Depends on what?"

"Training your mind with discipline to stay in control versus it controlling you."

For the first time, she took note of the bars. The force of her body dented them while her hands pulled two them apart, leaving a gap. She had done that.

"For now, just keep practicing breathing exercises," he stood before grabbing the chair and setting it up against the wall by the door, "I'll check in with you later."

Before she had a chance to say anything, he was already out the door as it closed firmly behind him.

Chapter 4
Vince

He was actually surprised how well she took the news. Her reflexes to the blood had been what he expected, but she had recovered fairly quick afterwards. There was still so much he hadn't told her, but it needed to be slipped in, in stages. So far, learning she was a vampire didn't cripple her. He'd give her some time to process.

The thought of her upset over Camille repulsed him. If she only knew what he knew about Camille, she wouldn't have cried blood tears over her.

"How did it go?" Darius, his second in command, asked across from him, sandwiched between two attentive wolves with different pelts coloring of tan, black, and white mixed together.

"Better than I had envisioned. You okay to keep watch?"

He nodded.

"Even though?"

"You have my complete trust. If you say she does not pose an immediate threat, there's nothing for me to question."

"Thank you. If anything changes, don't hesitate to radio me."

"You are good at what you do. She'll be just like us, a pro in no time."

He nodded before shifting his attention to the wolves. "I can count on you both to have his back?"

In union, both wolves nodded in agreement.

He turned away and walked down the hall. Most of his guys were on edge after learning about the girl's presence. The wolves had nothing to fear from the girl, but the vampires did. She could lose control and attack any one of them. They were highly uneasy being anywhere near the holding cell and no one wanted to be the first to guard it.

The ones not on duty had argued with him when he requested that they fill a cup full with their blood. He was the first to demonstrate cutting a deep wound in his hand and letting the blood gush out before the wound sealed shut. He proceeded to cut wounds into his hands three more times before the cup was filled.

A few tentatively agreed, after bribing him not to be selected to guard her. He complied only so he could get a stash of vampire blood started for her. As long as she did not become extremely hungry, they should all be safe. She already had a good portion of blood in her from Camille. As long as her belly continued to be satisfied, they could coexist peacefully.

"You make any progress with Caden?" he stepped into line beside Lamont and looked into the padded isolation room with crossed arms.

"Nothing's worked yet."

They watched Caden, in wolf form, limp around on three good legs with his broken leg raised before he threw his body against the padded wall looking for a way out.

"We're going to make her tell us," he stomped away.

"You think she hasn't been telling the truth?" Lamont fell into line behind him.

"There's only one way to find out."

"Vince," Lamont reached out and brushed his arm.

"Save your breath. You handle the wolves your way and I handle the vampires my way," he shrugged Lamont off.

He heard Lamont sigh. He didn't care and continued to make his way to the integration room, pausing at the one-way see-through glass. Camille sat perfectly still, staring at the table, with her hands folded in her lap.

"Has she tried anything, Niles?" he asked his recruit.

"Hasn't moved from that spot since you left," he shook his sandy brown hair out from his eye.

His eye twitched. "Everyone stays out here."

"Vince," Lamont protested.

"Oh, this is going to be good," Niles commented, rubbing his hands together with anticipation for a show.

He approached the door and glared at the two wolves that stood guard next to it. They bowed their heads and flattened both ears as they backed away from the door. Unless Lamont told them otherwise, they were not going to challenge him.

He pushed down on the handle, stepped into the room, and slammed the door behind him. He saw a slight jolt from her, but she didn't look up. "I want you to look at me."

She made no motion to comply.

"Look at me," he flipped the long table to the right as it crashed loudly against the wall.

Her eyelids lifted as her brown eyes met his.

"You are going to tell me the truth, right now! How did you break the hypnosis?"

"I don't know."

"That's not good enough," he seized her neck, lifted her from the chair, and squeezed.

"It's all I know," she gurgled, but did not fight back.

He pressed harder as the image of her breaking Nadine's neck flashed through his mind. She was supposed to be Nadine's friend. Supposed to be there for Nadine. Should have been protecting Nadine, not betraying her.

"Vince, enough," Lamont barged through the door.

He dropped her, watching her fall back over the chair as she coughed excessively.

"I told you to stay out," he turned with angry eyes.

"You were going too far."

"She deserves it."

"Do you think this would be what Nadine wanted?"

"Don't you bring her into this," he roared.

"You already have. You should take five and clear your mind. Nothing good comes from anger."

His eyes darted to Camille. She was still lying on the floor. Just the sight of her made his blood boil. Her presence was toxic. A negative energy enveloping him just being in the same room as her. He never felt like this before. Not even around his own father, Vladimir. Her betrayal burned him and left an eternal scar. One so deep it ran to the core.

He bumped his shoulder into Lamont as he left the room. No one dared to get in his way. No one spoke. He marched to the closest door before slipping outside.

He walked with purpose in long strides. The ones guarding knew that walk. Knew it meant he was not to be disturbed as he moved past them all.

He stopped in front of the fence. The only thing he had left of her. Only it wasn't even truly her. It was a fragment of someone she had to become in order to prevail. The memory of who Nadine was before transforming into Nadia was not as clear. Every day, the image of her faded more and more from his mind. He desperately tried to hold onto it. Being able to see her attire as Nadia helped him to tune his focus to Nadine. Her long wavy brown hair. Her beautiful hazel eyes. The coloration of green on the outer ring blending into brown was stunning and even more attractive when there was a fire in them. She usually wore a vest, a silver one most of the time he spent with her, when he attended high school and then a green one later. Her signature appearance.

A tension pulled on his pants, around his thigh, before a weight pressed down onto his shoulder.

"Hello, Leo," he rubbed his finger against the orange tabby's check. He began to purr immediately as he butted his head into the side of his face.

He had forgotten that he did possess one thing from Nadine. Her cat. Although, Leo wasn't just any cat. He was a vampire cat. They had found him still in her house. Her mother was gone, but he had managed to survive the attack when it was discovered Nadine was the one marked.

Unlike him, Leo was able to move on without her. He prowled the surrounding woods of the facility, night and day. His diet consisted of animal blood. He preferred small prey. He didn't cause any trouble. Stayed away from human activity. He also wasn't fond of all the wolves, so he kept his distance from the facility. Leo usually came around when he was standing at the perimeter fence.

"She struggled with her anger too," Lamont paused beside him, "I know whenever she killed a vampire, the only face she saw was Jomar."

"But she got her revenge against him for Marc."

"Revenge wasn't why she declared war. When anger did not consume her anymore, she found her true reason."

"What made her overcome her anger?" his right eyebrow raised half an inch.

"You. You were the start of it."

He turned to him. "Doesn't change what Camille did to her."

"No, it doesn't, but Camille has to live with those consequences. Don't you think that's punishment enough?"

He looked away. He didn't want to think for one second his words could ring true.

"You told me what you feared. That you never wanted to become like Vladimir. You're starting to cross that line."

"She doesn't count," he protested, whipping around.

Leo meowed with annoyance, gripping into his shoulder to hang on before jumping off.

"She counts," Lamont challenged.

"Then let's put her to the test," he scooped Leo into his arms before strutting off.

Chapter 5
Amelia

A vampire? She was a vampire? This couldn't be real. They were supposed to be fantasy. If they weren't fantasy, why did no one know they existed? This had to be a dream. All a dream. She must have fallen asleep at the cemetery. It wouldn't be the first time. Her mother would be mad. She slept better when she was outside compared to her bed, especially after a late shift.

She pinched the back of her hand with her fingernails. The impression from the lines of her nails faded away as soon as she released her skin. As if they were never there in the first place. She pinched herself again and watched in amazement.

She turned over her right hand before lifting up her sweater and looked at her side. She was disappointed to see her scars were still present, especially the circular and oval ones. If wounds on a vampire were supposed to heal, shouldn't her scars have healed?

So, she was dreaming. Of course, she was dreaming. Only her mind would craft such an attractive guy who was actually nice. She didn't even know his name. Guess it didn't really matter. He was a figment of her imagination.

Only if she was dreaming, wouldn't she have wakened up by now? Good dreams never lasted long. They typically appeared and faded away just as quickly.

She walked over to the steel bars and reached out. Traced the imperfected bar on the left and then did the same to the one on the right. Her hands did that. Her small, meekly bare hands pulled them apart like they were nothing. She had been savage. An animal instinct had taken over. One at the scent of that sweet coopery aroma that wafted from the cup.

Blood.

She drank blood. A sweet, pleasant metallic taste that her body seemed to crave more of. The want was there. The need was not. Not like it had been when she was sucking the life out of that other girl. The girl which did the same to her.

Her mind flashed back. She was surrounded and scared. Didn't know what they wanted from her. Were they going to hurt her? The girl was on her with lightning speed, twisting her around, and held onto her firmly with an arm around her thin waist.

"Please don't hurt me," she had begged.

The girl was quick to cover her mouth with her hand to quiet her. There had been something wet and sticky on the girl's hand. When she removed it, she tried to get the bad metallic taste from her mouth. Distracted, she hadn't been prepared for what came next. It was like a pair of scissors had stabbed into the back of her neck. She squirmed under her hold with discomfort. The hooded figure and wolf just stood there, watching the ordeal.

"Help me," she cried out.

"My dear, it will soon be over."

Her body was losing strength. She was becoming lethargic. A feeling she often experienced after donating blood. She was being drained. If she didn't stop, she'd be killed.

"No," tears were pouring down her face. She was helpless. No one knew she was there. She was going to die all alone. Was scared. So very scared. She didn't know them. They didn't know her. Why did they want to hurt her?

She focused to the sky. The stars. The moon. She had no fight in her. Maybe if she closed her eyes, the nightmare would go away.

The cemetery had always been her sanctuary. A safe place she could go. A place she could feel free. No one could judge her there. No one could hurt her there. No one could degrade her there. She didn't have to hide who she was. She could breathe easy.

She didn't know anyone personally. She saw family names associated with her high school classmates, but never asked any of them. They already thought she was weird. She didn't need to give them any more reasons to think that.

She enjoyed the quiet. Just nature and the dead. She imagined what they were like before they died. Imagined who they were as a person from the sayings etched on the headstones. Such beautiful artwork to lift the ambiance of somberness.

There had been a moment of peace. A moment of lingering nothingness. The fear she had ceased to exist. She was warm. Loved. Felt light within.

The fear and dark crashed down upon her chest. She opened her eyes and saw the girl above her. She grabbed her wrist before slashing a cut into her palm with a pocket-sized knife. It did not hurt. It did not sting. Before her mind could register why she felt no pain, the girl slapped her own palm against her lips. She licked her hand. Tasted a sweetness. Activated a hunger she had never known before.

The girl stood back from her before slicing into her own flesh with the pocketknife. The aroma filled her oversensitive olfactory receptors. Without knowing what she was doing, she was on her feet sucking the life from the girl.

The memory didn't make sense. There was so much mixing of blood. Wasn't it just a bite that turned one into a vampire? What happened to the guy in the hood? The wolf? Were they all working together? What did they want with her? She was a nobody.

She walked back over to the bench and sat down. So many questions began to invade her mind. She was feeling that sense of being overwhelmed again.

Breathe.

She focused on his voice. On his guidance. Closed off her mind and concentrated on one thing. She wondered when he would come back. She was so alone without him. He helped her so much already. Were there more like them? How many? How long had he been like this? Did it get lonely?

She stood and walked back over to the bars. Her eyes glanced up and down the walls. What time was it? She had to get back home before her mother found out she spent the whole night out, again. She tried her best to avoid making her mother upset.

"Hello?" she called out.

She watched the door and waited, but it did not open and she saw no one peer through the small window.

"Hello? Can anyone hear me?" she called out louder.

She waited patiently a few more minutes, only there was no movement.

Invading thoughts circled her mind. She had to get a hold of someone. Anyone. How could she? She had to think. Think of some way to get somebody's attention.

She looked at the bars before down at her hands. If she had been strong enough to pull them apart, maybe she could break one off.

She grasped the left bent bar with her good hand. Hesitated. This was a bad idea. She wasn't sure what she was afraid of most, failure or success?

She tugged on the bar anyway and gave it everything she had in her. It snapped off immediately. The non-resisting force threw her backwards up against the wall. She cracked the bench in half, trying to catch herself. She sat on the floor dismayed, holding the bar up in her hand in front of her face, exchanging glances from the cell door to the steel rod in her hand.

She pushed up to her feet and walked back over before clanging the metal rod all around to make a loud noise. She dropped the rod and covered her ears. The sound was deafening. It kept ringing, and ringing, and ringing in her ears. She couldn't make it stop.

There was a light weight against her shoulder. She pulled back before looking. Saw a fellow, older than the one with blue eyes, kneeling to her level from the other side. He had dark-chocolate brown skin with a thin black hairline, dark brown eyes, a large nose, and large lips. He was immense as he rose, towering over her. Was extremely well-built and made her look so small; like an oversized teddy bear in camouflaged attire.

She crawled away from him. Saw his large lips moving, but she couldn't hear anything above the ringing. She had no idea who he was. If he was supposed to be here or not.

He raised a hand. She shuttered. She watched as he moved it back and forth. Towards him and away. She couldn't understand what he was doing.

Her eyes darted to his. His neck overstretched along with his chest before releasing. The sight was baffling until she realized he was breathing in and out.

She closed her eyes and began to do the same. In slow progression, the ringing began to tune out. Her sense of hearing seemed to return to normal.

"Better?" she heard a low, soothing voice.

She opened her eyes and nodded.

"Are you okay?"

"Who are you?"

"My name is Darius. I'm a friend of Vince."

"Vince?" she frowned.

"The one that was in here with you earlier."

"Oh." She could finally put a name to the blue-eyed face.

"What were you doing?" he eyed the hole in the bars before down at the missing piece on the floor.

"I was trying to get someone's attention."

"Why?"

"Do you know what time it is?"

Chapter 6
Vince

He waltzed back into the room. She sat in the chair once more with her hands folded in her lap. The table in the corner, broken in two. He paused to study her. Watched as she breathed steady breaths, like he had once taught her. When he knew her as a human, she had been a free spirit, wild, and always looking for a good time. She knew what direction she wanted to go in life. Had big dreams and it all mapped out. Now she was a shell of herself. Like she should be.

"Stand up."

She stood obediently, keeping her head down. She should be ashamed. Ashamed of her actions. She had betrayed her friend. Led the enemy right to them. He didn't understand why and he didn't care. She was supposed to love and protect Nadine, not kill her.

"What you did to her, I'll never be able to forgive. Right now, though, the only thing that matters is what's inside you and only he can see that."

She slowly cast her eyes up with confusion before they stopped mid-level on Leo in his arm. Her eyes widened as her lips slightly parted. "Is that, Leo?" she whispered.

Leo's tail flicked up and down. On the outside, she was a monster he could sense. Until he looked into her eyes, into her soul, he would not be relaxed around her. That was if he saw good in her. The last phase of reconditioning the vampires was to have Leo peer into their soul with his yellow-green eyes to see if they truly could be good. If not, they were terminated.

"Don't move," he didn't bother to answer as he bridged the gap. He hadn't thought it through until this moment. He would have to get close to her. Too close for comfort.

Leo growled in the back of his throat at the slow approach. He kept a firm hand on Leo's back. He continued to growl before hissing a warning. He was just as tense as Leo.

"It is Leo," she uttered astonished.

He didn't know how she knew that. Leo didn't have any unusual markings that he noticed. He was just another orange and white striped tabby. He saw many strays he crossed paths with in his lifetime with the same colorings. However, all cats, all animals, could look into the eyes and see into one's soul, good or bad.

Leo relaxed in his arm before launching into Camille's arms. He was in disbelief as he watched Leo rub at her face and purred. Felt slightly betrayed. Leo was supposed to see she was evil, not good.

"Take him," she turned her head away from Leo, holding him out.

He happily complied before walking to the door, opened it, and let him down. Leo hissed at the wolves before racing off. His eyes found Lamont, who raised his eyebrows in a knowingly gest. He crinkled his nose with revulsion. Did Lamont always have to be right?

He turned back to her and shut the door. "You said to me, 'Don't let him take her.' Why does he want her?" he paced about ten feet from her.

"He wanted to recreate a vampire like Nadine. Said she had been the key."

"The key to what?"

"I don't know. He was vague."

"Convenient," he growled folding his arms.

"He made sure I never saw his face and I never saw him during the day. He kept to the shadows."

"How many others?" he continued to pace.

She hesitated, "I can't say for sure, but she was the only one that was successful. I didn't have all the information he wanted until we came across that wolf. He provided the missing piece that I didn't know."

"What compelled you to carve the mark?" he stopped.

"I didn't know what to do. I just knew I needed to send a message and hope it would reach the right individual before it was too late."

"That was foolish to risk our existence to the human world," he lectured.

28

"I think it would have been a bigger risk not to. Had you not intervened, he would have her right now and you wouldn't know anything," she bit out with some boldness.

"What's stopping him from creating another?" he moved in closer to intimidate.

"He's not a vampire. He lost the one he had. He doesn't know where we are."

"What is he?"

"I think you already know that answer. He's not human. He's something else."

He did know. Felt it when he was in his presence. Something vaguely familiar he couldn't put his mind to. It frustrated him to no end, but he knew for certain whatever the hooded figure was, he was not vampire or werewolf or human.

"Now that he has what he wants, he'll be looking for her."

"He won't find her."

"Good," she nodded.

"Which means you can't leave, ever, because I don't trust you. I never will again. You can rot here in a cell, in eternity, wishing you were dead."

"It's what I deserve."

He spun away. "Niles."

The door opened at once as Niles proceeded to enter.

"Vince," she whispered.

"What?" he grumbled, hearing the seriousness in her voice.

"Don't let her near Caden."

"Why?"

"I don't know, it's just a feeling the result wouldn't be good."

"Take her to D-Block," he zeroed onto Niles dismissing her plea and didn't look back. He never wanted to see her again. He had all he needed from her. A lot of useless information. He would have to tell Parker to keep an eye out with very minimum facts. Black hooded figure during night hours. Not very helpful at all.

He dashed into the restroom as Lamont followed without a word and turned on every single faucet.

"So, what's next?" Lamont asked.

"We don't have much to go off of. I'll have Parker monitoring, but it will be a needle in a hay stack. I don't want to cause any more alarm with my guys. Do you think the ones that stayed behind would be willing to help?"

His mind traveled back in time as roughly seventy wolves choose to stay at the only home they ever knew, the underground cave. A place where they stayed undetected from the vampires when they were enemies. Lamont allowed it knowing change could be stressful in an unfamiliar environment. Those seventy weren't ready to move on, whereas the rest were eager to leave. To have a chance to see more of the world.

"I will always be their alpha. What do you need?" Lamont answered.

"We need to track him down."

"You're needed here. I'm not. I will take care of it."

"No, I need to find this guy to know what we're up against."

"You and I both know tracking will be difficult with no scent."

"What am I supposed to do here while I wait?" he tossed his hands in the air.

"I believe you have a novice on your hands."

"Darius can oversee her until we get back."

"If we both leave, again, everyone will know something is amiss. It would be wise to know what we are facing so we can provide answers, not a panic."

"I'm not good at this. She would know what to do. She always knew what to do," he gripped the porcelain sink.

"She did not lead without conflict. She did not lead without mistakes. Every decision has a repercussion. How you convey it is how others receive it."

He looked into the mirror at Lamont's reflection. What flaws had Lamont seen in Nadine? To him, she had always been flawless. She was a natural born leader. When he had a purpose, leading became natural to him. He gave his vampires a choice. Most already felt half dead inside and cast out from society so dying and being reborn a vampire made them feel more alive. They had a purpose again. Fighting to keep the world safe is what they believed in. Now that the threat was eradicated, he struggled to find purpose. Struggled to continue on leading.

"If I discover anything new, I'll send Noir," Lamont added.

He turned with a sigh. "Fine."

Lamont retreated, leaving him alone in the bathroom with the running faucets. He didn't want to stay. He wanted to go find the threat. A threat to their livelihood. They were making a new life after the downfall of Vladimir. One where they could work together in harmony, like Nadine promised. They all wanted the same thing. To live peacefully and not go to war, again.

Chapter 7
Amelia

S he sat on the floor, rocking back and forth with unease. It was after five in the morning. She had no idea how far from home she was or if she had a chance to make it back before her mother found out.

Darius promised he would send word to Vince, but that had been awhile now. She had no idea how much time passed since he left the room. It seemed an eternity.

The door opened. Immediately, she popped up to her feet and ushered to the bars. She took a deep breath. For a second, her mind stopped worrying when she saw him. He had a way of making her feel like everything would be okay and that she was safe. She didn't want to leave here. She wanted to stay, but she knew she couldn't.

"I need to go home. I have to get there before my mother finds out I was out all night," she rambled out.

He dropped his head. He didn't speak for several seconds.

"Please," she forgot to be courteous.

"You can't go back home."

"For how long?" she was trying to remain calm as the repercussions to follow crossed her mind.

"Ever," he looked her directly in the eyes.

She stepped back from the bars and looked down. "I don't ever have to go back home?"

"That doesn't upset you?"

"I'm not sure how I feel," she lifted her head before turning her back to him and processed what it meant not to ever go back home. She was supposed to be upset, but it didn't upset her at all. Instead, she was relieved. Why did it feel like a sin?

She heard the clasp of the door shift. "Please don't leave me alone, Vince."

He paused before tossing his head over his shoulder. "How do you know my name?"

"Darius mentioned it. Was he not supposed to?"

"No, it's fine," he released the doorknob, grabbed the chair by the wall, approached, and sat down a bit from her cell.

His blue eyes studied her. She tore hers away with self-conscious. She wasn't used to being the sole attention of another. Half the time, she thought she was invisible. The other half she wished she was.

"You're not as distraught over the news as I expected."

Her eyes briefly glanced to his and away again. "I'm still processing." She shrugged her shoulders, "I half believe this is all a dream that I just haven't woken up from yet."

"It's not a dream. It's real."

Her eyes sought his. This was her reality now. It truly was real. She never had to go home again. See her mother again. Go to school. Go to work. Go to church. Be stuck in a town she always wanted to get out from under. Why had she been fortunate enough to be chosen?

"What happened to the other girl?"

"She will never hurt you again," he stated with a briskness.

It was her turn to study him. Mentioning the girl brought anger to his eyes. Along with it an iciness. It scared her. She wanted to know what he meant, but sensed it was best to leave the topic alone. She didn't want to upset him any more than she already had. "How long have you been a vampire?" she changed the subject.

"For a very long time," he drifted away.

"So, vampires are truly immortal?"

"There are still ways we can die, permanently."

"You're not happy being a vampire?"

His eyes landed back on hers before shifting in deep thought. Maybe she shouldn't have asked him that. She could tell it disturbed him deeply. The last thing she wanted to do was offend him. He had been nothing but kind to her. She had the desire to want to comfort him. Comfort him like her father used to comfort her. Everyone deserved to have someone they could lean on. To take away their pain, even if only for a moment. To not feel so alone.

"I have to go, now. I'll send Darius in to keep you some company," he rose and slipped out the door.

She had upset him. Now she was upset. Hurting him was the last thing she wanted to do. Yet, she managed to do just that without

33

knowing it. She knew nothing about him. Wanted to learn everything. What made him happy? What didn't? How she could bring him joy instead of pain.

Darius entered the room, pausing behind the chair. She didn't want company anymore. She wanted to crawl up into a ball and be alone with her thoughts.

"You okay, Chica?"

"I'm fine," she walked back towards the cement wall, sat with her back leaning against it, wrapped her arms around her knees, and rested her chin on her leg.

"You don't look fine," he insisted.

"I offended him."

"Vince?"

She nodded.

"He's not one who offends easily," he twisted the chair around and sat facing the back of it with his arms propped.

"I think you're wrong."

"You, in a way, remind him of someone. Someone he genuinely cared about. Someone he recently lost."

"Oh," she met his dark brown eyes.

She knew what it was like to lose someone you loved. She had lost her father right before her sixteenth birthday. She wished she had had more time to spend with him. She only got to see him every other weekend since she was five. They made the most with every minute they were able to share.

She had been devastated when she found out he had lung cancer and in less than a year, he was gone. Just simply gone, like he never existed.

She cried so hard for days. He didn't even get a proper burial. Her mother paid for him to be cremated, as she was the only family member he had documented. She wasn't even allowed to have his ashes. She never got to say goodbye. Her mother hadn't grieved over him, not like she did. Her mother couldn't stand her sadness. Had told her big girls don't cry like babies. That it was his own fault for smoking so much when he knew it was a death sentence. He brought it on himself.

She knew that pain very well. It didn't just go away because someone told you it should. Every day was hard to enjoy the sunshine when everything inside was dark. Only everyone expected you to smile and move on. Forget the past. Forget about the one person who was your everything. How were you supposed to keep on living when you felt so hollow inside?

Only she had no choice. She had to move on. Pretend she wasn't sad anymore. Avoided all the triggers. Blocked all the happy memories. Fooled herself into believing that living in the dark was the only place for her.

"You deserve to be happy and dream big. When you turn eighteen, if you want, you can move out and come live with me. You don't have to stay in your mother's shadow for the rest of your life."

His words echoed in her mind. They were so prominent, as if she was there on the edge of the river bank with her fishing rod next to him. The only person who truly cared for her. The only person who wanted to give her nothing but happiness.

Her one ambition was counting down the days when she could be with her father. She didn't need to see the whole world. Didn't care about making a living. He would have been more than enough for her.

She never thought she'd get out of her hometown. Thought she would be stuck there for the rest of her life doing her mother's biddings. Watched as everyone left town to go to college and make a name for themselves while she was stuck with a job at the local convenience store. The only thing she supposedly would ever be good at.

Maybe her father was the reason she was chosen. Maybe he was still watching over and taking care of her without her realizing it. This was her second chance. A life to do what she wanted. A place where she could be free to be herself and be accepted.

She didn't have anyone to lean on when she lost her father, but maybe she was sent here for a reason. She could be there for Vince. To be someone he could lean on.

Chapter 8
Vince

Her voice echoed in his mind. Struck a chord inside himself that continued to hum. Was he unhappy as a vampire? No one had ever asked him if he was unhappy. He never stopped to question it himself if he was happy as a vampire. He had been a vampire for so long it was just normal to him. If he had a choice, would he choose not to be a vampire?

He never had a choice to begin with. On his eighteenth birthday, his father turned him himself. His father wanted him to be as sinister and cruel. He had Vladimir in his one ear and his mother and Kumal in the other. Even though he had been so young, his mother instilled into him politeness. Right from wrong. The good thing to do instead of the bad.

Throughout his childhood, Kumal continued to teach him what his mother had taught. How to be compassionate. How to be well-mannered. How to be kind. It felt wrong otherwise.

He became a stronger vampire because of Kumal. He taught him how to maintain control rather than the bloodlust controlling him. To ask permission before feeding. Taking only what he needed rather than all of it.

The only reason Vladimir allowed Kumal to live was because he wanted to punish him and Immilla. Didn't want them to be together again, ever. Wanted them eternally separated.

He never became the son Vladimir desired. Kumal had tricked Vladimir into believing he was the only one who would be able to find the marked one from the prophecy. A lie. In a sense, he was the only one who was capable of blending in with a human crowd without going off the deep end, surrounded by pumping blood. Kumal had passed that onto him. The first time he met Nadine, he had no idea she was the one from the prophecy. Not until later.

He reached out and grazed his fingers against the black material. He wanted to feel a connection to her so bad. All he felt was emptiness. How could someone he cared so much about just cease to exist? He could barely keep her memory alive anymore. He was trying so hard to hold onto every fragment.

He couldn't remember what his mother looked like anymore and it scared him that the same would happen with Nadine. The smell of sawdust was the closet he could get to his mother, who loved wood-turning. He could not see her, but he could feel her. Warmth would radiate from within, as if she was with him, knowing he was loved by her. He had that same feeling with Kumal when he smelled the overpower aroma of fish. There had been a time when he lived with them both on Tenerife. Kumal would always go fishing for their favorite dish. He smelled of the salty sea and fish. It had been so long since he stood by an ocean and smelled the salty water.

He turned to the rays of the sun. A new dawn had arrived. A new day into a peaceful era because of Nadine. If only he could actually feel the warmth from the sunshine. A new dawn had been what she fought for. For them all. Every little thing he could think of did not bring him warmth inside. She didn't love him. Not like he loved her. He still couldn't understand why. Why she could love Marc, but couldn't love him. Was he unlovable?

He strode off. It was time to make his rounds. Make himself seen, like any other normal day. From the corner of his eye, he saw small groups of wolves, relieved from duty, head into the woods. They were out to stretch their legs. Knew to stay out of sight. Some liked to hunt for fresh meat, even though he had enough meat delivered for them all. Fresh was always desirable. Even his vampires struggled with drinking expired or diseased donated blood that was gathered from blood banks within a hundred-mile radius. It didn't matter what kind of blood they drank, diseased or healthy. Blood was blood. Their way of life. Just as any drop of blood from a vampire kept the wolves from aging.

He paused at the main door. "Anything to report, Michael?"

"Nothing out of the ordinary, sir."

"Are you ever going to stop addressing me like that?"

"No, sir."

He sighed. Had told Michael a thousand times he could address him by his name only, not sir, but he continued to remain formal.

"Excuse me, sir."

"Yes?"

"The others were wondering about the progress of…" he trailed off.

"Amelia?"

"Yes, sir."

"The progress is good, no, the progress is very good."

"Good to hear, sir," he opened the door.

He stepped through and was overcome with chatter. Cells lined up and down on both sides, doubled up with inmate vampires. Wolves prowled the outside while his vampires delivered three-ounce dixie cups of blood to the ones behind bars.

He walked down the center, skimming each of the vampires behind bars. He was looking for any questionable behavior. Many abhorred him. Hated starving. They were used to the good life. A life of abundance on ones that went missing without a trace. Now they had to survive on scraps. He was giving them a fair chance to change their ways. Many did not see it that way. Only good behavior was rewarded. Good behavior advanced them to the next step in the process. The most difficult ones were transferred to D-Block. Were given blood with a drop of werewolf blood to test them further. To see if they found reason to want to change for the good. If nothing changed, then Leo would peer into their souls.

"Hey, Vince," Ryker rolled up to him. "Why don't you have that new girl locked up in D-Block?"

"She's not a threat."

"We know nothing about her and she drinks vampire blood. Of course, she's a threat."

"She'll get it under control just like Nadine," he stated, crossing his arms.

"I haven't seen Lamont since you all got back with her," Ryker is causal to mention.

"He's taking care of his own business," he was quick to answer. He saw eyes from the others interested in the public conversation.

"What kind of business."

"One that does not pertain to you," he slipped past him.

"We have a right to know," Ryker called after.

He kept walking. Made eye contact with the others, smiled, and nodded his head in acknowledgment. He should have known he wouldn't be able to pretend nothing was wrong. He heard their whispers. Their concern. They had a right to be. They knew nothing about Amelia. Until she maintained full control, they had to be on guard around her. If she was like Nadine, not only did she drink vampire blood, but she would also have the capability to compel vampires. Werewolf blood did not weaken her. He wasn't sure if she even had a weakness other than piercing into her life force. Something he wouldn't want to do unless he had no other choice.

He was glad when he made it out. So many bombarded him with the same question, what the prognosis was on Amelia. She was doing well. Too well.

He dreaded telling her she could never go back home. She took the news better than he expected. He didn't know what her home life was like. Apparently, it wasn't too good for her not to be distraught over it. In fact, she seemed to be relieved. Maybe she was a good fit with them. It was too early to know for sure. Plus, she wasn't a spitfire like Nadine. She was shy and reserved. The only female in a sea full of male vampires.

"You have any updates for me?" he asked Parker as soon as he closed the door.

"Got nothing so far. You do know it's going to take me some time. I don't have much to go off of, plus the sun is up now."

"I know," he sighed.

"You think he's going to come for her?"

"He created her for a reason."

"Well, the odds are stacked against him with her here."

"Yes, yes they are," he agreed as he skimmed over the monitors, sliding to different cameras around the immediate area and around the world.

"I'll radio you a 10-19 if anything changes."

"You trying to get rid of me?"

"There's nothing for you to do here," he shrugged, "except get impatient."

"I won't become like my father," he stated with an iciness.

Parker nodded before diverting his attention to his main screen and typing a command into his keyboard.

Many times, Vladimir had lost his temper and took it out on Parker's equipment. Parker's prized possessions. The thing he cherished more than blood.

Chapter 9
Amelia

The door opened before Vince walked in with a cup. As soon as she smelled the intoxicating aroma, she took in a sharp breath and backed up against the wall, releasing slowly. She feared she would burst through the bars this time and hurt him. She didn't want to hurt him anymore than she already had.

"You have strong willpower," he uttered with fascination.

"Is that a bad thing?"

"No," he shook his head before setting the cup on the floor inside the cell and stepping back.

She didn't move. She wanted to. Her mind screamed at her to, but she delayed.

"Don't be afraid. It's a necessity. Our way of life. As long as you remain in control, it will not control you. Not unless you allow it. Think of it as water. Humans cannot survive without water. When they become dehydrated, it's already too late. You don't want to put yourself in that position. Then you will lose control."

His words made complete sense. She knew what it felt like to be dehydrated. To think of nothing but water. To crave nothing but water. To become desperate and willing to do anything for just one drop of water.

She approached slowly. Fought against her mind to snatch it off the ground and instead delicately reached for the cup. Slipped slowly while her mind demanded to gulp. Now she knew what it was like to have an angel on one shoulder and the devil on the other. Only she could control whose voice was louder. Whose voice she wanted to listen to. Which voice mattered.

"I'm sorry about earlier," she flicked her eyes to his.

"Sorry for what?" he frowned.

"Upsetting you."

"You didn't upset me," he pulled a key from his pocket and unlocked the door.

"What are you doing?" she dropped the cup and backed up into the wall.

"I'd like to take you for a walk and show you around a bit."

"I don't think I'm ready," she shook her head.

"Trust me."

Her eyes lifted to his. She did trust him. She just didn't trust herself. What if something went wrong? What if he couldn't stop her?

"The control you have far exceeds the guys I've trained, combined. You'll be fine, I promise."

"Okay," she stepped forward.

She hesitated before lifting her foot over the threshold. Nothing happened. She didn't know what she was really expecting to begin with. Awareness entered her mind that she stood beside him. The first time she wasn't contained behind metal bars since she first met him. She couldn't feel if her checks were warm. Didn't know if they flared up red. Didn't know where to look, the floor, the wall, the ceiling.

"Follow me," he took the lead.

She was grateful she was behind him. That he couldn't see her face. She had no idea what she looked like. Did she look obvious?

She trailed behind him out into a hallway. There wasn't anything spectacular to note other than Darius and two wolves waiting on the other side. They sat on either side of him and locked eyes on her. She stepped back with concern.

"Transform yourselves," Vince uttered.

Both wolves refocused their attention before exchanging looks and in front of her own eyes began rising to their back legs, growing, until their fur turned to a type of material against a human form.

"What just happened?" she whispered in disbelief.

"James. Wyatt. This is, uh, Amelia, right?"

Her eyes shifted from the two guys, who were just wolves a minute ago, to Vince before down at her name tag.

"Actually," she looked back up, removing the tag. "You can call me Melia."

Only her father had called her that. She never had to pretend she was happy when she was with him. She hoped she could feel that happiness again here.

41

"Okay, Melia," he tested it out. "I believe the human terminology would label them werewolves."

She peered across from her again. The two of them had very similar features. Sandy brown hair, milk-chocolate brown eyes, a five-o'clock shadow outlining their jawlines. The only difference was one had his straight hair slicked back while the other had his parted down the middle where it stopped halfway down the length of his face. "This is still real, right?" she looked back.

"Afraid so, but you have nothing to fear. We all work together as allies."

"It's nice to meet you," she smiled and bowed.

"Welcome," they both uttered, nodding their heads.

"How about you all take a break while I show Melia around," Vince exchanged glances between James, Wyatt, and then Darius.

"Are you sure?" Darius asked.

"Yes."

She saw hesitation in Darius before he disappeared down the hall behind James and Wyatt. Something nagged in the back of her mind, but she wasn't certain what.

She followed behind Vince down the hall when she saw a sign for a restroom up ahead. She was itching to get closer. She had the sudden need. "Do you mind if I use the restroom, quick?"

"We don't need to use the bathroom," he frowned over his shoulder.

"Oh," she became aware of the truth in the statement. "Do you mind if I take a minute, anyway?"

As soon as he nodded, she was slipping through the ladies' room door and letting it close behind her. She rushed over to the mirror and looked at herself. She looked completely the same. Maybe a little paler, but nothing about her features changed. Her checks weren't even red. She sighed with relief. She pitched her checks in intervals, but there was no change at all. She was glad to see she hadn't made a fool of herself. Glad to know blood hadn't rushed to them to make her embarrassment known.

She looked at her wrist. Placed two fingers upon it to discover she had no pulse. She felt all around, but nothing pulsated underneath her skin.

Slowly, she placed her hand on her chest. Her heart did not beat. This was real. She had really died. Yet, she was still here, standing. Could see herself in the mirror. This was becoming more and more real. She looked like the same small, fragile human on the outside, but she felt so much stronger on the inside.

"Everything alright?" Vince asked as she reappeared.

"Yeah," she beamed.

"Okay, let's go," he set about.

She had a pep in her step. Was excited. Excited to get to see his world. Get to know his world. She wasn't alone. There were others like her. Others she couldn't wait to meet. This was a new beginning for her. A beginning where she had possibilities.

He pushed open a door. She saw bright sunlight shining over the grass. Followed him through. He continued to walk outside onto the grass. Into the sunlight. Her mind instantly began to fire off warning bells. The sun wasn't safe. The sun would burn him.

With instinct, she reached out for his arm and yanked him back. He slammed up against the outside wall, partially in the shade, as she shielded his body with her own. Shut her eyes tight, waiting to feel the sting of the burn as she went up in flames.

"What are you doing?" his voice vibrated in her ear against his chest.

"Sunlight."

"The sun doesn't harm us. That's a false myth."

"Oh," she tilted her head.

She realized just how close she was to him. She was thankful her checks did not blush. Hers would have been beet red otherwise. The sun may not burn her, but the heat she felt from her body touching his had her on fire inside. She stepped away. Never felt such an intense feeling before. She didn't know what to make of it. It was petrifying.

Now that she knew the sun was not her enemy, she welcomed the sight. The light was intense. She didn't know if that was from her adrenaline rush or because she saw it differently now with her vampire eyes.

She closed her eyes and tossed back her head. The sunlight was not warm to her skin. She could see it. Could embrace it, but it did not feel the same. It was a little disappointing. The most sensation she felt since she was a vampire was when she brushed up against Vince.

Chapter 10
Melia

She strolled beside him, around the exterior of a perimeter fence. It hit her hard grasping they were at a prison facility. She didn't understand why. Why they chose this life when they could be anywhere? Do anything they wanted. The possibilities were endless. Only they lived in confinement.

She noticed vampires and werewolves guarding the fence line in and out everywhere. Some faced towards them, others faced away. The werewolves were in human form. She suspected it had to do with the sun.

On the other side of the fence was wooden terrain. They called to her. How she wanted to explore them. Find a river, or a stream, or a creek and listen to the ripples of the water. To feel connected to the earth and to her father.

They came upon a courtyard. There were vampires walking around a track. Some playing basketball on the court. Others mild around in small groups talking. The vampires wore different attire. Some wore all gray, while others wore camouflage. The wolves wore their different skin tight suit of varies colors she now knew mimicked their pelts.

One by one everyone in the courtyard stopped what they were doing as they noticed her. She was thankful she didn't have the ability to blush. She never walked into any environment when the sole focus was on her. This was not a feeling she was used to. It was terrifying and yet also exhilarating at the same time.

"Resume your activities," Vince commanded.

At once, heads dropped or looked away. She still heard the silence, though. Hardly any chatter commenced. She could tell they were still interested in her. Before, they spoke open and loudly. Now, they whispered and congregated. At least the vampires in camouflage did. She wasn't sure what to make of the scene.

Up ahead, an outfit was splayed out against the fence. It faced the courtyard. She wondered what it was doing there. Seemed out of place. There was a sword behind the black one-piece suit. Something silver looped around the waist like a belt, but was the strangest looking belt she ever saw over top a corset belt. The legs of the suit stuffed in black boots. Above the attire was a sign attached to the fence with a symbol. She wasn't sure what the symbol meant. She never saw it before. It was an upside-down triangle with a 'Y' in the center.

"What's this?" she paused.

"A reminder," he stopped.

"Who did it belong to?"

"Her name was Nadine. She was destined to take down my father, Vladimir, the very first vampire. She was successful, but it did not come without tragedy."

Her mind was swimming with more questions, but she heard the pain in his voice. Saw the sorrow in his eyes. This Nadine was the person he lost. "I'm sorry for your loss," she reached out and touched the lower part of his arm.

His eyes flicked down to her hand.

"She's always with you though, right here," she placed her other hand on her chest.

His eyes slid to her hand, over her non-beating heart, before lifting to hers. "Did you lose someone too?"

She nodded, dropping her hand. "My father."

"I'm sorry."

"The memories get better with time. They're not as raw," she reflected. Thinking about him didn't automatically bring the tears anymore. For a long time, she had to fight them back to please her mother. Had to flash to an image she feared to stop them in their tracks.

"I'm afraid I'll forget what she looked like, just like I did with my mother."

"Memories fade but how she made you feel, that never will," she watched his eyes lower back to her hand still on his arm. He moved away from her touch and resumed walking. She followed.

They continued to walk the outer perimeter fence. The place was so dull. Like how she felt inside. She never thought she would get out from under her mother. Out of the only town she ever knew. She wanted to know what was out in the world. Not be confined. All her life, all she knew was confinement. Always had to do what was expected of her. Be a good girl and go to church. Go to school and get good grades. Be involved with the community and volunteer. Stay out of trouble. Don't go to parties. Uphold a nice girl reputation.

She knew there was evil in this world. She was now that very thing. An evil hidden from humanity. The possibilities were endless. She could do bad things with this gift, but she did not have the desire. Yes, she craved blood, but when her hunger was satisfied, she still felt like her normal self.

"What's the first thing you hear?" he stopped by a section of the fence not heavily guarded. It was just the two of them. In the distance, she could still make out a few guards maintaining security on both ends.

"Birds," she heard the chirping from the nearby trees.

"Close your eyes and tell me what else you hear?"

She complied and listened. "Branches scraping. Leaves rustling. A slight buzzing from the fence."

"Good. Now focus on one and concentrate on amplifying your hearing. Mimic the act of swallowing, but you don't actually have to swallow. Your hearing will kind of pop like you are at a high elevation. The more you tune into the sound, the more distance you will be able to tune into."

She focused on the birds. Amplified once. Twice. The chirping grew louder. Closer. As if they were above her. She heard wings flapping. Talons gripping wood. She amplified a third time. The light wind rustled what crisped leaves remained on trees. The flapping intensified as two birds screamed at each other. In the background, she heard water trickling.

She refocused back onto the birds. There were so many of them. So many different happy songs. Several branches scrapped against one another, creaking. The buzzing from the fence pulsated in her ear. Before she had heard it at a low frequency, but now it was higher. Now it was all she could hear. It buzzed throughout her body. She wanted it to stop. Didn't know how to make it stop. It was overwhelming.

She covered her ears, but it did nothing. She still heard it loud and clear. The sound was intense. She couldn't hear anything above the noise.

She jumped when she felt a weight on her shoulder. Her eyes snapped open as she uncovered her ears.

"Breathe."

Vince's voice boomed in her ear. She turned her head and shielded her right ear in an automatic respond. Her mind vaguely processed his word before she started to breathe even breaths.

"Better?"

She nodded.

"It gets better with practice," he reassured. "You want to try again?"

"Yes."

Chapter 11
Vince

She had a determined mind. She didn't easily give up when she failed. She had held her head up high and tried again. Many before her had been hesitant. Did not want to go into sensory overload after the first time. It was extreme. Like your head was about to explode. Could drive you mad.

He couldn't get her light, delicate touch from his mind. Or her honey-sweet voice. She shared with him what it meant to lose someone you loved. The pain. The heartache. The rawness.

He didn't like hearing her say memories faded. He already knew that firsthand. With his mother. With Kumal. And now it was starting to happen with Nadine. The picture was distorted like pixels. It wasn't as clear as he wanted it to be. He hated that he only got a glimpse for a second and wasn't able to hold onto it. He shouldn't be able to forget, ever.

She was right about not forgetting how Nadine made him feel. Nadine had given him purpose. Had given him a reason to fight. Had opened his heart to feelings he had only remembered having around his mother. He never knew how strong they could grow. How powerful they could become. That was until she crushed him.

Now he was afraid. It was happening again. Happening too soon. He was still mourning Nadine and yet Melia's gentle touch terrified him. A light warmth swelled within. She was nothing like Nadine. She was an innocent bystander. Her life cut short for no reason. This was no place for her. Only there was nowhere for her to go. For her to survive on her own. The only way of life was right here with them all.

Melia was beneficial, though. He could let her drain the vampires that resisted without restraint. Would this way of life be enough for her? Would she be happy? He was okay with being miserable for the rest of his life, but that was not fair to her. He didn't know what the right thing would be. However, that did not matter right now. What mattered was finding the hooded individual who wanted her in the first place. Once that threat was eliminated, then he could worry about her future. Until that time came, she still had to work on her control which would keep her busy.

Movement caught his eye on the parking lot monitor. He narrowed his eyes at the screen and watched the black SUV park. At once, he left the control room and met Lamont outside. "Anything?"

"Nothing." Lamont shook his head.

"Why did you come back so soon?"

"There's not much to do during the day when my presence is necessary here."

He sighed with disappointment.

"How is she doing?"

"Better than I expected."

"She's safe here, but you know you can't keep her locked up forever."

"Yeah, I know," he sighed. "She doesn't belong here. She shouldn't have to live this life. This is no place for her."

"This is the only place she has all that she needs and not to have to endure it alone. Loneliness takes you to dark places."

"Like it did for Nadine?"

Lamont studied him. "Trying to psychoanalyze her decision does your mind no good."

"Melia is due for more blood," he shelved the discussion and turned away.

"I'd like to meet her," Lamont called after him.

He paused mid-step. "I'll meet you there."

As he mindlessly walked, he wondered what job he could task Melia with. His guys were easy. Most wanted in on the action; to rehabilitate the other vampires. Many had a background in the military, so they knew order and did not question authority.

Melia was different. He couldn't subjugate her to that. It was no life for her, especially when she was maintaining control herself. Life at the correctional facility would be dull and boring for her. She deserved better and it was up to him to decide her future here. He hated it.

There was one thing he was failing her with, leaving her alone inside that cell. He couldn't be there with her all the time. He also needed Darius back at his post.

He heard humming coming from the kitchen. As he entered, he saw Niles stocking a shipment of donated blood into one of the large silver refrigerators. He was oblivious.

Niles was one of the few he turned himself. His family made him enlist hoping he would come back changed into a man. Hoping his interests would change once he went through basic training. They didn't and his family couldn't accept he was different. He hated fighting, but hated being knocked down even more. Niles was someone Vladimir would never want to gift an eternal life. He didn't care how Niles identified himself. All Niles cared about was being accepted for who he was. He could give him at least that. He couldn't speak for the others that were turned, mostly by Darius, but most did accept Niles. The ones that didn't, well they knew to keep their opinions to themselves.

He liked that Niles was always positive. Saw the bright side of everything. He would be a ray of sunshine for Melia in such a gloomy place.

"Niles," he stepped forward clearing his throat.

The humming silence as Niles froze in place. "How long have you been in here?" his gaze darted.

"Only a moment."

"You gave me a fright, don't do that to me," Niles placed a hand on his chest.

"I want you meet Melia and hopefully assist with her progression."

"What? I'm too fabulous to die," Niles placed a hand over his forehead.

"You're not going to die. She is stable."

"How do you know she won't, well, you know," Niles clawed out with his hands and growled.

"She has not shown any hostility since she's been here, plus she doesn't know the type of blood she needs to survive on."

"You haven't told her?" Niles perked with a seriousness.

"No. It's not necessary. Not yet."

"You want me to lie?" Niles's voice rose an octave. "You know I'm not good at that. What would I say if it came up?"

"Right now, her only focus is on control of her senses. You know what it was like in the beginning. She doesn't need the stress of the type of blood she needs added on top of it. That's the last thing I will work on with her."

"Yeah, okay, makes sense," Niles nodded in agreement, "but I'm no teacher. I don't know what all Nadia was capable of."

"You know all you need to know which is all Melia needs to know."

"Oh, okay. If you say so."

"You won't be alone with her."

"Oh, good, that's a relief," Niles wiped his dry forehead.

"When you're done here, go find Oliver and meet me at the holding cells."

"Okay boss man," Niles gave a thumbs up.

He half smirked before grabbing a cup of vampire blood from the top shelf of the first refrigerator. He noted the stock was minimal. He would have to collect more afterwards.

As he turned the corner, he saw Lamont engaged in a conversation with James and Wyatt in human form. He wondered how Lamont managed to answer the bombarded questions. He never once saw any hesitancy from Lamont. Lamont was a natural born leader. He never thought one day he would fill his father's shoes and lead the vampires. All he ever wanted was to live in a peaceful world without his father. He never realized just what that would entail. When he built his own army, he mostly left Darius in charge and sought solitude when he wasn't training. Training gave him purpose.

He cleared his throat from a distance, as a courtesy, to announce his presence.

"I will get back to you on the matter. Now, if you would excuse me, I have business to attend to," Lamont recited with little effort.

He entered the room first, while Lamont followed and closed the door. He saw her sitting on the floor Indian style, in her new cell, with her eyes closed. She was still practicing. He was both astonished and worried. Had she overheard anything he wasn't ready for her to receive?

Her eyes snapped open and narrowed onto the cup of blood in his hand. She took in a deep breath through her mouth and slowly exhaled before her eyes diverted up to his and then over to Lamont.

"Hello," she greeted with her shy honey-sweet voice.

"Fascinating," Lamont commented in awe.

"What is?" her eyes diverted with confusion.

"Melia, this is Lamont," he took a step forward and gestured with his hand.

"I apologize for not properly introducing myself," Lamont dipped his head.

"You were in the car with us," she tilted her head before rising to her feet.

"You have a superb memory," Lamont smiled.

"You fought against the other wolf," she squinted. "What happened to him?"

Lamont exchanged a glance with him before answering. "He's perfectly fine."

"And he does not pose a threat to you," he added.

"He was just misguided," Lamont reassured.

"Oh."

He looked down, surprised when Lamont gripped the bottom half of the cup. Looked over with a frown as Lamont nodded his head. He was hesitant to release his hold, but he did.

"Do you remember anything about the man with the black hood?" Lamont advanced forward and handed the cup over.

"No, I never saw his face," she sipped the blood, "but he spoke to me."

"He did? What did he say?"

"He told me not to be afraid and that it would soon be over."

"What did his voice sound like?" Lamont probed.

"It was very rich and mesmerizing," she took another sip.

"Did he sound at all familiar to you?"

"No," she shook her head. "Am I supposed to know who he was?"

"No," Lamont assured.

"Do you?" she glanced between them.

"We don't know, not yet at least," Lamont admitted.

"What does he want from me?"

"There's nothing for you to worry about. You're safe here," he intercepted. He was annoyed with Lamont. Why would he bring the hooded guy up? He wanted her to forget about it, not dwell. He was making good progress, until now.

Chapter 12
Melia

She saw annoyance flash through Vince's eyes. He wasn't happy with Lamont. She wasn't sure why. Wondered which one of them was in charge. She thought Vince was up until now. Lamont had that superior disposition. Or maybe they were both in charge. Vince did mention something about being allies. Did they used to be rivals at one time? If so, what had brought them together?

When they both left the room, she closed her eyes, angled her head, and concentrated. Heard their voices on the other side of the door. She focused in on the words. A pang of guilt entered her mind. She knew it was wrong to ease drop. Should stop listening, right now, but she couldn't bring herself to do the right thing. She was curious.

"Why did you bring him up to her?" Vince whispered with a brashness.

"I was not aware that was a restricted topic." Lamont retorted.

"Well, it is. She has enough on her plate to worry about."

"Careful. Don't treat her as if she's naïve. The biggest mistake you can make is to keep her in the dark."

"I'm protecting her. She's not ready," Vince protested.

"Just make certain you are the one to tell her and that she doesn't find out on her own."

She heard footsteps retreating. Had no idea what they were talking about. Vince was protecting her? From what? Why did he feel the need to protect her at all? Hearing him say those words made her swell inside. Made her feel safe. No one ever felt the need to protect her other than her father.

"Good, you're here," she heard Vince's voice once more. "I want to give you some instructions first. Follow me."

She heard multiple footsteps this time. Wondered where they were going. She was always good at being quiet and just listening. Now she had enhanced capabilities. Knew first hand that it could be a dangerous thing. That you could hear something not meant for your ears that could scar you, but being the last one to know was even more damaging.

She had overheard a conversation earlier between, she now learned, Lamont, James, and Wyatt. She got the impression James and Wyatt were bored standing guard out in the hall. They wanted to know when they would get back to their regular duties. She wondered what their regular duties entailed.

The door swung back open. She ceased her pacing, redirecting her attention.

"Melia, I'd like you to meet Niles," Vince gestured to his right before his left, "and Oliver."

"Hello," she smiled, shifting her eyes back and forth between the two. From the clothing they wore, she figured Niles was a vampire and Oliver was a werewolf.

"You're smaller than I imagined," Oliver spoke.

She wasn't certain what to say while she took in his features. He had shaggy blonde hair, olive green eyes, thick eyebrows, and a square jaw. His skin-tight suit was tan and cream-colored.

"Hi, there," Niles uttered in a feminine-like voice.

Her eyes darted to his. He had blue eyes like Vince, but his eyes were a shade different. Baby blue. His hair a sandy brown that fell over his eyes. He was rail thin and wore eyeliner and makeup on his face. The type of guy her mother would shun. The type of guy she was supposed to dislike as well and not socialize with. According to the Bible, it was a sin, but also according to the Bible, it was not her right to judge. However, her mother wasn't here to preach to her. She would not be punished just by being nice to him. Not like she had been when the new guy, Spencer, had started at her school. No one had accepted him and word had gotten to her mother that she had walked him to the class they shared. Felt terrible when she told him she couldn't talk to him anymore. Even worse when the pressure had gotten to him, causing him to end his own life. She often wondered if he found peace even though the act meant he would spend eternity in Hell. He had already been living in it so how much worse could it be? She'd like to believe he would still be forgiven, even when he was at his lowest point.

"They're here to give you some company," Vince informed before turning and staring them each directly in the eyes. "I expect you *both* to be on your best behavior."

They both nodded in agreement before Vince left, closing the door behind him.

"Finally, thought he'd never leave," Oliver grinned.

She couldn't help but share a smile. He looked like trouble. Trouble was something she always avoided. At least she tried. The harder she tried, though, trouble always seemed to find her.

"So, how's it going?" Niles shifted in place.

He seemed nervous. Maybe he wasn't comfortable meeting new people like she was. It was always awkward. She never knew what the right thing to say or do was.

"Okay, I guess," she shrugged her shoulders.

"Dude, lighten up. She's not going to eat you," Oliver shoved Niles.

Niles gave him a stern look with wide eyes.

"He's right. I don't think vampire is listed on the menu," she joked along.

They both looked at her, then back at each other, before bursting out into hysterical laughter. She giggled along with them. She didn't think her joke was that funny, but it definitely lightened the mood.

"I like her already," Oliver proclaimed.

"So, what do you guys do for fun around here?" she asked.

"Fun?" Niles raised an eyebrow.

"If we told you, we'd have to kill you," Oliver cuts in.

She noted Niles hesitation.

"How long did it take you before you had full control?" she bunched up her skirt before sitting Indian-style on the ground in front of the bars.

"Everyone is different," he mimicked, sitting a bit of a distance from the cell, followed by Oliver. "It took me several weeks. Some things can be overwhelming."

"Yeah, hearing everything all at once is intense."

"Vince taught you how to do that already?" he tilted his head, stunned.

"How did that go?" Oliver asked with an eagerness.

"Okay, I guess. The first time, I tried focusing on just the birds, but then I became disorientated from the buzzing of the electric fence. I got better each time I practiced."

"Well, you're already more advanced than most of the guys. Even I didn't want to try again right after the head rush of noise," Niles commented.

"I am?"

He nodded.

She felt hopeful inside. Hopeful that she would fit in here. That she was doing a good job. So far everyone was nice to her. Treated her kindly. She wasn't used to it. Maybe she could make true friendships here. For once, she didn't feel alone.

Chapter 13
Melia

S he adored Niles. Now that he had come out of his shell, he was funny and honest. She liked that. Could be herself around him with no judgement. He didn't make her nervous. Not like Vince did.

Niles had been in disbelief that she never wore makeup or nail polish. Her mother never allowed her as she was always to adorn a modest apparel. He immediately dashed away and brought his bag of goodies. She was surprised he had makeup stashed away somewhere.

He let her pick the color of nail polish she preferred. Apologized that he didn't have many colors to choose from, but he had the color she desired anyway, green. More of a pine green, but it was still the color she liked. An earthy tone.

"That stuff smells awful," Oliver pinched his noise.

"Not to me, I love the smell of nail polish," Niles brought the bottle under his nose and inhaled.

She laughed at the gagging face Oliver made.

"All done," Niles announced while capping the bottle.

"Finally," Oliver walked over, but was quick to retreat at the lingering smell.

"Now, let's put some color on your face," Niles removed a large brush and dipped it into a pinkish powder.

She followed his instructions, turning her head right and then left as he lightly stroked her cheeks with the brush. When he was done, he moved onto her eyelids.

She was both excited and anxious. Had always wanted to know what it felt like to wear makeup, but her subconscious also screamed that it was wrong. She never understood why. She had no idea what she looked like. She craved to look at herself in the mirror. Her face was weighed down, along with her nails. At least she could admire them when she was allowed to have her eyes open. She felt like a different person. So wrong, yet it was also exhilarating at the same time.

"What is that terrible smell?" Vince waltzed in.

"See, I told you it was horrid," Oliver exclaimed.

"Just giving our girl here a makeover," Niles chimed. "All done."

Slowly, she opened her eyes. She saw Niles packing up before flicking them over and meeting Vince's eyes. He was staring at her. Staring strangely. She lowered hers at once with a bit of discomfort. Why was he staring at her like that? Was the makeup too much? Was she ugly? Maybe there was a reason she wasn't supposed to wear any.

"Hungry?"

She hadn't realized the hunger until Vince mentioned it while holding out the cup in his hand. It was a larger cup. At that moment, everything else in the room faded. It was just her and the cup of blood. The blood her mind demanded. The powerful smell of nail polish faded into the background. It was still present, but the aroma of blood was the only thing her nose inhaled.

She opened her mouth and took in a breath. The longing was still there. She couldn't tear her eyes from the cup. She wanted to reach out and snatch it only she stayed in control. Gently reached out for it as he handed it over. She wasn't as modest when she drained the contents.

Satisfied, she became keenly aware of Niles standing as far away from her as possible, clutching his bag of makeup. A pang of hurt cut through her. She thought they had bonded and yet he seemed wary of her.

"How about some fresh air?" Vince inquired.

"Sure," she nodded.

He unlocked the door and swung it open. She saw the worried glance Niles exchanged with Oliver before Oliver positioned himself in front of Niles.

She wondered why he was acting strange. Vince never acted like that around her. Why would she pose a threat to him? They were both vampires.

When she saw the sign for the restrooms, the desire to view herself in the mirror pushed Niles odd behavior aside. "May I have a minute, please?"

Vince looked over his shoulder with narrowed eyes. She flickered her eyes to the bathroom door. As soon as he nodded, she darted inside.

She stared at herself with awe, admiring both sides of her face. She felt like she was caked in makeup, but it was lightly brushed on. Her pale face wasn't as pale anymore and just a hint of pink showed on her cheeks. The soft green eyeshadow made her eyes pop. She hardly recognized herself. Now she understood why Vince stared at her off guard. She was enhanced, elegantly.

"Oh Niles, I love it. Can I give you a hug?" she burst through the door.

"Umm," he hesitated, looking beyond her to Vince. "Sure."

She threw her arms around him and hugged him tight. She was so happy. No one ever made her feel special before.

"Umm, Melia. You are kind of constricting me," he uttered.

"Oh, sorry," she pushed back, tucking a lock of her long blond hair behind her ear.

"Where's my hug?" Oliver protested.

She rushed over, not wanting him to feel left out, and was mindful how hard she squeezed this time. Hugging them both reminded her of her father. She wasn't even sure what possessed her to want to hug them in the first place. The only hugs she ever received were from her father.

When she looked over at Vince, he was quick to avert his attention as he continued down the hall. She followed in line, behind him. They passed the door he took her outside earlier. The hall seemed to be endless. They passed other doors that led to who knows where.

Finally, they walked out into an open lobby where two guys sat behind a large desk interchangeably laughing until they saw them enter and stopped.

"Graham, Dante, meet Melia," Vince introduced informing her Graham was on the left and Dante was on the right. She took in Graham's short curly blond hair, light blue eyes, and dimples on his baby face when he smiled politely, whereas Dante had mocha skin with matching eyes, pinkish lips, and short shaved dark hair. They were both young looking, but a maturity older than she was. She identified them both as vampires.

She was only now becoming aware nothing but masculinity surrounded her. Where were the female vampires? She hadn't seen any female wolves either.

She followed Vince out the front door into an empty parking lot. The sun was long gone. The night was clear. The air crisp and quiet. Stars glimmered like diamonds. There were so many of them. She wasn't sure if her sight was enhanced or not. The night was not as dark as when she was human. Her eyes reflected from the starlight.

"Close your eyes and tell me what you hear?" Vince requested.

She did as he commanded and tuned into the night life. The first thing she heard was popping noises from the trees in the wood. A sound she never heard them make before. More like a cracking sound within the tree. She also heard a hoot and then focused to a soft, low frequency chirping. It was persistent. Sounded in distress. It tugged at her.

Chapter 14
Vince

He hadn't been paying attention to her as he scanned the trees, looking for anything or anyone out of place. He had grown confident in her. She had a strong will. Most struggled with the transition, but she already appeared much of an expert.

He hadn't been prepared when she shot off across the parking lot towards the trees. A place he couldn't be certain if it was safe. The wolves prowled when off duty, but they were not informed to be on the lookout.

"Amelia!" he shouted.

She heard him. Stopped dead in her tracks. He saw the look of confusion on her face when she looked back his way. Was standing in the middle of the road wondering how she got there so fast.

A pair of headlights pierced the night. They aimed her way. She just stared, horrified, as the tractor-trailer truck headed straight for her. The horn blared, but she stood frozen.

He raced after her. The horn kept blaring as the brakes hissed. The truck jolted as the tires squealed along the blacktop. There wasn't enough time for the truck to avoid colliding with her.

He looped an arm around her thin waist, held tight, and pulled her along with him to the trees. They disappeared into the dark woods as the truck skidded to a dead stop.

Facing her with her back against a tree, he placed a finger against his lips before craning his head around the trunk. The driver was out of his truck, surveying the area with confusion. After a few minutes, he climbed back into his truck and drove off.

He relaxed before a rush of warmth invaded his mind at the realization his hand was pressed just below her shoulder. He removed his hand and stepped back.

"I'm so sorry. I don't know what happened," she cupped her hands over her mouth in distraught.

He had been furious when she took off. Was mostly furious with himself. She had no idea what she was doing. Had no idea danger could be lurking. He should have been paying more attention. "What possessed you to take off?"

"I heard something crying," she lowered her hands and looked into the distance as she remembered.

He studied her. How could he be mad at her for even one second? She was so innocent. Hadn't meant any harm. All she wanted to do was help whatever she heard in need. She had no idea she could run as fast as the wind. Or even faster. She was too good to be damned to a life of a vampire. Too good for someone like him. He still couldn't get over how her features were enhanced with just a little makeup applied. She was already a good-looking girl, but she seemed a bit more self-assured in her skin. That was what he loved about Nadine. How confident she was in knowing who she was and not caring what others thought.

"Oh, no," her sweet voice was laced with sorrow bringing him out of his own head.

"What?"

"The poor thing has a broken wing."

She scooped something off the ground from the litter of scattered dead leaves. Whatever it was, had blended in. Was a frosted shade of reddish brown. Tuning into the sounds, he now heard what she had. A low frequency chirping.

"Does vampire blood heal?" she looked at him with hope.

He wanted to tell her to leave it. To let nature run its course. He should tell her no. Avoid the risk of creating an actual vampire bat, but who would exactly want to bite a bat in the first place? All she wanted to do was heal the bat. He couldn't deny her.

"Yes," he nodded once.

"Really?"

He nodded again.

He watched, discouraged, as she pulled back the sleeve of her sweater and bit into her own flesh. By the time she placed the bat in her arm, the wound was already sealed shut. He should stop her, but he just stood there dumbfounded as she sat on the ground, placed the bat in her lap, and sliced into her flesh again with her razor-sharp teeth.

Instincts guided her. She was determined to help the bat. As soon as she removed her teeth from her skin, she swiped blood onto her finger before the punctures closed and offered it.

"What is that thing?" Niles shrieked when he appeared, along with Oliver in wolf form.

"A bat," he answered.

Oliver grumbled.

They all watched as it began to stretch out its wings and flex them up and down.

"All better now," Melia uttered, ignoring them and scooped up the bat, extending both her hands out.

They watched as the bat took flight. It flew high and low, swooping down before flying back towards Melia and landing on her shoulder. She smiled, stroking its tiny head.

"Guess she made a new friend and doesn't need me anymore," Niles jested.

He glared over at Niles a moment. "Melia, we should go back."

She looked up. Her eyes danced between them all, stopping at Oliver in wolf form. She placed her hand over the bat while twisting away from him. Oliver snorted with dissatisfaction. "May I take Rosa with?"

He raised his eyebrows perplexed that she had named the bat. She was already attached. He saw no harm though. "Sure, now follow me."

She rose to her feet, keeping a hand over her shoulder. He took the lead as she fell in line behind him while Niles and Oliver brought up the rear.

He looked both ways at the road and listened for any nearby traffic in route. Heard nothing close and crossed out into the open. He surveyed the surrounding front of the facility, but neither saw or heard anything out of the ordinary. He didn't like how vulnerable he felt with her out in the open. It was taking all his willpower not to grab her and run back to the lobby. Didn't want to cause her anymore alarm.

"It's snowing," she squealed with delight.

They were nearly to the parking lot from the patch of grass that separated the facility from the road. She had stopped to watch the small snowflakes slowly falling down. It was the first snow of the season. Well, at least where they were located.

"If you focus, you can see each unique shape."

He watched as she concentrated hard, following several flakes of white snow that floated down beyond her nose. He saw her demeaner change watching in fascination at one particular snowflake. It was so long now, but watching her brought back the memory of the time he was able to truly see the unique shape of snow. He had stared in wonder. As if everything slowed down so he could see all the differences of ice crystals falling down from the sky. A time when he was innocent and pure.

Chapter 15
Melia

She had requested to be put in the end cell that had a small window which faced the woods behind the facility. She watched Vince punch a fist through the glass. Cool air, she presumed, invaded the cell as the wind picked up. She made sure to show Rosa the way out when she wanted to leave. For now, she was content clinging to her sweater on her left shoulder.

"I can't believe you brought that thing in here," Niles complained with arms crossed, leaning against the far wall. "It could have rabies."

"Don't say that. You'll hurt her feelings."

"How do you know it's a girl?" Oliver asked.

"I don't know. I just do," she stroked Rosa's back. She was glad she wasn't the only female anymore, even if it was of a different species.

A swirling of snow blew in through the open window. She had always believed snow to be magical. Her mother despised it and only saw it as a burden. She always had to contain her excitement when it snowed. She didn't have to do that anymore. It felt wonderful to announce it with glee. She wasn't sure how Vince felt about snow, but he hadn't frowned upon it. Instead, he opened her eyes to the beauty and wander of it. To a human's eye, it was just a white flake. Now that she had advanced eyesight, she could see each irregular, symmetrical ice form. The snow was even more magical.

She had allowed each and every unique shape of snow to fall upon her face. They tickled her checks, but they did not melt against her skin. She had spun around watching all the frozen crystals drop down from the sky. She wanted to stay out longer, but she also sensed Vince's edginess.

He had yelled at her. Called her by her given name. It baffled her. She was even more confused when she stood in the middle of the road.

Had no idea how she got there. One second, she was standing next to him and the next she was about twenty yards away.

"Can I ask you a question?" she approached the bars and peered at Niles.

"Um, sure."

"How did I get to the road so fast?"

He relaxed at once. "Oh, that's easy. We're all able to run extremely fast."

"How fast?"

"Faster than a cheetah. You could triple or even quadruple it."

"Wow. What about the wolves?" she redirected her attention to Oliver.

"How about a race next time we're outside and you'll find out?" he grinned.

"Only if it doesn't cause any trouble."

"Trouble? Oh, honey, don't you think that for one second," Niles proclaimed.

She glanced away. He wasn't being entirely honest. She had read his body language. Had learned early on how to keep her mouth shut and pay attention to nonverbal cues. He wasn't exactly comfortable around her. "Did you know Nadine?"

"Nadine?" Niles shared a bewildered look with Oliver.

"You mean, Nadia?" Oliver interjected.

"Oh, right, yeah," she covered over her own misperception with a small smile.

"I never got a chance to know her, but she was not one to be trifled with," Niles paused. "What was she like when she was with the wolves?"

"I never got to know her either," Oliver dropped his head. "We all avoided her. She was, after all, a vampire. Our natural enemy living among the pack."

"Why was she living with the pack?" she inquired.

"Our alpha, Lamont, was keeping her hidden from Vladimir until she was ready to take him down," he raised his head.

"What about the other vampires?" her eyes darted to Niles.

"They were all Vladimir's disciples."

"What was different about her?"

"Umm…" Niles hesitated.

"Vladimir was known to be vile. She was willing to stand up against him with an army of werewolves and vampires that Vince created himself," Oliver jumped in.

"Why did Vince create an army of vampires?" she had the sense she was still missing a big piece of the puzzle.

"He wanted Vladimir to be defeated," Niles answered.

She could tell they were being cagey. She wanted to know more, but didn't want to annoy them with more questions. The only thing she did know for certain was Nadia or Nadine or whatever name she associated with was someone of importance. If she had been successful with Vladimir's downfall then why wasn't she here with them? Vince mentioned something about tragedy. What had it cost her to defeat Vladimir?

"Enough about gloom and doom, tell us something about yourself," Niles inched forward.

"What do you want to know?" she stepped back. Now she was the one on guard.

"Is that all-natural hair?" his eyes skimmed her golden locks that fell down past her waist.

"Yeah."

"Wow, isn't it like, heavy?" Oliver commented with raised eyebrows.

"Yeah, and tends to get in the way a lot," she sighed.

"Why don't you pull it back into a ponytail or a braid?" Niles questioned.

"I'm not allowed to."

They exchanged looks.

"Why aren't you allowed to?" Niles scrunched up his nose.

"My religion forbids it."

"Oh," Oliver uttered with a skewed frown.

"Aww, that's a shame," Niles sighed, disappointed. "I would have loved to get my hands on it. I love hair."

"Were you a stylist?"

"Professionally? No. When I was younger, I experimented on Barbie dolls and then upgraded to wigs. Sometimes the girls at school would let me braid their hair. My parents hated that I was different and never understood me."

She knew what he was talking about. Living in a world where you didn't fit in. Surrounded by those who had high expectations for you. Couldn't handle that you might think differently. Might question things not meant to be questioned. Were told to follow blindly a path not necessarily one you wanted to follow.

Chapter 16
Melia

When the door opened, she expected to be greeted by Vince's presence. Instead, the wolf leader, Lamont, entered. He carried a cup of blood in his hand. She wasn't the only confused one in the room. She noted both Niles and Oliver's expressions.

"The two of you shall take a break," his smooth, deep voice instructed.

"Did this come from Vince?" Niles inquired.

"An order is never to be questioned."

"Okay," Niles retreated, as Oliver closed the door.

They were both mystified. She was curious. No one visited her without Vince. Clearly, he had come alone. She wondered if Vince was aware.

"I see you made a new friend," he glanced over to Rosa, who was sleeping upside down on the highest bar in the dark corner.

"She had a broken wing. I healed her."

"That was generous of you. Are you thirsty?" he raised the cup.

She nodded.

"Why don't you come get it?"

She met him with a blank stare. "Umm, I'm locked up."

"Are you?"

Was this some kind of trick question? Unless he had the key, she was unable to get out of the cell.

"What happened here?" he shifted to his right and stopped in front of the bent bars.

"I had a minor accident."

"So, you did this?"

"Yes."

"How?"

She flashed back to the moment she had gone savage. She had not known her own strength. All she desired was blood. She would have gone to any length to get it. "I'm strong enough to break through metal?"

"Why don't you try and we shall see?"

She approached the door, reached out, and gripped the metal with her right hand, but hesitated before releasing. "I can't."

"Why do you think that?" he challenged.

"I'm in here for a reason."

"What reason?"

"To protect the humans."

He tilted his head. "Close your eyes and take a nice deep whiff."

"But," her eyes darted to the cup of blood in his hand.

"Trust me."

She breathed in deep through her mouth, letting it slowly release before complying and gradually closed her eyes. Her mind was firing in rapid succession. She was scared. Scared she might hurt someone when she caught the scent of blood.

"Relax," he encouraged.

Her eyes had been jolting beneath her eyelids. She hadn't been aware as she procrastinated in using her sense of smell. Took another deep breath through her mouth and loosened up. Angling her head back, she breathed through her nose. The smell of blood from the cup instantly invaded her nostrils. She commanded her mind to ignore the smell and focused on other smells in the vicinity. She smelled his blood beneath his skin, but she did not desire it.

"I don't understand," she reopened her eyes.

"There are no humans here, but I think some part of you already knew that."

She dropped her head. She had noticed, but hadn't questioned why she would be locked up if there was no threat here for her to lose control.

"Now, let's try this again. Open the door."

She stepped closer once more. Had a sense of security inside that she accepted. Now, this was a defining moment. One she was scared of.

"Don't be afraid," he whispered.

She met his brownish-yellow eyes. How did he know what she was feeling? The conflict inside. Was she an open book? She studied him

69

for a brief moment. He carried himself differently. He didn't show caution like everyone else. He knew what she was. What she was capable of better than she did and it did not deter him.

She placed both hands and griped the metal bars. She wasn't sure how much pressure to apply. The only goal was to open the door. She pulled hard and ripped the whole door off. She stared in disbelief.

"Very good," he praised.

"I shouldn't have done that," she placed the door off to the side.

"Your abilities are not meant to be limited. Now come, let's go for a walk."

She reluctantly stepped over the threshold. She should refuse and stay in her cage like a good girl, but she also wanted to see more of the world she was now part of.

James and Wyatt still guarded the door outside. They both grumbled in protest when Lamont gestured for them to stay. She felt bad they had to stand by at her expense. Didn't know why they were instructed to watch outside in the first place. Were they there to make sure she didn't get out or to make sure someone didn't go in?

She followed him out to the main lobby. Graham and Dante's voices hushed as soon as they appeared, watching with suspicion. She hated the awkward silence when she walked into a room.

Lamont led her outside. The sun was up and to her disappointment, there was no snow sticking to the ground. He led her to the right, across the grass.

She heard traffic on the road. Paused and watched cars drive by. Her mind processing that humans were operating them. She shouldn't be out here. It wasn't safe.

"Stay calm," he turned to face her. "Your mind is much stronger than you are aware. You already have control of it. It does not control you."

"How do you know?"

"You've already mastered the hardest part."

"What's that?"

"Accepting that you are a vampire."

She hardly knew Lamont. Yet, it was as if he saw right through her. She was terrified of making mistakes. Scared of hurting someone she didn't want to. Was still learning, but everyone was kind to her. She hadn't been unhappy when she found out she became a vampire. Was relieved. It was her way out. An escape from a life she thought she'd never get freed from. She was now a creature of the night. A creature known for darkness. She didn't have to be dark. She could use her abilities for good.

As they rounded the fence, a large black bird took flight from a tree across the road, running perpendicular close to the grass. A loud caw emitted. Her eyes bulged as it flew dangerously close. She covered her head and ducked low to the ground.

"Noir won't hurt you," he chuckled.

She warily peaked over her fingers and saw the crow perched on his shoulder preening her feathers as if nothing happened. "Why did she act like she was going to attack me?"

"She can be a bit of a diva," he stroked her. "Her respect does not come easily."

"How did you earn it?" she rose.

He pushed forward. "When she was a fledgling, a hawk knocked her from the sky stunning her. She wasn't able to fly right away and landed in a vulnerable area. I stayed with her until she was able to take flight again. She's remained loyal to me ever since."

She resumed following. Took in the outside of the facility. It was not as massive on the outside as she pictured it to be. She wondered just how many vampires and wolves were occupied inside. Wondered why they chose to confine themselves. If it was possible to stay in control, which she was starting to know firsthand, why limit themselves?

"What's on your mind?"

She narrowed her eyes at the suit in the far distance. "Did you know Nadine or Nadia?"

"I did. And they are one and the same."

"Huh?" she frowned.

"I knew her as Nadia, the name she took on when she became a vampire. As a human, she was Nadine."

"Oh." Now she had a small piece she could put together in the puzzle that made sense. It was still large, but it was a start.

"You, in a way, remind me of her," he continued.

"I do? What was she like?"

"She was fierce. She didn't wear her heart on her sleeve, but she was loyal to those she truly cared about."

"What happened to her?"

"She succumbed to her injuries sustained during the war against a malicious vampire."

"Is that how you got your scar?"

"No. I wasn't always the pack leader. The first wolf, Gabriel, put me in my place when I challenged him. A life lesson to be reminded of every day."

"You're not self-conscious of it?" she rubbed at her palm.

"No. There's a story of character behind it. A story of what I've overcome and shows that I'm not perfect, but I am wiser and stronger from it."

"What's going on here?" Vince demanded through clenched teeth as he strolled up behind them.

Chapter 17
Vince

As soon as he caught a glimpse of them on the camera, he was beyond pissed. What was Lamont thinking taking her out in broad daylight, outside the fence line, alone? He was risking her safety. Why not tell him? Why go behind his back? What was he up to?

"We're out for a walk, care to join us?" Lamont answered in a calm manner while Noir flapped her wings uttering an alarm.

"Please don't be mad," Melia shrank into herself.

His focus had been on Lamont, but as soon as he heard her tender voice and saw her sun-kissed eyes, his anger subsided. He didn't like seeing her cringe. Didn't want her to ever be scared of him. "I could never be mad at you," he slipped two fingers under her chin.

"Walk with us?" Hope radiated from her eyes.

"I'm not an imposition?"

"Never," her smile was sweet.

He positioned himself on the other side of her, scanning the tree line. Was still not comfortable with her out in the open, but she seemed happier and livelier. He was going to make it his mission to keep her protected at all costs. She gave him purpose again. Like Nadine had.

"I see you met Noir. I hope she wasn't too intimidating," he broke the silence.

"Well, she did take me by surprise."

"Don't take it personally. She does that to everyone."

He had gotten a reprieve, though. The one time she had showed hostility, Nadine separated them. Noir had been aiming for Nadine, but Leo stopped her short. With Leo around him most of the time afterwards, Noir kept her distance. In the end, Nadine had earned Noir's respect. The image appeared in his mind's eye; Nadine with

Noir perched on her shoulder. Fearless and fierce. Ready for war. Nothing was going to stop Nadine, not even him.

He had been selfish. Didn't want her to engage. He couldn't find her just to lose her again. Wanted Nadine to promise him she would survive. Should have told her who he was from the beginning. The son of a monster. Feared she could never love him knowing the truth. He was always prepared to defy his father, but wasn't prepared to fall in love with the one who was meant to take him down. He wanted to find another way, but never had a chance. He had failed Nadine.

A light touch brushed against the back of his hand. He looked down and found Melia's small delicate palm on his. He met her sympathetic eyes. Just a simple touch brought him out of his gloom. He wanted to avoid being dejected around her. Was trying to avoid being unhappy around them all. He was the leader of the vampires now. He couldn't show weakness.

"Whenever I was feeling down, I went to the river that flowed through my town. My father and I would go fishing there. I always felt more connected with him. Even though I couldn't see him, I knew he was there with me," Melia spoke quietly, slowly pulling her hand back.

He scanned his memory bank, trying to come up with a place he shared with Nadine that would make him feel more connected to her, but he fell short. The only place that came remotely close was the equipment room at the school's gymnasium. Several nights he spent with Nadine, aiding in practicing fighting skills. He fell harder and harder. He had tried to stay away from her when he realized he was developing feelings after calling her Nadia, only to annoy her. It had backfired. He had offended her. He knew he never wanted to be the one to upset her like that ever again. However, the equipment room was also the place where she felt the need to distance herself from him. He had been heartbroken, but he knew it was the right thing for her to do. She was supposed to move on with her life when she graduated from school while he disappeared from her life. Only she never made it to graduation. He had been selfish in going to prom to have one last moment with her. A dance. Maybe things would have turned out differently if he had never gone.

"There's a creek not too far through the woods," Lamont proposed.

"Really?" Melia looked over at him.

He nodded.

"Maybe we can go there sometime?" she glanced back.

"We could go there now," Lamont stated.

He sternly glanced Lamont's way. Why was he deliberately hindering him? Outside the fence line was bad, but completely away from the facility was a recipe for disaster.

"May we?" she tossed her head back in his direction with excitement.

He didn't have the heart to crush her. Not when she just told him that was a source of happiness. He couldn't deny her that.

"It would be an opportunity to really stretch those legs," Lamont commented.

"What do you mean?" she asked Lamont.

"Running without holding back," he answered.

"Oh, like last night?" her eyes redirected.

"Exactly."

"I don't know how I did that though," she hesitated.

"There's nothing to it, you just move," he reached out and clasped her hand. "I'll run with you."

"Okay," a bright smile lit up her face.

"On three. One. Two. Three."

They took off together towards the trees and navigated through them. It had been a long time since he felt the airstream rush against his face. To feel free. To leave his worries behind.

He held back at first while she gained speed. Now she was pulling him along as he struggled to mask her swiftness. She halted at the edge of the creek as he evaded running into her and stumbled into the water.

"Sorry," she quickly apologized with both her hands covering her mouth.

A Cheshire-grin spread upon his lips as he scooped up some water and tossed it towards her.

"No," she squealed, backing away before giggling with glee.

"What's fishing like?" he climbed out of the water.

"You've never fished?"

He shook his head. "I attempted spearing once upon a time."

"I could teach you. I always enjoyed the serenity of it. It was my father's way of bonding with me in the beginning. We didn't have to catch anything. We just enjoyed each other's company."

He never had a bond with his father. The bond he had was with Kumal, who he wished was his father. He taught him how to be strong.

Taught him ways in how to stay balanced. Although, his mind and soul had grown unbalanced.

He reacted with swiftness when he heard a twig snap from the woods putting himself in front of her ready to fight. When he saw Lamont reveal himself, he resumed a normal posture.

"Vince?" he heard her voice laced with concern.

"Why don't you see what you can locate under the surface of the water," he turned to her with a small smile.

"Okay," she eyed him wearily before retreating.

He watched for a couple of minutes as she concentrated hard. His smile widened when excitement lit up her face.

"I see one!" she exclaimed.

"Keep practicing," he encouraged, before nodding his head for Lamont to follow. He travelled a small distance from her stationed next to the tree line, ensuring to keep her in his sight.

"She glows with joviality, doesn't she?" Lamont glanced over his shoulder.

"I don't appreciate you not consulting with me first before making a decision that puts her at risk."

"How long do you plan on keeping her locked up?"

"Don't change the subject one me," he hissed.

"I only ask because I don't want to see you make the same mistake I did. Isolating and confining her will do no good to her mentality."

He studied him while absorbing his words. "Do you blame yourself for what happened to Nadine?" He never gave it a second thought about how Lamont might have felt when he divulged the truth how Nadine succumbed.

"By restricting her, I allowed her to dwell in her darkest self. Allowed her to resent what she had become."

"How do I avoid that with her?" his eyes diverted to Melia.

"Don't treat her any differently from the others and trust in her."

Chapter 18
Melia

For a moment, she had seen a lightness in Vince's eyes down by the creek. She hadn't expected him to spray water in her direction. Running with him had been exhilarating. She really liked how his hand felt in hers. Time almost seemed to stand still when it was just the two of them. She hoped he enjoyed being in her company as much as she enjoyed being in his.

She was both confused and flattered when he felt the need to take to her defense when Lamont emerged from the woods. No one had ever done something like that for her before. It was a nice feeling to experience. That he cared enough about her that he would shield her from harm. He valued her life over his.

"So, what is it you exactly do here?" she looked between Graham and Dante, who sat behind the front desk.

"Technically, our job is to redirect any unexpected visitors," Graham answered with a slight smile that exposed both of his dimples.

"We don't usually get anyone though, so we spend most of our time playing games or watching Netflix," Dante added.

"You guys playing anything cool that you could add a third player?" Oliver asked, leaning over their shoulders. Dante answered him as they began a side conversation.

"Most people want nothing to do with the inmates they believe are imprisoned here," Graham continued maintaining eye contact.

"Where does the blood come from for everyone?" she inquired.

"We have a crew who collects expired blood from hospitals within a hundred-mile radius."

"How many vampires are here?"

"The supply is adequate, no need to concern yourself," Niles dismissed.

He was dodging the question. She wasn't sure why he was uncomfortable or why certain topics were off limits. She couldn't tell if he was uncomfortable around her or just anxious about answering her questions and revealing something he shouldn't.

"Can I ask for a favor?" she bowed her head. She noticed Oliver and Dante's heads pop up from the side of her eye.

"Sure," Niles narrowed his eyes with suspicion.

She had been uneasy just thinking about it, but she still desired the experience. Had been denied her whole life of something so basic. Was made to believe in the religion she grew up with, but she also believed that some things went too far.

"Would you braid my hair?" The words rushed out before she could take them back.

"Of course," Niles's voice rose an octave higher as he rushed over and demanded Graham to stand as he took his chair.

She made his day as his guard went down. This was something he didn't have to stress about. This was something he enjoyed without overthinking.

He began to hum as he finger-combed her hair. It got a bit tangled from her escapade. She hadn't brushed it since she got here. It seemed a lifetime ago.

"I love your hair. It's so soft," Niles paused and took a whiff, "and smells so good."

"I use Herbal Essences honey shampoo, but it's been a while since I last washed it."

"It still smells fresh to me," he began braiding.

She never felt pampered before. She couldn't remember a time when her mother ever did her hair. His gentle touch was so soothing.

"You should braid my tail next," Oliver joked.

"Dude, I'd like to see that," Dante laughed.

She giggled along with their silliness. Was at ease with them all. Like she belonged. She never felt that before. Her mother would hate who she was hanging out with. Only she had to stop thinking about what her mother would think. She was never going to see her again. Didn't have to think like her anymore. Didn't have to care. She could be friends with whoever she wanted to be friends with. Wear make-up and pull back her hair. Simple things she had always desired. She didn't have to be riddled with guilt. She wouldn't be punished here for it.

"Are there any female vampires here?" the question popped out. She felt Niles pause down the middle of her back. "No."

"How come?"

"I'm not really sure," he resumed braiding.

"What about female wolves?" she met Oliver's eyes.

"There are a handful, but none of them came here," he answered.

"Why not?"

"They choose to stay back at our original home."

"What about the vampire that turned me? What happened to her?"

"You're all finished," Niles patted her on the back.

"I am?" she reached back and patted the length of her hair. It was twisted in interlaced strands.

She wasn't sure how she felt. All her life she saw so many other girls with different hairstyles. She was never allowed to do anything with her hair in her mother's presence. She never owned any hair accessories. Sometimes she would pull back her hair and hold it up while looking in the mirror, only for a second. In that stolen time, she felt like a completely different person. A person she wanted to be able to know even if it was a dishonor. She was always guilty afterwards and prayed for forgiveness. A part of her questioned why she felt compelled to pray. It was hair. Simply hair. Why wasn't she allowed to do what she wanted with it?

"May we go to the bathroom so I can see in the mirror?" she craned her neck to look at Niles.

"Umm," he hesitated with vagueness.

"I will take her," her eyes, along with everyone else, drifted over to Lamont's voice.

She sensed the shift in the room. The others were stunned by his presences while Niles appeared stiff as she flickered her eyes around the room.

"James, Wyatt, you may accompany us. The rest of you may stay here," Lamont declared, before gesturing for her to follow.

James and Wyatt quickly exchanged a look before following. Half the time she forgot they were in the same room as them all. They remained in wolf form and stood like statues by the front entrance on opposite sides.

She had more questions on her mind, but she didn't want to be the cause of getting him in trouble with Vince, again. Lamont was different from the others. He didn't seem afraid of what she might ask

79

and struggle to answer. He was more authentic. The back of her mind was warning that she already was asking too many questions. Her mother despised that about her. Would wash her mouth out with soap.

She was surprised when he entered the women's bathroom ahead of her. James and Wyatt remained outside the door. Like a good girl, she kept her mouth shut and walked over to the mirror, positioned her backside to it. Again, she looked like a completely different person. A battle took place inside herself that this was wrong, but she wanted it to be right. She just wanted to figure out who she was for herself.

"You want to meet Camille?" he asked.

Chapter 19
Melia

She should have told him no. She just couldn't muster up the word. Knew this was wrong, but she was tired of pretending to want the opposite of what she desired. She wanted to meet the female vampire who changed her life, but didn't know what she expected. What answers she wanted.

Lamont took her to an area she had never seen before. They descended a set of stairs. She hadn't realized there was an underground lower level.

He paused before rapping on a steel door three times. The door opened, revealing a familiar face. "Hey, Chica," Darius nodded his head with a humble smile.

"Hi, Darius," she beamed back.

"What brings you here?" he refocused his attention.

"We're here to see Camille," Lamont unveiled.

Darius's thick bushy eyebrows rose, shifting his eyes to hers briefly, before looking away.

"I take full responsibility," Lamont reassured.

She wasn't fond of the words he uttered. It became clear to her that she probably shouldn't be here. Yet Lamont brought her anyway. She should decline going any further. She didn't want to upset anyone if she wasn't allowed, especially Vince.

Darius stepped aside and permitted them entry. No words found their way out of her mouth. Without a fight, they ushered forward.

Lamont led the way. Ten cells were lined on both sides with occupants. Vampire occupants. They appeared drained. Shells of themselves. The life in them faded. A caged animal. They all watched her with interest. She felt bad for them. What had they done to live in this kind of condition?

They stopped at the very end. She noticed one cell on her right remained empty. The cell next to the light gray cement wall was dim due to the burned-out light. Within the cell sat the girl, Camille, she saw from the cemetery, huddled in the far corner. Her legs pulled up to her chest, with her arms wrapped around them. An orange tabby cat sat to her left, staring up at her before rubbing his head against her lower leg. She didn't stir. Didn't acknowledge the cat. She just stared straight ahead, unseeing.

"*Sorry,*" Camille had whispered in her ear before she experienced that moment of peace as the memory resurfaced her mind.

Camille hadn't taken pride it what she did to her. She had been remorseful. She wore sorrow on her sleeve. Only it appeared deeper than what she did to her. The light in her snuffed out.

"Hello, umm, Camille, is it?" she spoke in a gentle tone.

The glaze over Camille's eyes disappeared as awareness entered that she was not wherever she had drifted off. She slightly inclined her head and narrowed her eyes.

"My name's Amelia, but I prefer Melia," she babbled.

"Why are you here?" Camille asked in a thick, chalky voice.

"I wanted to come and see you."

The cat rubbing Camille's leg began to purr loudly. "Okay, you saw me. Now go on and tell me how you really feel."

She jerked back, baffled. What was she expecting from her? "I don't understand."

"Whatever you want to do or say, you have a right. I know you hate me."

Hate was a strong word. Hate was a negative energy. Nothing good ever came from hate. She had always practiced a positive mindset. The things that scared or harmed her she didn't consider as hating. There were things that happened she disliked, but was it enough of a dislike that was regarded as hatred? When she looked at her, there was one thing she knew for certain. "I don't hate you."

"Only a fool would believe that," Camille humphed in the back of her throat.

"I don't think you're a fool."

Camille tilted her head and gave her an odd look.

"Is that your cat?" she flicked her eyes.

"No."

"He seems to like you."

"Yeah, well, feeling's not mutual," Camille pulled her leg away.

"There's a saying about the eyes being the window to the soul. Do you think that's true?"

Camille stared with pursed lips. "What is it that you want?"

"Maybe he senses that you are lonely and need a friend."

Camille's eyes baulked before she covered over it with a half chuckle. "I'm not someone you want to be friends with, trust me. I'll only disappoint you in the end."

There was something that haunted Camille. She felt this urge to reach out and help her unload the burden she carried.

"If there's nothing you want, I'd like for you to leave," Camille dismissed.

"Why me?"

"What?" confusion crossed Camille's ashen countenance.

"Why did you pick me?"

Camille heaved a sigh. "You were an easy target. A loner. Out late with no one around. Someone who most likely wouldn't be missed."

The words stung. They were all true, yet it still hurt her inside to hear. Did her mother miss her? Did she even notice or care? Did anyone in her town? The only person who would cause an uproar was already gone.

"I think it's time for you to go now."

She didn't move. She wasn't ready to go.

"Leave!" Camille shouted with fury, standing at the bars with dilated pupils and lengthened teeth.

She backed away, horrified by her monstrous appearance. It frightened her then and it frightened her now.

In a matter of seconds, Lamont pulled her back, shielding her, as Darius pressed some kind of device against Camille, causing her to fall and convulse on the concrete ground.

"What did you do to her?" she cried out in alarm.

"Tasered her," Darius answered.

"Why?"

"To incapacitate her from trying to harm you."

"I can assure you it does not hurt her. She will recover momentarily. It's just a shock to her system to immobilize her," Lamont turned and looked her square in the eyes.

She heard Camille moan. Her eyes darted over and saw that her convulsion had stopped. She moaned again as the cat took the opportunity to rub his face against hers before she pushed him away, gently.

"I should take you back now," Lamont placed a hand upon her back and escorted her away.

She was upset. Didn't know how to process it. She had pushed Camille too far and because of it, had been punished. It was her fault not Camille's.

"I'm sorry you had to see that," Lamont voiced in a soft tone.

She didn't know what to say as they crested the top of the stairs. She focused on the rhythm of the nails clicking behind her from James and Wyatt.

"Where did you come from?" Vince demanded as they intercepted him in the hall.

She didn't have the energy to care if she caused more trouble between the two of them. She just kept walking.

Chapter 20
Vince

He felt a frosty shift of energy when he entered the open space of the lobby. All eyes were down, refusing to meet his. Her absence was hard to miss.

"Where is she?" he zeroed onto Niles.

"With Lamont," Niles answered while pretending to pick dirt from under his fingernails.

"Where did he take her?" he paced forward.

"The bathroom. She wanted to see how her hair looked after I braided it," he glanced up, shrugging his shoulders.

"How long ago?"

"A while," his head dropped as he continued to pick at his nails.

"What's a while?"

"I wasn't really paying attention."

He narrowed his eyes at Niles. Skimmed over to the others, who pretended to be busy with whatever was on the computer screen. He set the cup of blood down on the front desk with enough force to make a prominent sound. Niles cringed.

"What aren't you telling me?" he folded his arms against his chest.

Niles threw up his arms. "Remember, I am just the messenger."

"Niles," he drawled out.

"Well, while I was braiding her hair, she asked about, which I believe Lamont might have overheard," he paused, shrinking into himself before whispering, "Camille."

He marched away. No one dared to say anything or follow. What could Lamont possibly gain by taking her to Camille? He wanted nothing more to do with Camille and yet she found a way to be a thorn in his side, continuously jabbing him. He didn't know why he was keeping her around in the first place.

He saw them enter the hall from the stairway. He was hoping he was overreacting, but the fact of the matter was evident. "Where did you come from?" it took every ounce of willpower not to start yelling. At least not yet. Not in front of Melia. He didn't want to alarm her.

Somber eyes flicked to his for a fleeting moment. She tore them away just as quickly as she walked onward.

He followed with his eyes as she walked past him without a word, followed by James and Wyatt. She was clearly upset. He didn't like seeing her that way. "What did Camille do?" he lashed out with a snarl.

"I made a mistake. It was too soon," Lamont hung his head.

"She shouldn't have been taken at all." He shoved past him to the stairs and leapt down the first flight.

"Vince," Lamont called after him.

He ignored him and leapt down the second flight to the bottom and stomped forward. He pounded on the door hard enough to make a dent. As soon as it opened, he proceeded in. Darius stood back without being told. Tony, the other vampire, and the wolves stayed out of his way.

When he reached her cell, he was not expecting to see Leo with her. It only made him angrier before he kicked in the cell door. She lifted her head at the sound and watched as he yanked a bar clean off with sharp edges exposed. Slowly, she rose to her feet.

"I'm ready," her eyes closed.

Seething with revulsion, he entered the cell and pulled back his arm with the bar, prepared to strike. She signified nothing but pain and anguish. She did not deserve to breathe the same air as any of them. She deserved to burn in Hell.

Lamont cut him off, in wolf form. He growled a warning, locking eyes with him.

"Get out of my way."

Lamont stood his ground, deepening his growl.

Neither one was prepared when Leo launched an attack. He was confounded as the cat bit into his arm. The bar slipped from his hand, clanging against the floor.

He looked down at his arm, shocked, as it continued to bleed and did not instantly seal. Leo had never shown him hostility after he looked into his eyes. He was always warm with affection. Had even surprised Nadine, who thought he had compelled Leo after she found out he was a vampire.

His eyes diverted to the bar on the ground. He had been prepared to impale Camille. Impale her like his father's favored method. He staggered backwards, disgusted with himself. The one thing he feared he might become, he almost did. His thirst for revenge blinded him.

"Vince, are you okay?" Darius asked with caution.

He was deeply ashamed. Didn't want to be seen as he made a mad dash back out the door. He just kept putting one foot in front of the other. Felt constricted. Needed air. Fresh cold air to burn his lungs.

He ran until he reached the suit. Breathed heavily. He never felt this intense sensation before. Not even with his own father. The more he fed it, the more it consumed him.

"Why did you have to leave me? I don't know what I'm doing," he shouted.

He had been suppressing how he truly felt. It was now surfacing. He was guilty for it, but he couldn't deny it from himself anymore. He was mad at Nadine. Mad that she took her own life. Mad that she left him behind.

"Vince," Lamont placed a hand upon his shoulder.

"If you expect me to apologize, I won't," he snapped.

"I didn't come here for that. I came here for you."

He hung his head, uncertain how to respond. He didn't know how to feel. They were enemies by nature, but had learned to come together for a purpose. That purpose was gone, but they chose to remain allies. Neither one of them wanted to fight against each other again.

"Even if you had killed her, the pain wouldn't have gone away," Lamont asserted.

"Why was my love not enough for her?" he whispered.

"That's not something I can answer."

He knew Lamont couldn't. Only one person could and she was gone. He would never get closure. "I don't even know what we are doing here. I can't see myself ever trusting any of those vampires out of their cells."

"Maybe a new generation is meant to carry us into the future," Lamont countered.

He processed the words Lamont spoke before the radio from his belt crackled to life.

"Vince, do you read me?" Dante's voice shouted over the radio in a panic.

"I read you," he answered on full alert.

"We have a situation," he paused before adding, "Melia took off."

Chapter 21
Melia

The image replayed over and over again in her mind of Camille falling to the ground, shuddering. It disturbed her. She didn't know her story or any of the other vampire's stories who were locked up. Locked up like caged animals, shells of themselves.

Camille's hostility hit her in a way she hadn't expected. Was that what she looked like when she had desired blood? A look of evil? Was there evil inside of herself? Was she capable of mass destruction? Did becoming a vampire change who she was?

"Would you like to talk about what happened?" Niles stopped in front of her.

"No. Not really," she continued to stroke Rosa clinging to her chest.

"Okay," he dropped down beside her on the floor and sat there quiet with her.

She wasn't sure what to make of the sincere gesture. She never had a friend to show her an act of kindness when she was visibly upset. Never had a true friend at all. Everyone who she thought were friends only used her for their own guiles. The first sign of trouble they would run the opposite way. She never had anyone to talk to other than her father and even then, there were things she just couldn't tell him.

Rosa took flight and flew around wildly at the front doors, searching for a way out. She pushed up to her feet and walked over to open the door. When Rosa used her echolocation that showed her the way out, she was gone. Her heart ached watching her go, but she deserved to be free. Maybe she would come back or maybe she wouldn't. She wasn't meant to be tamed.

She lingered at the door, tuning into the low frequency chirps Rosa emitted as she hunted in the ascending night. Faint sunlight hung low on the horizon keeping darkness from overtaking.

She narrowed her eyes as the chirps became frantic. A large bird, an owl, was chasing after her with outstretched talons. She watched in horror when the owl snatched Rosa from the sky.

"No," she shouted and took off after them.

"Melia," someone called after her.

She ignored them. Her only focus was to follow the owl. She didn't think, she just acted as she raced into the woods across the road letting Rosa's chirps of distress guide her.

"Let her go," she shouted to the sky.

She maneuvered around the thick trees, darted across another road, returned to the trees, and bypassed another road back into the woods again. She heard a herd of deer race away from her in a panic. She wasn't exactly being stealthy. She couldn't see the owl above the thick treetops.

She shot out into the open in someone's backyard. Her eyes located the owl circling a short distance away. She rushed after it and crossed yet another road and hopped over a creek. She paused at an open field where rows of plate markers stuck up from the ground.

A graveyard.

Her eyes caught sight of something small falling. The owl soared into the trees as Rosa fell to the ground. She rushed after her and caught her in cupped hands. She felt her tiny heart beat racing in her palms.

"I've been waiting for you."

She jerked her head towards the trees and saw a dark figure hidden emerge from the base a tall one. He was covered head to toe in black. The voice of the hooded figure resurfaced her mind. It was the same voice.

"What do you want?" she stuttered, glancing all around. Realization dawned that she had no idea where she was or how to get back. She was completely alone and vulnerable.

"My dear, I mean you no harm. I only want to see you reach your full potential."

"What do you mean?"

"You are capable of far more than you know. Only I can show you the way, if you allow me."

"No, no, thank you." She didn't trust him.

"All in good time, my dear, but you should know you have not been told the entire truth about yourself. When you do, I will find you again."

He was gone.

She swept the area before she spun around in a circle, but there was no sign of him. She had no idea what he meant. What truth was being kept from her?

"Melia," she heard Niles's voice before water splashing.

She turned to his voice and saw Oliver in wolf form leap over the water, matching Niles's pace as James and Wyatt closed the gap to her before blazing past.

She never noticed the dark strip down Oliver's back. The rest of his coat was tan mixed with cream, the only exception was his ears, which were completely tan.

"Melia, you gave me a fright. Don't do that to me," Niles placed a hand dramatically on his chest while Oliver sniffed the surrounding area.

"I'm sorry, but Rosa needed help."

She looked down and found her hands empty before looking further and found Rosa climbing up the front of her sweater. She didn't appear to be hurt, just shaken.

"I see you found her. Is she okay?" Niles inquired.

"I think so," she looked down and nodded.

"We should get back," he encouraged.

Out of thin air, Vince appeared with Lamont in wolf form. His eyes swept the area before settling on her with a sigh of relief. She wondered why everyone seemed to be overreacting.

"How's Rosa?" Vince asked.

"She's safe now," she stroked her lovingly.

"You went quite the distance. Never saw this place before," his eyes wandered some more. She wondered what he was searching for. Or who he was searching for.

She looked over her shoulder and watched as the wolves sniffed around the immediate area, including the trees where the hooded guy had stood. She didn't say anything. Something in the back of her mind prevented her. She wasn't really certain of anything. She found herself even more confused. One thing she knew for sure, though, Vince was keeping something from her. They all were. She had noticed how they always treaded carefully around her, but ignored it. Now she was going to pay extra attention. She wasn't sure what the right questions to ask were, but she was determined to find out what they kept secret.

Part 2
The Dark

Chapter 22
Vince

He side-eyed Melia with wariness as they walked back. She had been unusually quiet. She kept her head down and continuously stroked Rosa as she followed. James and Wyatt scouted ahead as Niles followed behind her, with Lamont and Oliver bringing up the rear. The bat was an omen. He doubted it to be a coincidence it got carried off by an owl to the cemetery, unharmed. He was eager to speak with Lamont to find out if he had picked up on any scents, but his focus right now was to get Melia back.

The worst-case scenario crossed his mind as soon as he learned the details. Thought she'd be gone without a trace. He still had no idea what they were up against. Allowed his despair to get the best of him.

"Did something else happen to you at the cemetery?" he probed.

"Why do you ask that?" she countered, guarded.

"You just seem distant."

She didn't answer.

"You know you can talk to me about anything, right?"

Her head jerked. Her lips slightly partied, but closed just as quickly as her eyes flicked over her shoulder.

"Would you prefer to speak in private?" He could tell something was clearly on her mind.

Her eyes met his before dropping her head with a slight nod.

He turned to face the others. "Keep moving."

His eyes met Lamont's wolf ones and nodded once. Lamont pulled forward and took the lead while Niles and Oliver followed after exchanging a baffled look.

He waited silently for several seconds, listening to their movements along with any other abnormal sounds. When he was certain no prying ears were listening, he focused his attention on her. She looked so small. So fragile. So vulnerable. The complete opposite of Nadine.

Nadine had made it clear she wanted no part in becoming a vampire despite being marked to fulfil his mother's prophecy. Only she became one anyway, despite her mind set against it. The worse part was she had no one except the wolves to help her transition. Something he would always regret.

Melia wasn't given an option. The choice had been made for her. He wondered what her decision would have been if she had been fortunate enough to have a say in the matter. He never saw such control from a newly changed vampire.

"It's just us now. You can ask anything you want," he said in a gentle tone.

"Well," she pulled her braid over her shoulder and twirled a finger around the end. "You've all been very kind to me, but why do I always require someone to accompany me everywhere I go?"

He hesitated. It was a loaded question. One he didn't want to give too much away with his answer. She was fishing for something. He wasn't certain what happened to her in the cemetery, but he knew he had to give the right answer or risk losing her. "They're there to accompany you while you transcend, as well as for your protection."

"Protection?" her hand released her hair as her eyes lifted to his, probing.

"You were turned into a vampire for a purpose. A purpose I'm still trying to find out why."

"So, you didn't want me to become a vampire?"

"Not if it was against your will."

"I was supposed to be given a choice?"

"Yes."

"So, the one in the hood went against your wishes?"

He nodded. "Did you see him tonight?"

She massaged her temple while in deep thought. "What does he want from me?"

"Listen to me. I'm not going to let him do anything else to you against your will, I promise," he stepped forward, placing his hands on her upper arms.

"Why would you keep this from me?" fear ebbed its way into her voice.

"I didn't want you to be alarmed. You have enough to worry about just being a vampire."

She fell against him and embraced him tightly. He had not expected the move as he stood stiff at first before relaxing and wrapping his arms around her, patting her on the back. He was conflicted with the moment of affection as it brought back warm memories of his mother who hugged him tight every night like it might be the last time because, he now realized, she knew one day it would.

He sighed. "We should get back."

"Okay," she stepped away.

"Do you still feel energetic?" he smirked, reaching out his hand.

She smiled that sweet smile of hers before placing her hand in his. Together, they shot off into the night. For a moment, everything dissolved away. It was just the two of them navigating the woods. A whistle in the wind. A stretch of enjoyment.

When they emerged into the open, facing the front of the facility, it all came crashing back down on him. He longed to turn and go back to that peaceful spell. Only he could not afford to put his guard down. Her safety was his top priority right now. He needed to find answers, fast, in order to keep her safe from the threat he knew was out there.

He pushed the door open hard enough for it to slam against the wall and found Lamont already speaking with Parker. An area map was pulled up on one of the monitors.

"You find anything?" he asked.

"I checked the surrounding area for any surveillance cameras, but nothing. I was able to tap into a security door camera at the house across the street, but it wasn't the right angle. There's nothing more I can do technically," Parker answered.

"I couldn't pick up on any scent. You think he was there?" Lamont inquired.

"I have no doubt that he was." He whirled to face Niles. "Did you see or hear anything?"

"No," he shook his head, "but I wasn't completely aware of anything else except finding her."

"What was she doing when you found her?"

"Standing in the open with Rosa in her hands. She seemed a bit disorientated," Niles answered.

"Anything else?"

"No. She was insistent on helping Rosa."

"Okay, thank you," he nodded his head, dismissing him. He waited for Niles to leave the room and close the door before redirection his attention. "I don't like this. Somehow, he knows where she is and got too close to her tonight," he began to pace.

"I'm soon due to check in with the other members of my pack. I can have them come here and set up an outside perimeter by tomorrow night," Lamont advised.

"You don't think we should move her to a different location?"

"No. Uprooting her is not in her best interest. She needs stability. Something to keep her mind off the disturbance."

"Like what?" he frowned.

"Whatever makes her happy," Lamont departed.

Chapter 23
Melia

Her eyes danced around the room. They were only friendly to her because they were supposed to be protecting her. Could she even really consider them as her friends? All she ever wanted was to be accepted for who she was and just be enough as is. Now she doubted if they really accepted her as one of them. Was she a burden?

No one knew what to say. No one knew what to do. The room was stiff. She realized Niles was the one who lightened the mood, but he was currently missing. He had followed after Vince. She wondered where they went and what they were discussing. She was most likely the topic.

She had mixed feelings in what Vince proclaimed. No one ever felt the need to want to protect her. The word protection didn't make her feel completely alone. If only she had someone in her life like that when she was human. Her father was the only person she ever felt truly safe around, but her secret was too big of a hardship to load its weight onto him. Every second she spent with him, she wanted only to embrace happy memories. Capture the essence of freedom when they fished. The ground beneath her feet. The breeze feathering through her hair. The lullaby of the babbling water. A connection with nature she shared with him.

She doubted she would be permitted to go outside right now. Not after the mishap. She wasn't sure where she wanted to go, but she just knew she couldn't stay in the lobby.

"Are you going somewhere?" Dante was quick to ask as she walked a straight line.

"Bathroom," was all she uttered as she heard the clicking of James and Wyatt's nails as they followed.

She walked the length of the hall, but stopped short. Stared at the door that lead to the stairwell. She looked away, trying to find a reason to convince herself to keep walking, but nothing came to mind. Without realizing it, she reached out and pulled the door open before continuing. She paused and heard confused noises emitted behind her from James and Wyatt, but they didn't stop her.

She descended the stairs and paused with reconsideration, but pushed the unease back and continued. When she reached the door, she knocked three times before she had a chance to stop herself. "I'd like to see Camille, please."

It was hard not to see Darius's surprised look. "Does anyone know you're here?"

"James and Wyatt," she glanced over her shoulder.

"Chica, I don't think it's a good idea for you to be here."

"Okay," she dropped her head, disappointed.

As she started to turn away, Rosa pushed off from behind her shoulder, partially hidden by her loose braided hair, and flew into the room.

"Rosa," she ducked under Darius's arm and pursued her.

"What is that?" a vampire guarding the cells with Darius asked, but she didn't know his name.

Rosa flew directly to the end and into the dark cell. She stopped short as she took in the scene. It was empty with the door ripped off.

"Back again so soon?"

She turned her head to the cell directly to her right and saw Camille sitting with her back against the wall like she saw her last time. "What happened?" her eyes deliberated the other cell.

"A misunderstanding," Camille shrugged.

"It's because of me, isn't it?"

"It's got nothing to do with you," Camille dismissed.

"I'm sorry."

Camille's eyes narrowed. "You have nothing to be sorry about. If anyone should be sorry, it's me," she drifted off as she continued to speak, "but sorry doesn't change anything. Sorry, doesn't take back what I did. The deed is unforgiveable."

She kneeled to her level. "I forgive you."

"Don't," anger flashed across Camille's face. "You're naïve right now. It's just a matter of time before you learn the truth that I don't ever deserve anyone's forgiveness."

She was intimidated by her anger and leaned back before trying to analyze the depth of her brown eyes. Anger was a defense mechanism that suppressed deeper emotions. She was broken inside. Broken beyond the hope of repair. Shattered into a million little pieces. There was a fragment she could empathize with. "Everyone deserves forgiveness, including you."

Camille looked away, disgusted.

She perceived Camille wore her pain as armor allowing it to weigh her down so she could drown in it.

"Leo," Camille shot up and snatched the orange cat, hanging three-fourths up the side of the cell bars. The cat yowled in protest, reaching up with his paw.

As her mind comprehended that the cat was stalking Rosa, everyone else in the room reacted hastily. She was yanked to her feet as Darius shielded her with his taser gun pointing at the ready as James and Wyatt stood on guard with growls.

"No," she placed her hand on Darius's massive arm.

"The first reaction to any regarded threat is to use excessive force," he uttered, keeping his eyes trained on Camille.

"But she didn't threaten me."

The door burst open. Her eyes expanded as she hunched down and positioned herself on the other side of Darius. There was a fury in Vince's eyes. It was terrifying as he closed the gap.

She watched intently as his eyes flicked over to Camille with revulsion while his hands flexed into fists at his side, assessing the scene.

Camille stood expressionless, with her eyes to the floor.

"This is no place for you, Amelia," she shrank when his attention redirected to her. "You're not allowed here, ever again!"

"I'm sorry. I didn't know," her voice was jagged even to her own ears.

"Let's go," he grabbed her arm forcefully.

She lowered her head and took a hesitant step before stopping with a gasp, whipping her head over to the mangled cell. "Rosa."

"James. Wyatt. Take her while I get Rosa," he propelled her forward.

She wasn't fond of that decision, but complied as James took the lead and Wyatt fell in line behind her. She looked over her shoulder at Camille. She still held onto the squirming cat, still interested in

101

Rosa. Camille sneaked a glance in her direction before back down to the floor.

Rosa took off in a hurry, away from Vince, as soon as he entered the threshold of the cell. She heard her distinct chirp as she located her target before she landed on her back and crawled behind the base of her braid.

Before she looked away, she saw the sheer hatred in Vince's eyes as he noted the proximity he was to Camille. There was history. Hurtful history. Something more than just Camille turning her into a vampire.

Chapter 24
Vince

It took every fiber of willpower he had not to lose control, again. He didn't want Melia to see that primal side of him. That darkness in him scared even himself. It craved to take over. Craved to take control. It had a taste and it wanted more. Wanted to consume him.

"You are not to permit her access again. Do I make myself clear?" he growled in a whisper next to Darius's ear.

"Understood," Darius confirmed.

He gave one last death glare to Camille before strutting away. She was the source of the darkness within. The source of the negative pull. His intentions were to never see her again as she rotted away in her cell. Yet for some reason, Melia continued to return to her.

He saw Melia's eyes. He had frightened her. Hated himself for it. Hated that Camille had such a spiteful effect on him as he sat on the stairs with his head in his hands. He didn't know what the right thing to do was. Should he give Melia some time? He probably should. She probably wanted nothing to do with him right now, but he also didn't want to be alone. Normally, he had Lamont to lean on and talk to.

In some strange way, Melia grounded him. Whenever he was around her, the pain and agony seemed to take a back seat. He needed that right now. Needed to take his mind off the hurt.

He pushed up to his feet, spun, and climbed the rest of the stairs. Out in the hall he picked up on her honey scent, but it did not lead back to the lobby. He turned the opposite direction and followed her aroma. It led to the holding cells.

When he opened the door, he observed James on guard to his left before he relaxed and sat back down. As he entered, he noted Wyatt was on the other side of the door, whereas Melia was sitting on the bench in her old cell with her feet dangling and her hands gripping the edge.

"I like to apologize for being harsh," he stopped before her.

"You scared me."

"I didn't mean to. I just don't want her to have the chance to hurt you again."

Her head lifted. "Is that why you hate her?"

He looked away. Was that how he felt about Camille? Had he felt that way about his father? If he had truly hated his father, then wouldn't he have had the strength to kill him? He always despised his ways. Yet, when he came face to face with him, he held back. He hadn't realized that until now. He never wanted to become like him. Only the bitterness in him was growing out of control when he was around Camille.

It mortified him that Melia had caught a glimpse of his darkness when she was so honest and pure. He didn't want her to be afraid of him. Didn't want to give her a reason to run. Her innocence was refreshing. Maybe she was his second chance.

"Hatred will consume you unless you learn how to forgive."

His eyes darted towards hers. "I could never forgive her. She doesn't deserve it."

"Why do you believe that?" her head tilted.

"Only a true monster would be capable of killing her own friend."

She frowned while momentarily processing. "She has to live with that decision every day. You don't. Forgiveness isn't just for her, it's also for you. To let go of the pain and move on from the past that has a grip on you and only holds you back."

There was an insightful part of Melia that reminded him of Nadine. Similar, yet different, at the same time. A quality he admired.

"The first step is to acknowledge," she added.

He was confused. What was he supposed to acknowledge? The hate? It was festering inside. Turning him into something he didn't recognize. Had this been what Nadine felt when she turned? Was this why she didn't want to be turned to begin with? Had Camille allowed herself to be lost to the darkness in order for her to be able to complete the unspeakable act? In that moment, when he had lost control, all logic was erased from his mind. He had never struggled with that part of himself before. He had Kumal to support him and stay on the right path. Something Camille hadn't had much of when they found Nadine. He hadn't been as supportive of Camille as he should have been. All he cared about was Nadine and overlooked Camille. With that moment of acknowledgement, the realization emerged that she wasn't fully to blame.

Camille was never supposed to get caught up in his world to begin with. When he found her, changed, all he could think about was getting to Nadine. Camille had been a mess. She hadn't taken the news well to begin with when she found out he was a vampire and then, when she woke up to discover she had been turned into one as well, she was completely devastated. She struggled to cope with her new reality, but he had her push aside the trauma in order to pursue Nadine. When they found Nadine, all his attention went to Nadine when he should have given Camille the full attention she required as a newly turned vampire. It was easier to put all the blame on her to avoid the added weight of his own guilt.

"I'm to blame as well," he collapsed on the bench with the added heaviness on his shoulders.

Without a word, Melia placed a tender hand on his.

"I was so caught up with Nadine I dismissed Camille and how she was affected in the presence of Marc, the one that turned her." She had a reason to loath Marc as much as he did. His anger didn't help her festering resentment. If he had been paying more attention, maybe he would have seen some kind of sign.

The weight on his chest magnified. Shame washed over him as he glanced over at Melia. She had a right to be scared of him and run away. If she knew what he had almost done to Camille, she would be appalled and not want to be in his presence. He was disgusted with himself. He couldn't blame Nadine not being able to love him anymore, he was a horrible being.

He slipped his hand from under her warm one and walked away. He felt so cold inside. He was just like his father. Just a different kind of monster. Everything Nadine sacrificed was for nothing.

He stepped out into the darkness. That's all he was. That's all he ever was. A darkness that walked into Nadine's life. A darkness that destroyed Camille. No matter how many times he pushed it away, it always stood at the ready to take over. He could never outrun it. Could never overcome it. Now he understood why Nadine would take her own life.

"I'm so sorry," he fell to his knees at her suit. "It's all my fault." He hunched over and felt such shame. He had been angry with Nadine for taking her own life. Blamed Camille on everything. It was easy to do so the pain wouldn't consume him. Easy to blame Camille's actions as betrayal without taking any accountability. Easy to hate her.

A warmth rippled over his shoulder. He looked up and saw Melia standing in front of him. "I've done terrible things," his face was sticky.

"Everyone deserves redemption," Melia spoke softly as she kneeled across from him and pulled him into an embrace.

He surrendered. He didn't deserve her comfort, but the gesture was warm and welcoming. Her hug helped to relieve some of the pain he had been concealing, even from himself. It was a weakness he couldn't afford to show as a leader in order to maintain control. He had felt so alone and abandoned. Even Lamont didn't know the extent. Yet, somehow, Melia was able to see right through him and not run away from his demons.

Chapter 25
Melia

She saw beyond the sadness in his eyes and knew he had a tormented soul. Hid behind a mask. Knew he dwelled in the past, living with the pain and agony. Saw the hatred in his eyes. Heard the anger in his voice. She had been afraid, but she also knew it was a cry for help.

He griped her tightly. His pain was her pain. Saw the moment he realized the truth he buried. Acknowledged what he refused to see. All she knew was if Camille had been sorry when she took her life, she had to have regretted taking her own friend's life. A friend who happened to be Nadine. She was becoming aware that Nadine had an effect on everyone here.

"Nadine never wanted to become a vampire," he mumbled.

Her eyes traveled to the suit. She wondered what Nadine was like. She was a legend. Someone to look up to. She would have loved to meet her if she had had the chance. It was clear that Vince loved her and why he was so broken inside.

She didn't know the whole story. Only had pieces, but the picture was growing clearer and clearer with each day and night. There was a lot of hurt here and a lot of wounds that needed healing. Something she could help with. Something preached to her for her entire life. That was why she was here. This was her purpose.

A tiny splash of moisture landed on her cheek. She looked towards the blackened sky and felt another land on her skin.

Rain.

She loved the rain. The tranquil sound it made. The feel of it on her skin. It was a bit different to her now, but better. Amplified. A vibration of beautiful white noise. A magical symphony.

"I guess we should go inside before we get soaked," Vince pushed back, his face stained in red.

"I don't mind. Rain is cleansing," she pushed up to her feet and tugged on his forearms.

Reluctantly, he rose.

"Relax and embrace it," she closed her eyes and tilted her head. "Let it rejuvenate you."

The rain picked up and caressed her face. She loved how soothing it felt to her mind, body, and spirit. The comfort it provided her. It helped to wash away her own pain. She only hoped Vince could find that connection too.

She peeked one eye open and saw Vince had mirrored her. He was beautifully broken. It was a privilege to help him. She could help them all. Help them fight their demons, if they wanted her help. Everyone had demons. Some could be hard to face. Some were unknown.

She closed her eyes and spun in a circle with her arms high to the sky. She let the rain wash away her doubts. It didn't matter what they might be keeping from her. She should have never questioned why she was here in the first place. Some mysteries were not meant to be understood.

"What are you doing?" he asked.

She stopped spinning and opened her eyes. He was staring at her with curiosity. "Twirling."

"Why?"

"You've never done it?"

He shook his head.

She reached out and grabbed both his hands. "Just let loose and let your body free."

She circled slowly with him with a small smile. His posture was stiff as he followed her lead. Little by little, he relaxed. His eyes locked on hers. There was no sadness. There was no pain. There was just him here with her in this moment of positive nourishment to his soul.

His hand curled tighter in hers. Her smile brightened. He was fully relaxed now. Embraced the energy she flourished onto him. She was able to give him some peace. It was the best kind of sensation she thrived on. Helping those in need.

"What's this?" he stopped to turn over her right hand and stroked her flawed palm with his thumb.

"It's nothing," she yanked her hand back.

"Did someone hurt you when you were human?"

Her eyes narrowed as she tried to decipher his words. Why would he think someone had hurt her when she was at the human stage of her life?

"The wounds that healed naturally before you become a vampire never go away," he added.

Now it all made sense; why she thought she had been dreaming at first. Any wounds inflicted after she became a vampire would disappear as if they were never there, but her human scars still remained.

"I don't want to talk about it," she moved past him. The moment they had was gone. Now all that remained was the fact that she was soaked beyond a doubt, weighed down by her wet clothing on her back. There was beauty in the rain. Beauty and sadness. There were many times she welcomed the rain only so she could walk outside in it and let it wash away her tears.

She was here to help Vince. Not unload her hardships on him. He didn't need any more pain to be added on top of his. She always dealt with her pain alone. She learned how to manage it and be strong. Her pain did not compare to some of the people she had met when she volunteered with her mother at shelters during the holidays. People who lost everything. People who were just dead inside coming for a hot meal to fill their caving bellies with children younger than her. Many times, she caught the look of disgust in her mother's eyes who went out of her way to avoid contact with those low on life covered in filth. Would tell her, in private, those kinds of people were just looking for handouts. Played a part of the unfortunate to get something free and looking for pity. Would tell her that nothing comes for free in life and when it knocked you down, you had to pick up your feet to earn everything you had, like she had to.

Her mother told her countless times she had not been ready to have a child. Had felt pushed into having her when she was married to her father. Pushed into starting a family. To be a housewife. To give up on her dreams.

Her mother discovered the ultimate betrayal. That her father had cheated on her when he left for a business trip. Her mother thought she would surprise him by visiting when she caught him with another woman. Demanded a divorce. Wanted sole custody, but the courts decided otherwise. She was grateful the court allowed him to spend time with her even if it was only every other weekend. She cherished every moment she spent with him.

Her mother had to pick herself back up after the divorce when her family cast her out. She was all alone with a child she didn't even want to begin with. She turned to a different church. One that welcomed her with open arms. Followed their ways and made a name for herself.

"When you're ready, I'm here for you," Vince's voice brought her back to reality.

"It has little significance," she stepped out of the rain back inside.

Chapter 26
Vince

She had completely withdrawn. He saw the concave scar on the palm of her hand. Wondered what could have made a wound like that. Three semi-circular reddish discolored rings. The one thing that came to mind was burn marks. He didn't know what would make that kind of mark. If it was a burn mark, who would have hurt her like that? How could anyone want to hurt someone like her? She had the kindest soul.

Compassionate.

Thoughtful.

Caring.

She had seen a glimpse of his demons which frightened her, but she didn't run away. She helped him take a step to face them. Something he had been avoiding. He still had a long way to go, but it was a start.

He stood outside the dented door to D-Block. Raised his fisted hand, visualizing knocking on the door. He just couldn't bring himself to actually knock. How could he look Camille in the eye after what he almost did to her? She hadn't exactly tried to defend herself. It was almost as if she expected it. Wanted him to go through with it. Disappointed when his path to her was blocked.

He wondered how she even happened to align with Jomar in the first place. Jomar, who envied him and thought him unworthy to be the son of the vampire he worshiped. He recalled the painful memory he tried to close behind a door; Jomar had not desired Camille to break Nadine's neck. In fact, he had been angry. He didn't know what had transpired afterwards. There had been no time to mourn when he picked up on wolves storming the area. He barely made it out with his own life.

Even though he was acknowledging more of the details, he just wasn't ready yet to face Camille. To speak to her. Or to forgive. She should have had Nadine's back not have been the one to stab it. Nadine would have never done what she did.

"Vince, do you copy?" Parker's voice boomed over the radio.

"I copy. What is it?"

"We have some visitors."

He frowned. "I'll be right there."

He secured the small radio back onto his waist as he headed up the stairs. His mind spun with the possibilities. Who was visiting and why?

He barged into the surveillance room and saw on the big screen three wolves standing outside the fence of the loading and unloading area waiting to be buzzed in. He wasn't familiar with two of the wolves, but the third had a light brown and tan pelt who he recognized.

Cameron.

"Why are you all wet?" Parker frowned, wheeling back.

"Let them in," he turned away before Parker entered a keystroke to open the gate.

He swept through the lobby without uttering a word, ignoring the whispers as his mind was focused on his mission. He didn't know Cameron well, but he had a bond with Nadine. Remembered the first time meeting him. He had fearlessly stood before him and his vampire army before shifting from wolf to human form, declaring Nadia had sent him. He led them the rest of the way back to the pack and waited patiently for the signal before a battle started. The battle before the war.

The last time he saw Cameron was in the atrium, where he struggled to make his way to the clock tower. Cameron had charged down the stairs, clearing a path for him. He had dispersed after that, never to be heard or seen again.

He opened the door next to the truck docking station, stepping back outside into the rain. He met them a quarter of the way. With Cameron was another male and a female with similar markings. Dark back fading to tannish underbelly and white legs. The female had more of a lighter muzzle and neck, whereas the other wolf had a darker muzzle.

The wolves exchanged looks before shifting to human form before Cameron stepped forward and crossed his arms. "Where's Lamont?"

"He's not here at the moment," he shook his head.

"Why did he send for me?"

112

"I didn't know he did, but it probably has something to do with Melia or maybe Caden."

"Who's Melia?" Cameron frowned.

"Why don't you all come in and I will explain."

"I'd prefer to hear it from Lamont," the female crinkled her nose.

"Helene," Cameron grumbled with annoyance.

"I don't know when to expect his return," he answered with brisk.

"We know how to wait patiently," Helene retorted.

"You can, I'm not," Cameron countered.

"I'll stay with her," the other male spoke.

Her brashness didn't daunt him. She could stay out in the rain like the wet dog she was if she wanted. They both could.

He nodded his head as Cameron followed. Why had Lamont not mentioned he wanted Cameron here? How did he think Cameron would be helpful? How did he know where to find him?

He was different now. He didn't project that same young innocence he had when he met him. There was more confidence. He also grew a bit from that oversized pup-like stage.

"What's going on? I left for a reason," Cameron persisted.

"I understand. The truth is, we don't know what's going on. All we know is, Caden is hypnotized, hostile, and locked up. Then there's Melia," he paused at the bottom of the step and looked over. "She's a vampire."

"So," he shrugged a shoulder.

"A vampire like Nadine."

Confusion crossed Cameron's face. He didn't recognize the name, at first, since he knew her as Nadia. Only it didn't take him long to put two and two together as his face faltered. "Why?" Cameron whispered.

"That's what we are trying to find out."

"Just where do I fit into all of this?"

"I guess that is a question you will have to ask Lamont," he proceeded up the steps.

Cameron did not follow as he assessed the area. "What is this place?"

"Technically, a prison. We're trying to rehabilitate the other vampires."

"This is not what she would have wanted."

His words wrapped around his heart and constricted it. He never knew what approach Nadine would have taken after. She hadn't confided in him. Had she confided in Cameron?

"I'd like to see Caden," Cameron interrupted his thought.

He found himself surprised. He thought Cameron would want to meet Melia first. He didn't know what history Cameron had with Nadine, but it was clear he cared about her.

As he led Cameron to the solitary confinement cells, they walked through the lobby. He noticed a strange look on Oliver's human face, but no one uttered a word. He also noted Melia had not returned. He was going to have to check on her later.

He paused outside the door and watched as Cameron glanced through the small window into the padded cell. He hadn't been down since after Caden was locked up that first night, but Lamont frequently visited. He heard thumping from inside.

"How was he hypnotized?" Cameron asking stepping back.

"There's someone, or rather something out there that wanted to recreate a vampire like Nadine. We don't know what he looks like. All Lamont and I saw was a black hooded figure when we found Melia. He was accompanied by Caden and a vampire, Camille."

"The one who betrayed Nadia?"

"She told you?" he shouldn't be surprised but he was.

"Kind of," he semi-shrugged.

"Camille had been under hypnosis too, but somehow broke free from it. She doesn't know how. She couldn't provide us with much intel, but it's clear he wants Melia for something. Something Nadine had been essential for."

Cameron grew quiet as he peered through the window once more, while a bunch of thrashing from inside could be heard. "I'd like to go in."

"I think you should wait for Lamont. He hasn't been successful with any of his approaches."

"Maybe because he doesn't know certain things that I know."

It was his turn to give a look of confusion. Lamont was the one that knew everything. What could Cameron possibly know that Lamont didn't?

Without another word, Cameron shifted and stood at the ready by the door. He sighed. He didn't like this. They both heard a thud before Cameron nodded his head. He had no choice but to trust Cameron knew what he was doing. He opened the door and pushed it open a gap. Only enough for Cameron to be able to squeeze through, but neither of them had anticipated Caden was also ready to squeeze out as he launched through the crack just as Cameron was rushing in and rammed Cameron.

Without delay, he reached out for Caden right as he snapped his jaws on his forearm, snapping the bone. He groaned in pain pulling back as Caden took off.

"No. Stop him," he exchanged a panicked look with Cameron.

Chapter 27
Melia

She shared a moment of bliss with Vince. A moment where it was just the two of them and each of their pain ceased to exist. Until he felt the scar on her palm. A memory she wanted to forget. A memory that would always haunt her mind because the scar would never heal. She would be forever reminded of the worst day of her life. A day she had felt truly alone. She had no one to turn to. No one who cared about her. She had to pretend nothing happened. Pretend everything was okay when she was dying inside. A time when she had felt so small. So insignificant. Just so beaten down.

She didn't want to go back to that point in her life. It was her lowest. The scar was a constant reminder. She was happier here. She had hope again. Hope her life would change for the better. She didn't want to dwell in her past. She wanted to be the beacon for those in need here. For Vince. Had been training practically her whole life. She knew how to help others overcome their misery. She knew how to uplift their spirits.

Her throat was starting to feel rough, like sandpaper. She couldn't recall the last time she drank some blood. Vince had been good at keeping up on that. She didn't know where the supply was kept. Maybe she could ask Niles to get her some.

As she rose from the bench in the cell, James and Wyatt rose to all four paws, watching her movements. She still wasn't fond of being escorted everywhere she went. She had gotten used to being alone. Welcomed it at times. She could actually relax and let her guard down instead of wearing a mask, pretending she was someone everyone else wanted her to be.

She exited the holding cells and stepped out into the hall while the clicking of the nails trailed after her. She was starting to dislike that sound.

"Finally. I was worried about you," Niles perked up and ceased pacing out front.

"You were?"

"Of course, I was."

There were many thoughts that crossed her mind she wanted to verbalize, but tamed them back. "Is that for me?"

His eyes followed hers to the cup on the desktop. "Yeah, thirsty?"

She nodded as she resumed her strides, grabbed the cup, and chugged down the lukewarm contents. She wondered how long it had been sitting out waiting for her. Normally, the blood was chilled.

"How are you?" Niles asked.

"Still a little thirsty."

"I can go get you some more blood."

"Can I come with?"

"No," Niles uttered sharply. "I mean no, it's better for you to stay here. You don't want to overdo it."

"I'll go too. I'm a bit hungry myself. You guys want anything?" Oliver looked over at James and Wyatt who both nodded their heads.

"We'll be back before you know it," Niles grinned before heading down the hall on the other side of the building.

She was bummed. Wanted to go with. To see more of the facility. She understood they were taking precaution with her around the blood, but it wasn't fresh from a human body. It was stored blood. Did they think she would drink the whole stash? She was certain there would be a point when she would have her fill even if she had lost control, but she had been maintaining control this whole time. Yet, they still seemed to walk a tightrope around her.

"What are you guys up to?" she redirected her focus.

"Watching *Black Panther*," Dante answered.

"What's that about?" she walked behind the desk.

"You never heard of it?" Graham asked, dismayed.

"I never watched much of anything."

"Well, we're going to have to fix that," Dante reassured.

She watched for a few minutes, but couldn't stomach the violence of two guys fighting each other. She didn't understand what the purpose was.

Her eyes wandered over to the door behind them. Her eyes stumbled across it before. Many times, she wanted to summon the courage to ask, but shelved the desire to know. She had already asked too many questions and her mother's voice continued to echo in her mind to stop.

"What are you doing?" she jumped at the sound of Dante's voice.

"I, I was umm, just curious where the door leads," she stuttered.

"You don't want to go in there. It's where all the unsafe vampires are locked up. They can be nasty."

"How many are there?" she inched her way back.

"Roughly four-hundred or so," Dante shrugged.

"How many good?"

"About half of that," Dante answered.

"There's more bad vampires than they're good?"

"We have the advantage with the wolves," Graham added.

"Who's hungry?" Oliver cheerfully inquired as he hugged an armful of meat.

She scrunched up her nose, eyeing the red raw meat. It repulsed her. She watched as Oliver dropped the pile of meat onto the floor before shifting and digging in along with James and Wyatt. They ate savagely.

"They're such wild animals," Niles jested.

She moved away from the door as the blood in the cup in his hand called to her. She was hungry herself. Wanted to devour the blood. There was an animal inside herself too. There was one in all of them.

"Niles?" a dark brown wolf appeared before charging from behind him.

"What?" Niles whipped around and dropped the cup of blood with a shriek as the wolf launched into the air.

She screamed as Oliver hurled himself against the other wolf and slammed him against the wall. The dark brown wolf grasped Oliver's nape and flung him across the room.

"Oliver," she shouted.

The golden yellow eyes of the dark brown wolf latched onto hers. There was an evilness glazed over them that made her shutter. He wanted her.

James and Wyatt cut the dark brown wolf off with deep-rooted growls. The dark brown wolf's eyes shifted to theirs with anger. The coarse fur stood up on the back of his neck as his muscles bunched.

"We're under attack! Vince, do you read me? We're under attack," Dante shouted into a small device as Wyatt launched an attack.

"Let's get out of here," Niles yelled, grabbing her arm and pulling her along with him in the opposite direction.

She heard a yelp and looked over her shoulder. Wyatt held up his front right paw as James and the dark brown wolf engaged upright before James got knocked down. The dark brown wolf leapt over and pursued her once more, only to be cut off by Dante.

"Don't look back," Niles insisted.

She was terrified. If she still had a heartbeat, it would be racing like she was running a marathon. She knew the wolves, at one point, were the vampire's enemies, but she never realized the brutality they could bring.

She stopped dead in her tracks. The smell of blood entered her nostrils. Fresh blood. A smell she was unable to ignore.

"Melia," Niles yanked her arm and put himself in the path of the dark brown wolf before he got knocked down.

The wolf locked eyes with her once more. She noticed four scratch marks scared the right side of his face. He jumped at her and nipped the bottom of her leg just before another wolf came out of nowhere and crashed into him.

While both wolves sparred, she felt an odd sensation from the puncture wound in her leg. There was so much going on around her, but there was only one thing her mind was focused on.

Blood.

"Melia?" Niles's voice was laced with concern.

Part of her heard him, but the other part was dominate as she pushed him up against the wall and sank her teeth into his neck.

"Melia, breathe," Niles begged.

She greedily sucked the sweet elixir. Her body and mind had been denied this boundless stamina. She was drunk in the madness of it. Only ever at half her potential. She wanted to devour it all.

"Melia, stop." The different voice sounded vaguely familiar, while a hand roughly shook her shoulder. "Stop. You'll kill him."

She didn't want to stop, but she didn't want to kill either.

"Amelia!"

She jerked away. Stared into Niles terrified eyes. He was afraid of her. Her eyes lowered to the side of his neck. There was a bloody hole. She backed away.

"Melia."

She looked over and saw Vince. She noticed he held his left arm close to his chest.

"Why did I do that?" she redirected her attention to Niles with alarm.

She heard Vince sigh. "You survive on vampire blood, not human blood."

119

Chapter 28
Vince

Her eyes met his. He could tell she was processing his words before glancing over to Niles. She placed a hand over her mouth as she slowly backed away, shaking her head.

"Melia," he reached out towards her with his good arm.

"Don't touch me," she pulled away. Her words were like a knife to his stomach. "Melia, it's okay…"

"No, it's not okay," she redirected her attention. "I never wanted to hurt you. I'm so sorry."

"I know," Niles whispered, with a hand pressed to his neck.

"It's not your fault, it's mine," he declared.

"How many others are like me?" she whirled back to him.

He saw the hurt in her eyes. Hurt and betrayal. He did this to her. Kept the truth. It hurt him to see that look in her eye as he hung his head with shame. His silence was answer enough as she bolted.

"Melia!" He ran after her. Should have known better than to take his eyes off her for one second. She was a flight risk. If things had just gotten bad before, now they had become worse. She was in a vulnerable state. He couldn't lose her. Not now.

She was faster. He couldn't keep up. Gave it everything he had, but she became more distant. He couldn't even see her anymore. All he could do was track her. Track her course until she stopped, giving him enough time to catch up. Did she even know where she was going?

His foot got tangled up in a branch. He couldn't overcome the momentum as he fell forward. Favoring his wounded arm, he turned to his good side and slammed against the ground, bouncing a few times as his head cracked against an exposed rock.

He turned over onto his back and looked up into the night sky between the trees. His vision was off. It blurred in and out of focus. He had no idea why. The only thing he did know was that she was not safe on her own. He had to find her before the hooded guy did. Even if she hated him now, he couldn't stop. Whatever was wrong with him had to wait. He had to keep going on.

He pushed himself back to his feet and swayed, while the woods spun. He shook his head and put one foot in front of the other. Had to focus on one thing, finding Melia.

A white blur cut him off.

"Get out of my way," he grumbled, stumbling forward.

"Vince, you're in no condition…"

"I have to find her," he hurled the words like fire, cutting Lamont off.

"We will find her. After you take care of yourself first," Lamont stated.

"You were right. I should have told her before she found out like this," he placed his hand on his head and felt a sticky substance. When he pulled it away, he saw it stained with crimson.

"How did she find out?"

His eyes widened. "Caden."

"What about him?" Lamont's head jerked.

"He got out and bit her."

He caught fleeting concern cross Lamont's aspect. "Where is he now?"

"Last I saw, Cameron was battling with him."

"Cameron's here?" Lamont perked.

He nodded.

"He may have answers we need." Lamont hooked an arm around the center of his back. "Lean on me." Lamont declared as he steered him in the opposite direction of Melia.

He wanted to fight him over the matter, but he didn't have the energy. His injury was severe. Wolf venom slowed his healing process. He didn't know how to function with one arm and his head was pounding. He needed blood. A good amount to re-energize.

Lamont's steps were eager. He was slowing him down. It was the first time he ever experienced Lamont unsettled. He always showed a calm demeanor. Didn't think anything ever phased him. How he was wrong. He didn't like seeing Lamont like this one bit.

They stepped through the doors of the lobby. He wasn't sure what he was expecting, but he wasn't expecting to see Caden in human form with the same four scratch marks on his face. The scar he got from

Leo on the battlefield when he attacked him, even though they were supposed to be on the same side. He had been trying to get to Nadine, but Caden had hindered him until Leo intervened.

"How?" Lamont shifting his eyes between Caden and Cameron.

"The same method Nadia used when she compelled him. A snapping of the fingers," Cameron answered.

"She compelled me?" Caden's husky voice asked in disbelief.

Cameron turned his head and nodded.

"What exactly did she compel him to do?" he probed.

"To kill her," Cameron met his eyes.

He stiffened against Lamont.

"Why would she want me to do that?" Caden asked, baffled.

"She knew you'd be the one who was capable of going through with it." Cameron shifted to Caden.

"All this time, I've had this feeling of being deprived of something. It's because she manipulated my mind and I could never carry out what I was meant to do. How dare her!"

Cameron dropped his head and kept quiet.

"That's why you left," Lamont uttered as Cameron raised his eyes. "You didn't want to bear witness."

"I don't mean to interrupt your reminiscing about Nadia, but what does this have to do with Melia?" Niles cut in.

"Nothing, yet," Lamont answered. "Caden, what do you know of the hooded guy? What does he want with Melia?"

"He offered to help me get what I wanted in exchange for helping him."

"What did he need help with?" he asked with annoyance. He wasn't fond of Caden then, and he wasn't fond of him now.

"All he needed was a key piece of information he didn't have. It was why his attempts to recreate a vampire like Nadia had failed."

"What information was that?" Lamont probed

"Drinking her own blood when she woke, changed."

"I never told you that." Lamont frowned.

"You didn't have to, I overheard it," Caden smirked.

"What does he want with her now?" he grew more impatient.

"He wanted me to bite her. Bite her like I did Nadia."

"For what purpose?"

"That I'm not clear on," Caden shrugged.

He slumped with disappointment.

"What I do know is, her blood tasted different, like Nadia's blood. Sweet, not bitter like when biting into an ordinary vampire."

"And healing," Cameron inserted.

"Vampire blood healing to a wolf?" Lamont tilted his head.

"You don't remember, but I do. You were wounded, severely, by a vampire defending Nadia."

Caden wrinkled his nose.

"She healed you, then she took the memory away. That's when she instructed you to stall Vince on the battlefield. When she asked you to terminate her after she terminated Vladimir."

"You knew she was suicidal and you did nothing to stop her?" he growled, stepping forward.

Lamont tightened his hold.

"You and I both know she was determined and no one would be able to change her mind," Cameron retorted.

"So, we're back at square one. We still have no idea what this hooded guy wants with Melia," Lamont declared.

Chapter 29
Melia

His words reverberated in her mind. She survived on vampire blood, not human blood. Vampire blood. She almost sucked the life out of Niles. That's why he was uncomfortable around her. He knew at any moment she could lose herself to the bloodlust.

She had been petrified. Everything happened so fast. Yet, the moment she smelled that fresh blood, she had lost control of herself. Something deep within had taken over. She forgot to breathe. Nothing else mattered but the blood.

She didn't want to hurt Niles. Or Vince. Or anyone else there. She thought for once in her life she found a place she could belong, but she had been wrong. She was different from the rest. It wasn't fair. It was cruel.

She had no idea where she was going. All she knew was she had to run and never look back. If she stayed away, she couldn't hurt anyone else unintentionally.

She was truly alone now. Had nowhere to go. She couldn't go back home even if she wanted to. Her mother would see her as nothing but a monster. Maybe that's what she was. She had been foolish to think otherwise.

She didn't know how long she ran. She stuck to the trees as best she could. Avoided open areas. Crossed roads when she had no other alternative routes nearby. Jumped over creeks. Bypassed civilization.

She slowed when she saw a little white church appear through the trees ahead slightly to the left. A place she had never seen or been before. The tombstones called to her. The only place she ever felt comfortable speaking what she buried inside was to the spirits of the dead. She didn't know them. They didn't know her. She didn't have to worry about them judging her. Didn't have to see their facial expressions or hear the whispers.

She sank to her knees. "Why? I thought I found a place where I would finally be accepted for who I am. I can never show my face there again after what I did. I'm so tired of being different. So tired of feeling so alone."

"My dear, you are not alone," a weight, light as a feather, bared down on her shoulder before being quickly removed.

She pushed up to her feet, spun around, and stepped back as she found herself face to face with the hooded guy. "What, what do you want?" fear froze her.

"I want to see you get what you want."

"What do you think I want?"

"To be appreciated. To be admired. To be respected as you are, completely."

She remained quiet.

"You hold yourself back abiding by the rules generations have made before your time. Rules that do not evolve, while the world around you continuous evolves anyway. Taught to live a certain way due to the fears of others. In doing so, you live an incomplete life. An unbalance one. You have always felt like something is missing because you live your life as only half of who you are. I can help you embrace your other half."

"I don't want to hurt anyone."

"My dear, it is time for you to stop allowing those to be able to hurt you."

"How do I do that?"

"Power."

She frowned. "I don't understand."

"They have power over you because they make you believe you are powerless."

She dropped her head at the magnitude of truth that rang in his words. All her life, she had been submissive. Never stood up for herself or spoke out in fear of reprimand. She never had the capability to defend herself.

"In order to reclaim power, you must face you past."

She jerked her head and began to shake it violently. She couldn't bear to think about ever going back. It made her sick to her stomach.

"My dear," he removed an object from his oversized sleeve, allowing it to rock back and forth. "Relax."

Her eyes narrowed to a spiral shell wrapped in some twine as it swung back and forth. He repeated the word over and over again until her mind, body, and soul felt at ease.

"I need you to find something."

"Find what?" she asked, with comfort.

"Something that's buried."

"How am I supposed to find it?"

"Close your eyes," his smooth voice instructed.

She obeyed without question.

"Reach out and listen to what calls to you."

She closed off her mind and focused. Focused on whatever it was she was supposed to be listening to. She had no idea what it was or what it was supposed to sound like.

She felt a warmth she wanted to seek out from the direction she had run from. Warmth like a ray of sunshine pointing to a safe place. She felt it, but it did not call to her mind.

"Find me," she heard a voice inside her head, calling that sounded much like her own. It pulled her in the opposite direction from the warmth. Her eyes snapped open as she looked straight ahead with a bit of concern. "What is it?"

"Magic."

"Magic exists?"

"It has always been in existence, but its use suppressed. You, my dear, have the ability to unbound it."

"There must have been a reason why it was contained."

"Fear, my dear, fear. However, just like you, magic is not meant to be caged."

She stiffened. Caged. Exactly how she felt. It was as if he could see to her very core. He saw things about her no one ever did. "What do I do when I find it?"

"The sun is nearly upon us. I will have to find you once the sun sets, as I can only travel in the shadows. Find the object which calls to you and retreat to a place no one can find you."

"I think I know where I can go. How will you find me?"

"Apparition. Where I desire, I can transport."

"So, you're like a ghost?"

"I prefer spirit."

"How does that work?"

126

"Another time, my dear. I must stress that you will have to take precautions as your new acquaintances will be searching for you," he warned.

"How do I keep them from finding me?"

"Mask your scent."

"How."

"Water is a good place to start."

He was gone. She was alone again. Beams of light were starting to break up the night sky. She had so many more questions now, but she had to focus. Focus on finding this lost magical element.

She closed her eyes again and listened. The pull was stronger now. She only had to keep going forward. She also heard something else. Thundering footsteps upon the ground from behind her. She picked up the scent of wolves. She couldn't let them find her. Focusing some more, she picked up on the sound of rushing water.

A river.

She bolted off to the right.

Chapter 30
Vince

One by one, they filed into the control room. He had pushed away from Lamont and pushed through the blurriness, with Cameron and Caden following. His head still pounded and his arm throbbed in protest, but he already lost precious time. He had to find her. Find her before that hooded guy did. That is if he hadn't already found her.

"What happened to you?" Parker's jaw dropped.

"I need you to do your thing and find Melia."

"Okay, what does she look like?"

The veins on his neck constricted.

"Never mind, I can pull up old footage. Hopefully, there's a good image of her on the cameras," his fingers typed lightning fast on the keyboard.

"What is this place?" Caden surveyed the room.

He ignored him.

"Found one. Okay, now, let's see what we can find that's current," Parker performed another search.

"I didn't know how much blood you needed, so I just brought a cart full," Niles entered with a bunch of blood bags.

He lacked to comment as he grabbed a bag and tore into it before grabbing another. He noticed the look of disgust on Caden's face. Gradually, his energy and strength returned as his bone fussed back together and his wounds sealed.

"I'm not getting any hits right now," Parker announced.

"Unacceptable," he threw the empty bag with force against one of the screens.

"Vince, I sent some of my guys out to track her. What you need to do is clear your mind and think. Where would she go?" Lamont calmly stated.

"I don't know. I don't know her that well," he threw up his hands.

"What do you remember?"

He closed his eyes and tried to recall anything significant from the times he spent with Melia. Only he couldn't focus. His mind fired a mile a minute. He was supposed to protect her. He couldn't do that if she wasn't here.

"She was heading south," Lamont encouraged.

"Want me to bring up a map?" Parker asked.

Lamont must have answered as Parker pulled up a map of the immediate area and widened the field. He just stared at it. There wasn't much to see south except greenery while his eyes pulled off to the left as a memory surfaced.

"The river."

"What about the river?" Lamont questioned.

"Parker, pull up the place we found her on the map."

He entered some text into a search field that automatically zeroed into a perimeter of a small town. It was south.

"She could be going to the river in her hometown. She told me she liked going there when she was feeling down."

"Then let's go find her." Lamont turned away and reached up for a pair of keys.

"This time I'm driving," he snatched the keys from him and waltzed out.

"What should I do?" Niles called after.

"Hold down the fort with Darius," he muttered over his shoulder.

"Me?" Niles aspirated.

He didn't care what happened here. All that mattered right now was finding Melia. If anything happened to her, he wouldn't be able to forgive himself. He should have been honest with her in the first place. He had learned nothing from his time with Nadine. Thought he could protect her by keeping vital information she deserved to know about. Both had ended badly. He couldn't go through this again.

"You two might want to fasten your seatbelts," Lamont suggested as he clicked his own into place.

He didn't wait for all the doors to close before he backed out, switched over to drive, and peeled out of the parking lot. Parker had been sensible enough to have the gate open without his request, otherwise he would have smashed through it.

He stomped on the accelerator and sped away. The sun was creeping up taking over the midnight blue sky. He knew his time was limited before the morning commute traffic.

"I don't understand something. Why would I defend Nadia? I despised her. That would have been against my nature," Caden griped.

"She wanted you to remember only despising her," Cameron answered while staring out the window.

"At what point did I ever stop?"

"We were taught to despise vampires. Told they were the enemy. Nadia changed that. It had been hard for me to even accept. It took me a while to see that she was the bridge meant to bring us together," Lamont acknowledged.

He glanced in the rearview mirror and met Caden's eyes. He saw anger masking his confusion.

"If you want your memories back, temporarily for twenty-four hours, from Nadine's compulsion, eat asparagus," he advised.

"What is that?" Caden's nose crinkled.

"A vegetable."

"A vegetable? You want me to eat a vegetable? You do realize I'm a carnivore that survives on meat," Caden protested.

"If you want to continue living in the dark, then by all means." He saw the look Caden gave him, but he did not retort. He knew what it was like to live in conflict. To be taught one thing that wasn't necessary right.

His eyes zeroed on the flashing lights behind him. He sighed with annoyance. He didn't have time for setbacks. He also couldn't afford a chase scene.

He pulled over to the shoulder as the cop parked behind him and sat in his cruiser for an unbearable amount of time as he drummed his fingers on the side door.

"Maybe I should drive afterwards," Lamont proposed.

"No."

He saw the cop open the door, climb out, and make a slow approach. He took in a deep breath and exhaled.

"License and registration, please."

"That won't be necessary. You will give me a warning about speeding and let me go."

"I'm going to let you go with a warning. Be mindful of your speed," the cop mimicked.

"Thank you, officer," he closed the window and took off.

He kept the speed ten miles over the limit when he wasn't slowed down by the traffic on the road. He zipped in and out, changing lanes to get ahead. His grip on the steering wheel tightened.

"If Caden didn't kill Nadia, and she successfully eradicated Vladimir, then how did Nadia die?" Cameron broke the silence.

He shared a brief look with Lamont, who nodded.

"She," he paused and swallowed hard, "killed herself."

"How selfish of her," Caden snapped.

He swung the car to the shoulder and stopped hard before kicking the door open, punching through the glass, grabbing a hold of Caden, and ripping him out through the window. He punched him in the face, hard.

"Vince," Lamont clasped a hand on his fist. "Let's not make a bigger scene.

"He stays behind," he yanked his hand away.

"How did she do it?" Cameron asked from the broken window.

He pierced Cameron's eyes with annoyance. Why did it matter how she killed herself? She did it. There was nothing that could be done now. She wasn't coming back, ever. "She impaled herself."

"With what?"

His eyes narrowed. What was he getting at? The image he tried to block flashed through his mind. How she stabbed herself with the broken end of his mother's wand. How she dissolved away into nothing but a pile of ash.

His eyes widened. The wand. It had been broken into two and thrown into the fire, yet it had not been destroyed. It had not been indestructible until Nadine pierced herself with it. His mother was a witch who created that wand. Nadine had been reluctant to even touch it.

The phone in the SUV started to ring. He rushed over and reached over the console for it.

"Yes, Parker?" he answered.

"I got a hit, but it's farther south from her hometown. I can't be certain as she's traveling in the river, but I think she's heading towards…"

"The asylum," he finished his sentence.

"Yeah. How did you know?"

"Can't explain. Got to go," he hung up.

"Vince? What's going on?" Lamont studied him.

The other half of the wand was still out there somewhere. "I think he wants to bring back magic."

131

Chapter 31
Melia

What once stood was now leveled into one big charred pile of rubbish. There was an enormous amount of negative energy that surrounded the place. A past history of violence and despair. An agony of pain she acknowledged only scratched the surface of her own. There was so much darkness here, even in the direct sunlight. It did not burn anymore, but the smell of toxins lingered. Smoke still trapped in the remains. An acrid aroma that repulsed her.

She wondered how many spirits remained here. Knew for sure now that they did indeed exist. She was uncertain how it worked. The only thing she was certain about was they were unable to linger during the day.

She didn't like being here, but what she was supposed to find had called her here. She walked across the blackened debris carefully. Part of her felt like she'd be sucked into a black hole that was hidden. She was always respectful in the cemetery not to walk over the top of someone's grave. Was she walking over someone's remains buried under? Was she walking over someone's ashes?

She stopped when her inner voice seemed to intensify. She kneeled and began to dig through the rubbish. The charred remains blackened her hands as she continued to rummage. She paused while lines creased upon her forehead. Beneath the burned rubble was half of a smoothed light brown, oddly shaped stick. It did not appear to be touched by the fire, even when everything else was burned to a crisp. Two sections were carved into with round interlacing grooved lines. The one end had jagged edges while the other end fit perfectly in her hand. There was a symbol carved into the handle. A symbol she had seen before. The same symbol above the suit that had belonged to Nadine. Had magic called to her too?

She turned the stick around in her hand. She could feel the pulsating energy within. Energy that wanted to be released. She didn't know how to release it. She wasn't even sure if she should.

She turned it around some more before looking at the end of the handle and was able to make out a spiral. A symbol that was sacred. A symbol that was linked to nature. One she found herself to doodle often. She had no idea if this was supposed to mean anything to her or if it was just a coincidence.

Now that she found what she was looking for, she could leave this dreadful place and hoped she never had to see it again. This was where the war had happened between vampires and werewolves. Once divided, now united, somewhat. She could have never summoned up enough courage to fight. Not like Nadia. A thought occurred to her. Was she a vampire like her? Did Nadia feed on vampire blood? She never understood why the werewolves had taken her in. Unless her enemy was their enemy. If only she had survived. Then she wouldn't have been the only one.

She swam up the river that lead to her hometown. It was easier to stay submerged when she didn't require oxygen. It was like she was in another world. One only she could appreciate.

She allowed her instincts to guide her. Watched above the surface for familiar terrain. She had spent so much time on the riverbanks that wind through her hometown and knew every inch. For the first time, she was able to appreciate what the river had to offer beyond her turf.

She swam just beyond her father's workplace. Hovered in the water to ensure no one was around before she pulled herself up on the bank. Her clothing clung to her and dripped as she squeezed the water from her hair. Listening to the traffic on the road, she waited for a break and dashed across it into the trees. She stuck to the trees, arched around the cemetery, and paused to take it in. A place where her whole life had changed. She had been hopeful that it was for the good, but now she was unsure. Being back in her hometown was discomforting.

She continued across the barren landscape until she was behind a row of homes. She proceeded to her father's rundown trailer. It sat on a half-acre lot and had seen better days. It sat uninhabited. Her mother couldn't do anything to it since her father had left it to her for when she turned eighteen.

She stepped up onto the small back porch. She didn't have the key, but she didn't need one. The doorknob twisted off right in her hand. She entered and closed the door behind her.

This was the first time she had been inside since her father had passed. There was a lot of dust and mildew her nose picked up on, but his scent also lingered. His scent brought so many mixed emotions of happiness and sadness.

She navigated down the narrow hallway and paused outside the door to her room. She let the door swing open and tilted her head to the ceiling, where a portrayal of *Starry Night* was painted by both her father and her hands. It wasn't perfect, but it was a memory to be cherished. She loved falling asleep as if she were under the stars.

She did not need sleep or was tired, but she walked over to her small bed and laid down, transfixed on the painting above. Remembered that day vividly. She had paint everywhere. On her face, in her hair, on her coveralls, which saved her clothing underneath, and on the floor. They had had a paint brawl that her mother would have disapproved if she had known about it. It was their secret.

The light through the window was starting to fade. She had no idea how long she spent in her room. Long enough for the sun to start slipping away.

She rose from her bed and slowly made her way back into the hallway. She stood there with hesitation before she summoned enough strength to approach her father's room.

His bed was still left a mess. He was never one who enjoyed fixing his bed. Saw no point when you were only going to untidy it when jumping back in.

A sad smile formed at the picture of her on his dresser in a yellow frame that read *You Are My Sunshine*. A gift she had given him.

She stared at herself in a trans-like state in the small mirror over his dresser. Stared without really seeing. Stared without really feeling. She was numb.

Movement caught her attention in the mirror. Another image had appeared. She rose and spun to face the hooded spirit on the other side of the bed across the room.

"Let it out, my dear."

She grabbed the framed picture and hurled it against the wall with an ear-piercing shriek before crumpling to the floor, hugging her knees, rocking back and forth.

"Why did you have to leave me?" she sobbed. She let the red tears fall. She was both upset and realized, angry. All this time, she had been suppressing her anger out of guilt. He was supposed to be here for her. Had promised her a place of happiness. He broke his promise.

Chapter 32
Vince

He filled them in about his mother, Immilla. How she went to battle with her own father, who had been siphoning dark magic from witches burned at the stake. That it was magic that had created them into the creatures they were today. How the magic was closed off and witches ceased to exist.

He didn't know who the guy in the hood was exactly, but he assumed it was Immilla's father. Somehow, he had come back from the dead. He didn't know for sure how his mother prevailed against him since she never wrote it down in her journal, but since there were no witches or magic around, she must have been successful.

When Nadine found half the wand hidden in Marc's hidden cave, she had refused to touch it. When he offered it to her before the war, she had been hesitant. At the time, he didn't understand what was causing her odd behavior. Now he was seeing it from a different perspective. Did she somehow know magic was still present inside of the broken piece? Was she able to access it? Was that the reason she killed herself? To keep the magic from being unleashed again?

The ground was still a heap of charred destruction. All the memories flooded his mind as if the war had just happened yesterday, not over six months ago. He still carried all the guilt and all the pain. It weighed down on his shoulders. He never thought he would come back to this vile place. Yet, here he was in broad daylight. Not even the sun could light up such a dark place.

"She's not here," Lamont returned from tracking the area along with Cameron and Caden.

He didn't need Lamont to confirm what he already knew in his heart. She had a head start. If she was traveling by the river, they wouldn't be able to pick up on her scent. The only thing they could do now was return to her hometown and see if she had returned by chance.

He heard the line picked up. "Parker, I need you to find everything you can on Melia."

"You have a last name?"

He stared blankly. He never asked. Had never thought to ask. Hadn't wanted to really get to know her in the first place. Realized he had been keeping his guard up around her.

"I can't do much without one," Parker continued.

"I'll get it for you," he disconnected.

"So, what now?" Lamont asked.

"Go to the place she worked."

"How's that going to help?" Caden asked sarcastically.

He ignored him. Didn't know why he didn't leave him behind like he wanted to in the first place. Could barely tolerate his presence and attitude.

He allowed Lamont to drive while he bounced his leg in the passenger seat looking out the window. He had been foolish. He should have spent more time with her and gotten to know her better. Instead he pushed her away. Withheld information. This was all on him.

"Pull over," he requested as they passed the cemetery where they found her.

Lamont complied, pulling into the parking lot.

He climbed out of the car and walked over to the spot where he had gathered her petite body into his arms. She had looked so peaceful in her slumber. What had she been doing at the cemetery in the middle of the night in the first place? An unusual place for someone to go.

She had only talked about her father, who had passed. He knew nothing about her mother. Did she live with her? Did she have a good relationship with her mother? He had this sense she wasn't happy here.

He climbed back into the SUV. No one spoke as Lamont slowly drove on. Within a few minutes, he had him pull into a spot at the food mart.

"Why were you so insistent to know how Nadine died?" he craned his neck around the seat at Cameron.

"I watched her struggle every day to hide the pain. She kept busy, so she wasn't alone with her thoughts, but there were times she was.

She'd cut herself after every vampire kill, always disappointed that no mark was left behind as a reminder what she had done," Cameron's eyes lifted.

"Becoming a vampire destroyed her wellbeing."

"No, becoming a killer did."

He never viewed it from that perspective before. Never understood why she was so adamant in not becoming a vampire. When times called for it, he didn't bat an eye. In his world, it was kill or be killed. He was starting to realize he hardly knew Nadine as well.

"She lost control, one day, not realizing her own strength when she was practicing throwing her dagger and caused a large chunk of rock to fall down from the ceiling in her chamber. It nearly crushed me, but she managed to pull me away just in time."

"I remember that day," Lamont commented. "I knew it wasn't just some random accident. I can't believe you lied to me about it."

"She always acted like she didn't care about anyone or anything, but in that moment, I saw she was lying even to herself. She did care and she couldn't turn that part of herself off," Cameron paused turning to Caden. "She knew you despised her yet she didn't want to see you banished. She even tried to stop you from going to the vampires and betraying the pack."

"Guess she didn't try hard enough," Caden uttered with a snark tone.

"When I get my hands on some asparagus, I'm going to shove it down your throat," his hands clenched into fists.

"My opinion won't change." Caden folded his arms against his chest.

"We'll see about that," he pushed the door open and stepped out of the vehicle.

Caden was infuriating. He didn't know how Nadine ever put up with him. He didn't even know why he had come with them in the first place. Melia meant nothing to him. He was regretting not leaving him on the side of the road even more. If they found Melia, would he try to do something to her?

He walked in and made his way to the first employee his eyes landed on. An older gentleman.

"Can I help you?" the man smiled politely.

"I'm hoping you can," he leaned forward and spoke low. "Do you know a girl named Amelia? She worked here."

"Amelia? Yeah, I know her. Sweet girl. Terrible about what happened. She just disappeared. Why do you ask?"

"I'm trying to gather some information. This was the last place she was seen, correct?"

"Yeah. Who did you say you were, again?" the man asked with suspicion.

"What was her last name?" he stared directly into his eyes.

"Sinclair."

"Thank you. Now, you will forget about this conversation," he walked away.

Chapter 33
Melia

S he stared at the surface of water collected in a small gully behind the woods from her father's trailer. She had not known about this place. It was a bit of a walk from the trailer a lot further than she had ever explored. She was not as apprehensive about becoming lost like she used to as a human. She had heightened senses now, so all she needed to do was focus to find her way.

"Are you ready?"

That was the question she kept asking herself over and over again. Even though she was a vampire, part of her was still skeptical that magic existed.

She rotated the broken stick in her hand. Felt the energy and heard the whispers. There was power in it. Immense power. She questioned if she should release it.

"My dear, do not let fear restrain you. What you hold in your hand is the possibility of seeing your father again."

She stilled and looked over. "Isn't there a rule about magic that no one can be brought back from the dead?"

"Cognitive magic has no limitations. What you desire you can achieve, but it takes a great deal of practice."

"You'll help me?"

"Of course, my dear."

She inhaled deeply before she pricked her finger on the jagged end. She watched compelled as the edge seemed to suction her blood before a jolt of energy rushed through her veins. It traveled down her hand, up through her arm, shot across to her other arm while down the rest of the length of her body. She never felt more alive inside. Like she was on top of the world, invincible. She had this newfound strength within.

"How does it feel?"

"Exhilarating," she was breathless.

"Good, now the real work begins. I want you to reach out as if you are touching the water, scoop up a handful, and suspend it in the air," his oversized sleeve reached out. "I'll hold that for you."

She nodded, handed over the stick, and noted it suspended in air from an invisible hand. She turned her attention to the water. Slowly, she reached out with her right hand and mimicked his words with disappointment as nothing happened. She inhaled through her nose and exhaled out her mouth before trying again, with no success. She sighed with frustration.

"Focus and visualize the motion."

She closed her eyes for a moment before reopening them and trying once more. Nothing happened. She repeated the motion over and over again. Each time was unproductive.

"Why don't you reach down and touch the water? Feel it beneath your fingers."

She bent down by the edge and dipped her hand into the water and watched the drips rain back down onto the surface with a rippling effect. She closed her hand, feeling the moisture before shaking off the rest and standing.

With determination, she visualized her hand dipping into the water, scooping it up in her hand, and holding it above. She felt a bit of energy pull into her hand, but once more nothing happened.

"When you were standing in your father's room, what emotions were you feeling."

"Mostly sadness, but also a bit of anger."

"Conjure up that emotion and reflect it in your motion."

She turned her head away from the water and from him. Didn't want to let that moment back in. Shouldn't have felt mad at her father. It wasn't his fault he got cancer. He had tried to quit smoking for her by limiting himself. If she should be angry with anything it should be with the cancer not him. Cancer is what took him from her.

This time, she stared directly at the water. Imagined her hand under the surface, lifting it up. Visualized it suspended above her hand. She felt a vibrant force gather to the palm of her hand. Her mind was completely focused on the action before her eyes recognized an orb of water suspended in the air. As soon as she saw it, her eyes went wide as it dropped back down. She covered her mouth with her hands in shock.

"I did it."

"Very good," she detected a smile in his voice. "Now, do it again."

She conjured up that feeling to put in motion the action as she scooped up an orb of water again and again. Some were small, but the more she practiced, the bigger the orb of water grew.

With each successful attempt, she felt her energy level depleting. The bigger the orb, the more energy expelled. She was uncertain of her limitations.

"I feel tired." The tiredness was not from a lack of blood. She had not felt this drained since she was human.

"Magic is heavy to the inexperienced. While the sun is up, you shall rest while the sunlight revitalizes you. I will return at dusk."

Without another word, he was swallowed by the shadows. She had not been paying attention to how long they spent outside in the dark. Now she realized dawn was nearly creeping in.

She took off through the woods back to her father's trailer. She was astonished she had the energy to run with her vampire speed. It was an odd feeling to feel drained, but also alive at the same time.

She crept through the trailer, pausing at her room and assessed the environment. Her room faced the front and had a small window that did not have a lot of access to sunlight. She continued down to her father's room. His room faced the back with a larger window that allowed more sunrays in. She opened the curtains completely. She basked momentarily in the direct sunlight.

She walked over, picked up the broken frame, and set it back on the dresser before cleaning the shards of glass from the floor.

She fixed the bed, smoothing out all the wrinkles. Once satisfied, she turned her attention to the dresser. Pulled the first drawer open and saw single socks littering the bottom. She pulled out the drawer and dumped the contents onto the bed. A small wooden box tumbled out as well. Inscribed on the top of the box was the name *Synklar*. She opened the box and found a yellow-gold carved spiral made from wood. It hung from a black waxed cotton cord. Never saw it before and wasn't sure if it meant anything, but it belonged to him. It had to be meaningful somehow, plus it was something she could carry with her every day and cherish. She didn't have to hide it. Could wear it visibly with pride. In her mother's world, she was never allowed to wear jewelry. She wasn't in her mother's world anymore. She was in a different world now. A world that had its own rules, but not as strict as from the one she came from.

She turned on the stereo on his dresser, bypassed the radio and pressed play. Waited to hear what CD he had left inside as she fiddled with the spiral in her fingers. She smiled as she fell back onto the bed when she heard the first three chords of the Evanescence song off the album *Fallen*. It was both their favorite album and artist, which had been released exactly on the same day as her second birthday.

She used to be terrified her mother would find out. She knew she would have been livid and completely disapproved of her listening to this kind of music. It was dark. It was sinful. Yet, she had a hauntingly deep connection to the instrumentals and to the majority of the lyrics. It was as if the artist knew how she felt inside and allowed her to be able to express what was trapped.

She allowed the music to play on repeat as she soaked up the sun and inhaled her father's scent. She felt at home. Felt at peace. She lay there with her eyes closed, transported back in time as her strength rejuvenated.

Chapter 34
Vince

He pulled into the small driveway facing the small white one-level ranch home and parked. He didn't move. This is where Melia had lived. It hadn't been too far from the place she had worked. Parker hadn't found much on her. She was a respectable girl who never missed a day of school or work. Had above average grades, but nothing exceptional. Went to church faithfully every Sunday. She was a good obedient girl.

"You want me to go with you?" Lamont asked.

"What if I'm wrong? What if she didn't come here and we are just wasting time?"

"Where else would she go?"

"That's just it. I don't know. I don't know anything."

"What are you afraid of finding out?" Lamont asked pointedly.

He looked over at Lamont. Was he afraid? Of what?

He pulled the handle and bumped the door open with his elbow before slipping out. As he closed the door, the garage door began to open. He paused, watching the door rise. Heard the passenger door close before he saw a woman appear with a box in her hand, heading to the open trunk of her white Altima. She stopped in her tracks, eyeing them wearily.

She looked similar to Melia, except older and rough around the edges. Her blonde hair was thinner and sandy looking compared to Melia's lavish honey-blonde hair. Her eyes were dark brown and cold looking.

"Who are you?" her eyes shifted between them.

He found no words.

"Are you Jocelyn Sinclair?" Lamont asked.

She walked the rest of the way to the back of her car, set down her box, and folded her arms. "Who's asking?"

"My name is Lamont. This is my partner, Vince," Lamont took the lead. "We are detectives assigned to your missing daughter's case."

"Are you now? Mind showing me some credentials?"

"Absolutely, Vince?"

He saw it. A slight lip curl at the mention of her daughter. She didn't seem to be too upset that her daughter was missing. Melia had never talked about her mother. He now realized he was afraid to find out what their relationship had been. Knew what it was like to feel unloved by a parent. Didn't want to uncover that she experienced that kind of pain as well.

"I've got it right here," he reached into his pocket while closing the gap. "You will invite us in for a little talk."

"Why don't you two come inside?" she turned and headed for the open side door in the garage.

He followed while his eyes drifted to the box in the trunk that was filled with a bunch of clothing. He inhaled, picking up on Melia's scent on the material. His hands turned into fists as he took in a deep breath before he stepped into the kitchen, with Lamont following behind him.

"What would you two like to talk about?" she crossed her arms.

"Your daughter, Amelia, went missing several days ago, correct?" Lamont verified.

"Yes."

"What do you think happened to her?"

"I don't think. I know. She ran away. Ran away because she is self-centered."

"She's anything but self-centered," he lashed out.

"Vince," Lamont warned.

"You say that as if you know her," Jocelyn studied him.

"If you think she ran away, where would she go?"

"I don't care. She's not my problem anymore. I had to give up my life because of her and she was never grateful for what I had to sacrifice. She better never come back here because she won't be welcomed."

"So, you're just going to erase her? Go on with your life as if she never existed?" he spit out with bitterness.

"If only it was that easy, but I still have to be reminded every day. The community still prays for her safe return. All I ever hear about everywhere I go is about her."

"So, you have not seen her since she disappeared and you don't expect her to come back?" Lamont paraphrased.

"Like I said, she wouldn't be welcomed. Not in my house. Not after everything she's put me through. She's so eager to be a grown-up and make her own foolish choices, so be it."

"Thank you for your time. We'll see ourselves out," Lamont nodded.

"The least one of you could do, since you wasted my time on that selfish person, is carry out my box of canned goods to the car," Jocelyn pointed at the box on the table.

"I got it, I'll meet you at the car," Lamont hinted a small smile in her direction before meeting his and nodding his head.

"I'll get it," he bumped his shoulder into Lamont and cut him off.

He snatched the box as the can goods shifted around. Took stock of what was inside. Noted cans of soup, beans, mushrooms, vegetables, jars of jelly, small cans of tuna, a bottle of honey, and some containers of spices. "You got a lot packed in here. Did you save any for yourself?"

"I don't eat any of that stuff, so it's going to the church as a donation."

"I understand why she ran away from you. You are the selfish one," he stepped down into the garage, tossed the box in the trunk and thundered away.

"How dare you!" She shouted after him.

He opened the door, chucked a can of asparagus at Caden before climbing in, yanked the control into reverse and pealed out of the driveway as Lamont closed his door beside him.

He sped down the narrow lane and blew right past the stop sign and disregarded the yellow warning slow sign.

"Vince, slow down," Lamont begged.

He ignored him as he gripped the wheel. Had to get as far away from Melia's mother as he could before he did something he would regret. Saw the same look in Jocelyn's eyes that his father had in his.

Loathing.

Disgust.

Unloving.

She valued her life more than her daughter. He knew what it was like to feel unwanted. To be a bother. To lose the only person who ever truly cared for you and be stuck with a parent who shunned you. Knowing there was nothing you could ever do to win their love.

"Where do we go now?" Cameron boldly asked.

He eased off the accelerator. Melia's mother was a loose cannon. He doubted she would ever go back to her. The only person she would go to was her father, but he was deceased. He felt completely helpless. How was he supposed to find her? She could be anywhere. Why hadn't Parker found her on a camera? How could she just disappear?

"How about we wait for nightfall and we can search the area," Lamont suggested.

"We are just wasting time here."

"All is not lost. We will find her. It's just going to take more time than you like."

"How can you stay so positive all the time?" a car horn blared behind him.

He flicked his eyes to the rearview mirror and saw Jocelyn's Altima. He gritted his teeth before making a right onto the main road next to the elementary school and watched as she turned in the opposite direction.

Fresh blood never felt so tempting before.

Chapter 35
Melia

She opened her eyes as the light began to fade. She was re-energized. Eager to learn more as she stood by the window and waited for the sun to fade. Wondered what she would learn next as she glanced down at her hands. Power pulsating within. It was exciting and scary at the same time. To feel this power. To hold this power.

"Are you well rested, my dear?"

She turned towards his voice. She was still not used to him appearing at random. "Yes."

"Good. This next lesson will require all of your strength, but first you must acquire an emotion to relate with."

"What do you mean?" she frowned.

"There's a great deal of weight inside of yourself that grounds you. That unbalances you. In order to let it go, you have to face the one who failed to nurture you."

"No," she shook her head, backing up against the wall. "No, I can't."

"You must," his voice rose an octave.

"Please, don't make me."

"I'm not making you do anything you don't already want to do," the rock wrapped in twine swayed. "You know deep inside in order to be truly free, you have to face your past."

"I don't know where to begin."

"I will guide you, for you are not alone."

She grabbed a hold of her necklace for added strength before summoning the courage to put one foot in front of the other. Her destination wasn't far. Before she lost her nerve, she kept on the move and stayed hidden as much as she could in the woods. Crossed a street and snuck behind homes closer to town. She paused behind the one-level ranch style home. A place she never thought she'd have to see again. A place she never thought she would return to.

She walked over to the side garage door and pushed her way through. It was dark and no car present. She walked across the length of the garage and entered. All the lights were off and no one was home.

There were Bible verses hanging over all the kitchen walls, along with a portrait of Jesus. A warm, welcoming, and positive environment. Her eyes wandered over to the stove, knowing it was a lie.

She made her way through the house. Every inch carried a verse. Carried a story. Stories she never shared that she kept secret. Stories of despair.

She found her bed neatly made with fresh, clean beige sheets with no wrinkles to be seen. She walked over to her dresser and stared down at the thick Bible. Believed with her whole heart everything that was written, but she didn't believe in her mother's ways. In the church's ways.

She opened each drawer and found that everything she had ever owned was gone. As if she never existed. Someone easily erased. A forgotten memory.

She sat in the small kitchen quietly. Part of her was itching to run and never look back, but there was another part, a stronger part, that made her stay.

The door creaked open as the lights flicked on. Her mother, with her long dirty-blonde hair trailing behind, paused as she took her in.

"You think you have the right to come back here after humiliating me with your stunt?" her mother's arms crossed in front of her chest.

Her automatic reflex was to cringe at her callous tone as her eyes peered to the next room still griped by darkness. His dark hood aided in blending unseen by a human's eye, but not to hers. His words chanted in her mind.

"Stupid girl. You look like a whore. First thing you do is break every rule. You're a disappointment. Always were. You're going to burn in Hell and you deserve it."

"I haven't broken every rule," she stood. "Not yet."

She grabbed the pair of scissors lying on the table. In one fluid motion, she pulled her loose messy braid forward and cut off a big chunk of her hair. She looked at her hair dangling in the air in front of her for a moment before letting it drop to the floor.

"You selfish little..." her mother advanced forward with her hand raised.

She caught her mother's wrist in mid-air. "No."

Her mother stared at her, shocked.

"I won't allow you to hurt me anymore. You were supposed to take care of me. Nurture me. Protect me," she paused, "Love me. Instead, you were manipulative. Controlling. Abusive."

"Oh, you poor thing. Is that why you came back? You found a little confidence and now you want pity?" her mother yanked her arm away.

"You did this to me." She held up her scarred palm.

"Because you lied."

"I didn't lie. You just didn't want to believe it was true."

"I want you out of my house now!"

"You pretend to be this perfect moral person to everyone you meet, but you have a malicious heart who hates her own daughter."

"I'm calling the cops," her mother grabbed the cordless phone off the counter.

"He," she swallowed hard. "Raped me, and you silenced me by burning my hand on the stove."

"I'll do it to your other hand," her mother charged, grabbing her left arm and pulled her over to the stove turning the dial to high heat.

"I won't let you hurt me again," she ripped her hand away and showed her gruesome face.

Her mother shrieked, backing away. "Get away from me. You're the devil."

" '...as he has caused disfigurement of a man, so shall it be done to him,' " she recited. "You burned my hand, now I shall burn yours."

Her mother screamed in agony as her skin sizzled and singed against the red-hot coil. She released her hold as her mother yanked back and whimpered in pain. There was a part of her that hurt inside for hurting her own mother the same way, but it was far in the back of her mind.

"How does it feel, not to be in control? How does it feel, to feel powerless?" There was nothing more to say as she exited through the door into the garage and back out the side door before taking off into the woods.

"You did good, my dear," he materialized in front of her.

Mixed emotions overwhelmed her, but she heard the pride in his voice. He was pleased. She liked the way it made her feel. To be enough as she was.

"She poisoned your mind and your soul. Sucked the life out of you. In letting go, you are able to regenerate. Touch the ground and let new life emerge."

She breathed in and out slowly before kneeling to the leaf littered forest floor. Delicately, she placed her left hand on the ground. She wasn't sure what he was looking for. Her hand pulsated to the same lively rhythm beneath the surface. Life buried beneath. Life that wanted to burst free.

She summoned the sentiment of the encounter with her mother. She was now unbound. Never had to go back to that way of life, restrained.

She felt that same vibrant force release. She opened her eyes and saw a path of wildflowers emerged, including many Black-Eyed Susan, her favorite.

"Walk the path."

Chapter 36
Melia

She reminisced about the feel of the flowers beneath her bare feet as she walked across them. With every step she took, new flowers blossomed underfoot. When she looked back, they had shriveled up and wilted back into the earth. A representation of her past relationship with her mother.

By mid-afternoon, the sunrays were invaded by dark gray clouds. She had gathered enough energy to be recharged. She felt it. Hadn't expelled as much energy overnight. She was awake and so alive.

She looked down at her long skirt. There was one more thing she had the need to change. Change from who she was. Change into who she always wanted to become.

She headed to her dresser. It was still filled with all her forbidden belongings she received from her father. A book about Wicca. She had always felt connected to nature. Felt its energy. Took time to appreciate it. Respected it.

Continuing to rummage, she searched until she found her favorite casual stretchy hunter green pants. She removed her skirt and slipped them on. Wearing them had always felt like a sin. She only ever wore them in the house. Never outside. She couldn't risk being seen by anyone who would report back to her mother. Didn't have to worry anymore. She never had to wear a skirt again.

She admired herself in the bathroom mirror. Her hair was a choppy mess just pass her shoulders. She brushed through it. She didn't recognize the face in the mirror. Wasn't sure who she was anymore. She was free now, but still felt alone. Something was missing. She felt incomplete.

She walked back into her room and gawked at the skirt she had tossed on the bed. With a sigh, she slumped down on her bed and stared up at *Starry Night,* but wasn't really seeing.

An idea surfaced her mind. She rolled off the bed and grabbed her skirt. She entered the kitchen, grabbed a pencil along with the pair of scissors from the drawer, and walked into the living room sitting down on the floor spreading out her skirt. She studied it carefully before sketching lines around the front. When satisfied, she cut along the lines around the skirt until the front half was removed, stopping just below the elastic of the waistline. After cutting off frayed threads, she rose and pulled it back on. The front was open while the back trailed behind her. She spun in a circle. It didn't feel exactly the same, but she liked the feel when walking as the momentum of her speed waved it behind her. She was satisfied.

When she heard raindrops beat against the roof, she headed towards the small back porch that sloped to the ground. She watched the rain fall peacefully. Closed her eyes and visualized what she desired before flicking them open, reaching out with both her hands, and pushing them apart. The rain parted like a curtain following her hands, leaving an untouched space where it did not fall upon anymore. As soon as she lowered her hands, the rain resumed falling normal.

"That came to you more effortlessly, my dear," his voice came from inside.

"I can see your hands," she saw large translucent hands down by his side.

"Yes, it appears the magic you harness enhances my form."

"I'm sorry. I just realized I never asked you your name."

"Why do you want to know my name?"

"To know what I should call you," she frowned. "I don't think I ever gave you mine. I'm Melia."

"If you insist in calling me something then call me Max."

"Max," she smiled. "It's nice to meet you Max."

"The pleasure is all mine, my dear."

"How long have you been a spirit?"

"I believe you need to focus on your next task," he withdrew the rock wrapped in twine. She could now see it clasped in his hand, gently moving back and forth. "It's time for your voice to be heard."

She didn't know when the rain had stopped. Didn't know when she trekked away from her father's home to the outskirts of town. Felt sick to her stomach seeing the red brick church from the bushes across the field of grass. Watched a few stragglers climb into their car and leave the evening service until all the cars were gone.

She waited patiently as the breeze picked up, blowing strands of her hair across her face tickling it. She was still getting used to how light her head felt with less hair. When he stepped out the side door, she advanced.

"Amelia, you've come back to us," his angelic voice churned her stomach even more.

She stared at Pastor Samael swallowing down the bile that always mustered as a reflex in his presences. She wanted to run and never look back. Run as far from here as she possibly could, but her legs did not listen. They remained planted in place, where she stood.

"What happened to you, my child?" his eyes had that way of violating her.

"I'm here to confess."

"Of course, come," he reopened the side door and hung back.

"You first," she didn't move.

The lines on his forehead creased in confusion. He pushed his glasses back up the bridge of his nose before reentering.

Slowly, she took one step at a time and paused, observing inside, before entering. She closed the door behind her.

"Has someone hurt you, child?"

"Stop calling me child. I'm not your child," her hands clenched into fists.

"We are all God's children."

"Yes, I'm a child of God, but not yours."

"I sense some hostility within you."

She walked out of the room and into the hall, listening to his every sound behind her as he followed. Continued past the pews and stopped at the bottom of the steps that led to the altar. Kneeled, folded her hands together, and prayed in her inner voice.

"You cut your glorious hair," he reached out.

"Don't touch me," she leaned back, stepping up and away.

"You have changed," he smirked.

"No, I am liberated. Free to be who I want to be, not bound by anyone's rules, especially yours."

"His rules."

"No, you take His words and twist them to suit your needs in order to gain control."

"I can assure you that He speaks through me. I'm distraught to hear you have doubts."

"My doubts have always been in you, not Him. I don't need to come here in order to believe."

"So, why did you come here?" annoyance crossed his face.

"... *'But if you do what is evil, be afraid'*."

He tossed back his head and laughed cynically. "Afraid in my own house?"

"You forced yourself onto me in what was supposed to be my safe haven and you left your mark," she lifted her sweater, revealing the three cigarette burns. "Now I'm going to show you what evil truly looks like."

The smirk on his face faltered when she allowed her teeth to lengthen and eyes to blow out of proportion.

"You've been possessed," he turned and ran down the aisle.

She darted to the opposite end, blocking his path to the exit.

"Stay away from me," he picked up a Bible and hurled it at her.

She snatched it from the air. Saw the fear in his eyes before he took off in the opposite direction. Stumped her foot on the floor as the ground trembled beneath. He stumbled catching himself on the back of a pew pushing himself up to his feet. She closed her eyes and concentrated. All the windows in the room shattered into a million pieces as a wind forcefully entered. One by one, pews started ripping up from the floor and projectile across the room smashing into the walls, splintering into pieces.

"Amelia, please, I have children," he shouted over the noise hunched over in a ball protecting his head.

She let the wind gather underneath her and lift her into the air above him.

"Confess," she demanded.

"Forgive me Father for I have sinned," he began.

"No," she cut him off as another pew smashed against the wall near him. "Not to Him. Not to me."

"But my reputation will be ruined."

"Punishment as it should be for destroying every young girl's life you could get your hands on in this town."

"Please, don't make me do this. My wife and children need me," he sobbed uncontrollably.

"What they need is the truth," she brought her hands together and pushed air into his direction, causing him to fall back. "And to know that you will never be able to hurt anyone again."

She motioned with her left hand, scooping up a shrapnel of glass letting the airstream carry it before letting it drop down with vigor between his legs.

His agonizing scream was so ear-piercing she had to tune down her hearing.

"You're not in control anymore. And you never will be again," she propelled herself out the open window riding the current of wind she commanded.

Chapter 37
Vince

When darkness came as a cover, they searched for her scent on both sides of the river that wound through town and the cemetery where they found her, but came up with nothing. He tried not to be disappointed, but he was.

They hung out at the food mart where she had worked and asked those coming and going if they knew anything about Amelia that they didn't know before. Basically, what they were told was all the same. She was a sweet girl and helpful around the community, only they didn't know much about her personal life. All information provided he already knew.

"There's one place we know for sure she will return to eventually," Lamont mentioned in a casual tone.

"Where?" he stared at him in dismay.

"There's only one place she can go to that will satisfy her hunger."

He blinked, stupefied. "Why didn't you say something before now?"

Why hadn't he thought about it in the first place? She didn't feed on human blood. Could she even survive on human blood at all when vampire blood was not present?

"You're not exactly one who likes to wait around twiddling your thumbs," Lamont answered.

He couldn't argue with that. "Yeah, well, I don't appreciate you withholding vital information that could end up risking our chances of finding her sooner."

"I know she can survive for up to three days without blood, just like you can."

"So, does that mean we are going back? I could use to replenish energy myself," Caden inquired.

"If you're so hungry, eat the asparagus," he scoffed as he pulled onto the road and headed out of town.

157

"I much rather continue to dislike everything about your kind."

"So, why did you come with us?" Cameron challenged.

He saw the disconcertment Caden gave Cameron before turning his attention away without another word. Wondered about that himself. He made it clear he didn't like Nadine and Melia meant nothing to him. Had also dispersed from the pack after the war. What had he been doing all this time before the hooded guy found him? He should question him further, but he was Lamont's problem and not one he wanted to get involved in. At least not yet. The only thing that mattered right now to him was Melia.

The first thing he did when he returned was pay a visit to Parker, only to be let down that there were still no leads. He made his rounds and checked in, being questioned every step he took. He hated it. Being questioned. Being the center of attention. Having no answers. Letting the ones who grew fond of Melia down. He felt like such a failure.

He stood at Nadine's suit. The only place he could go to get away from everyone. The evening was exactly how he felt inside.

Gloomy.

Melancholy.

Without sunshine.

Cameron's words echoed in his mind the evening before. *"You honor her by the very thing that destroyed her?"* He never thought he could be even more wounded. Even more ashamed. This had been her transformation of a killer. The very thing she fought so hard against. Why had he been so naïve?

"I was a blinded fool, wasn't I? Was so busy trying to fix everything that I never listened. Now I fear I made the same mistake."

He reached out and touched the material. Felt nothing but emptiness. The aromatic scent it used to carry had faded, blown away by wind and washed off by rain. It hardly had a scent at all.

What he once thought of as a symbol of remembrance was instead a symbol of fear to hold over the vampires. He was holding onto an image of her that was distorted.

He ripped the suit from the fence and let it fall to the ground. Ripped the Dragon's Eye symbol and chucked it over the fence. Turned and walked away without looking back.

As he walked through the facility, the environment was different. He didn't like it. Couldn't comprehend what was buried beneath that was trying to surface. The familiarity was off.

He rapped three times. When the door opened, he was greeted by Darius. He obediently bowed his head and opened the door wide to allow him entry. His loyal comrade. The very first one he turned. Homeless and on the streets. Had wanted to become a marine like his father, but had been disqualified for being over eighty inches. After disappointment, his mother had fallen ill, so he had taken care of her while the medical bills piled up and worked whatever white-collar jobs he could find. When she passed, he was left with nothing.

"Anything new on Melia?" Darius inquired.

"Afraid not," he sighed.

He liked the fact that Darius did not push him further, unlike the others who bombarded him with questions. Had no idea what the future might hold. If she would pose a threat to them. If she truly was the key in bringing magic back. Something he kept to himself in order not to cause any more panic.

He positioned himself in front of Camille's cell. There was still bitterness inside of him. Leo was still with her. He had managed to make her surrender her guarded posture. She sat Indian-style with him curled in her lap, stroking the back of his neck while he purred with glee. He didn't know what relationship Leo had with Camille when she was human, but he now clearly saw that Leo was consoling her.

"He has her, doesn't he?" she whispered without breaking stride with her strokes.

"Why?" his radio crackled. He never got clear reception in D-Block.

Her hand stopped hovering above Leo's head. Slowly, her eyelids flicked as her brown eyes met his. Her mouth twitched before her eyes lowered. "I was jealous."

"Jealous?" his head jerked. "Of what?"

She looked away. "She had a choice, mine was taken. She had both of you who were fond of her, I had no one. She stood firmly without anyone being able to influence her. I stood on shaky ground."

He turned away, disgusted at her admission. How could she have been jealous of her friend? He heard the honesty in her voice and the humiliation. Something he wouldn't have picked up on before. His mind would have been quick to turn to anger as it took hold of him, pushing aside all reason. Anger, a defense mechanism. Anger, that could control him if unleashed. Anger, that could blind all logic. A response from jealously. He had tunnel vision when he was face to face with Marc. Had shoved Nadine out of his way just to get to him.

159

Only saw him as a vile monster he wanted to destroy and would have gone to any length.

He diverted his attention when he heard a knock on the door. He watched Darius make his way over, unlocked it from the inside, and cracked it open. Without warning, he jolted back and crashed to the floor as the door burst wide open. The wolves clashed with three wolves that stormed in.

"Melia," he stared, dumbfounded, from across the room. She was different. Not only in her physical appearance, but also something unrecognizable in her eyes.

"Drink up boys," she tossed blood bags to the vampires behind bars.

"Melia, no," he shouted.

"She's hypnotized," Camille declared on her feet.

He stood memorized as she lifted into the air over James, Wyatt, and Oliver in combat with the other wolves before landing in front of him.

"Out of my way," she shoved him with force.

He slammed up against the back wall as she ripped off the door to Camille's cell. "Amelia, stop."

"Amelia is no more. She's dead. I seek to requite," she flung the cell door at him.

He caught the door and tossed it to the side. He wanted to let her have her revenge. It was only fair. Camille had taken her life. Now she was prepared to do the same. "No," he inserted himself between Melia and Camille.

If Melia was in her right frame of mind, she would not want to harm Camille. She had forgiven her. Had wanted him to forgive her. To overcome the hurt and move on. Not dwell in it.

A gale of wind thrust him to the side as his head banged into the bars. He whirled around as Melia sliced into the side of Camille's neck. Camille did not fight. Did not resist. She awaited death as her punishment.

Melia pushed back from Camille and spat out the blood in her mouth as if it were sour. Flabbergasted at the sight before he became aware blackened eyes were on him.

"You," Melia glared. "What did you do to her blood?"

She was on him lightning fast. Her strength overpowered his own. She was angry and thirsty.

Chapter 38
Melia

The taste in her mouth was like sour milk. It made her stomach churned. He poisoned her blood somehow. Poisoned it to prevent her from taking it. She had not come for anyone else except the one who had killed her. It was her right to seek justice. He took that away from her. Now she was angry. Angry and hungry. He was going to regret trifling with her.

She ripped into his neck and tore off a chunk before she sucked the sweet elixir. A replenishment of the life force she required. It had been a few days. She was getting low on energy. A necessity.

There was something about his blood she couldn't quite wrap her mind around. She wanted to stop, but her hunger greedily took charge. She couldn't think. Couldn't understand why she felt the need to want to stop, but the thirst drove her to take more.

Breathe

The back of her subconscious urged. She had the desire to want to take a breath, but couldn't find the strength to pull away. She was consumed by her desire of wanting the necessity she needed.

"As long as you remain in control, it will not control you." The words surfaced her mind. She was not in control. The bloodlust was. It wanted it all. Every last drop. Only she did not require it all. She was already rejuvenated with life. She did not need to take one in order to survive.

She tore away and froze, captivated by familiar blue eyes staring back at her. Her eyes fell down to the hole in the side of his neck before drifting back up to meet his.

Her mind was cloudy as her eyes wavered. There were bits and pieces and the uncertainty if it truly happened or if it was a figment of her imagination. She wanted this to all be a dream, but she was afraid none of it was.

She glanced over and found Camille standing against the wall. She also had a tear in the side of her neck.

"What have I done?" She turned away, prepared to bolt, but his hand caught her arm and held firm. "I never meant to hurt anyone," she choked out.

"I know," he slipped his other arm around the small of her back and pulled her close.

She surrendered and sobbed into his chest. She had no idea what was going on. No idea what she was. She could have killed him. He should be afraid of her. Only he consoled her instead.

A loud whine escaped one of the wolves. She looked over and saw one laying near them covered in bloody gashes. He was badly wounded, yet he jumped back onto his feet as Oliver's wolf form stalked closer.

"Tell them to stop." Vince gripped both her arms, holding her out at arm's length.

Leo screamed loudly as he inserted himself between the wolves with extra-long canines.

"I don't know how," she shook her head vehemently.

"They are under your control. They will listen to your commands."

"Stop fighting," she cried out.

Oliver's raised hackles lowered as his attention directed to her. James and Wyatt also ceased fighting against the other wolves. They assessed the situation with confusion before they began licking each other's wounds.

She cupped a hand over her mouth when she noticed Darius kneeling by Tony, squeezing out every drop of blood that remained in empty blood bags. Blood was pooled on the floor beneath him from a wound in his stomach. Half the cells were empty. She had caused this madness. "I'm so sorry."

He pulled her close again, hushing her while patting the side of her head. "The fault is mine," she heard the vibration of his voice in her ear against his chest.

She wanted to argue the matter, but she was just so mentally drained while images continued to flash through her mind.

"Everything is going to be okay now," Camille whispered.

She swiveled her head and looked at her with doubt as the memory resurfaced. "Are you sick?"

"No," Camille frowned.

"What's wrong with your blood?"

Camille's eyes darted to Vince, back to hers, and then away. "I've been consuming animal blood."

"Where have you been getting animal blood?" Vince asked in dismay.

She had no idea what it meant for a vampire to drink animal blood. The only thing she knew for certain was she could not stomach that type of blood. It repulsed her.

"Sir," a vampire barged in, hopping on one leg, pausing to take in the scene.

"What is it Michael?" Vince asked.

"We have a situation."

She felt Vince's body stiffened. The image flashed through her mind, ordering Niles, Graham, and Dante to gather blood and provide to those imprisoned at whatever cost. If he didn't hate her now, he was about to.

"I need you all to come with me," he paused. "Michael, stay here with Tony and Camille."

He reached down and slipped his hand into hers as he tugged her along. He wasn't allowing her to leave his side. She dreaded the scene to come.

He rushed up the stairs, down the hall, through the empty lobby, and pushed through the door she had never entered. There was another door on the other side he barged through before stopping in his tracks. Rows and rows of cells were on the floor level and an upper level. There was so much violence ensuing within. So much blood spilled everywhere as wolves and vampires continued to combat.

"Stay with her," Vince demanded before swiftly climbing the stairs to the second level.

She gasped as he charged through the battle. What if he got even more hurt because of her? She'd never be able to forgive herself. She had disrupted all of their lives. She should have stayed away.

A loud alarm rang out with flashing lights and water raining down from sprinklers above. Her first reaction was to cover her ears, along with everyone else who stopped fighting.

"Everyone, stop," Vince's voice boomed above the noise.

A few unsuspecting imprisoned vampires took the opportunity to make their great escape as they veered her way. Darius pulled her away, shielding her with his body while the wolves that came with them blocked the path to the exit along with a sinister Camille.

"Let them go," Vince declared.

All eyes raised to his. The vampires didn't delay as they jumped over the wolves and pushed Camille out of the way, taking off out the door.

She held onto Darius. When she felt him relax, she slowly opened her eyes and caught sight of a small gathering of wolves.

"Lamont?" she slowly took a step forward.

Everything around her faded away as she walked through the spray, falling from the ceiling, stopping when she was upon the white wolf who panted. Blood oozed out of a wound from his chest. He was barely hanging on.

He had always been so kind to her. Never bothered by any of her questions. She hadn't known him long, but he was as warm and inviting to her as her father had been. He saw something in her she still had yet to figure out. Now he was slowly dying. It was all her fault. She was helpless.

"Melia," Vince reappeared as the water stopped falling. "Your blood can heal him."

A flicker of hope flooded within as she sliced into her arm, kneeled down by his muzzle, and offered him her blood. He grumbled before tilting his head away from her.

"Lamont, it's the only way," Vince kneeled next to her.

"Please," she sliced into her arm again, scooping up some blood onto her fingers, and reached out.

He shifted his paw over the back of her forearm with a slight whine. His breathing became labored until he took his last breath as the last bit of light faded from his eyes.

A mournful howl startled her, followed by a light brown and tan wolf. In union, all the wolves joined in howling their sorrows.

She was tortured with guilt.

Chapter 39
Vince

He was gone. The life snuffed out like a candle. They had been too late. He never imaged one day he would have to live in a world without Lamont. He kept him grounded. Trusted him with things he never shared with anyone else. Lamont saw him at his good and saw him at his worse. Helped him work through some of his demons. Was always there to catch him when he fell. Was always there to guide him. A friend. They worked together as equals. Something he never thought one day vampires and wolves would do.

He didn't know when the howling stopped. Didn't know when the growling began. Didn't know the reason for it as his eyes skimmed the faces of the wolves near him. Their eyes locked. He followed their line of sight to Melia, who backed away from Lamont's lifeless body.

"Stand down," he rose to his feet and pulled Melia behind his back, kept a sturdy hold, and shifted slowly around, eyeing every possible threat with a fierceness ready for a fight if it came down to it.

"Let them have her. She's the reason for this disruption in our lives. Everything was fine until she came along. We would all be better off without her," Ryker protested from behind on the ground.

"You'll have to kill me first," he declared, listening keening and watching every movement possible in his peripheral.

"Not before me," Camille followed, moving to his right.

"And I," Darius moved to his left.

"Me too," Niles rushed forward, along with Graham and Dante.

At once, James, Wyatt, and Oliver positioned themselves in front of them as Cameron positioned himself in the lead.

"You heard Vince. You will all stand down, now," Cameron spoke to the wolves in human form.

"Unifying with the vampires was his downfall. They can't be trusted, now or ever," Helene shouted after transforming to the left of them.

"You will hold your tongue," Cameron commanded.

"Who are you to make such a demand?" Helene challenged.

"I expect you to respect me as you did Lamont."

He was taken aback. Cameron had left the pack. Had not wanted to be a part of the pack anymore. Now he had become the new alpha? What had he missed?

"Who are you to declare yourself as next in line?" Helene persisted.

"I can attest that it was Lamont's last request for Cameron to ascend," Caden answered, in human form, as he approached and took a respectful bow.

He was astonished Caden did not argue the matter like Helene. Rather, he accepted it. He made it known he detested vampires. He had expected further argument from him.

"What? No, you are what this pack needs, not a vampire worshipper like him," Helene protested.

"Enough," Cameron raised his voice. "This is not the time to fight among ourselves and pick sides. There is a threat far greater out there. An entity we have not seen before. All will be lost if we become rivals again."

"What about the vampires that escaped?" Ryker questioned.

He stepped forward and fell in line beside Cameron. "We will deal with them, but first we must understand our bigger threat."

A slow clapping was heard from the doorway. His attention shifted along with everyone else. The black hooded guy stood just inside with his hood down around his shoulders. He quickly pushed his way back to Melia, positioned himself in front of her, and wrapped his right hand behind her back, keeping her close to him.

The hooded guy was younger than he imagined. Had dark shoulder length hair, bushy eyebrows, and a cleft chin. There was something off about him. He wasn't quite solid like they were. He could almost see through his head.

"A wise choice to focus on me," he stopped clapping. "What a pathetic life you live, merely existing. You are all far more superior and yet you allow weak humans to live supreme unaware of your existence. They should bow down to you. It was yours for the taking.

That right belongs to you no more. A storm is coming. Allow me to demonstrate."

He vanished at the last word. Reappearing in a cell to the far right of the first floor. Several metal bars were stripped floating in the air before they were launched down the rows to the vampires that still remained inside. One by one, they fell. Impaled clean through their stomachs as the life force bled out.

Again, he vanished before reappearing with crackling laughter on the opposite side on the first floor, repeating before moving onto the second level, continuing his attack until all the vampires still confined in a cell were terminated.

He stood frozen in place. He didn't know how to proceed. No one did. The guy was fast and brutal. How were they to stand up against magic? They were powerless and defenseless. They were at his mercy.

He reappeared at the doorway. "I caution you all to choose wisely which path you want to take because when the time comes, there will be no turning back."

"Vince," Melia whispered.

He looked over his shoulder and saw her eyes were heavy before she slumped over. He quickly caught her and lifted her into his arms.

"You are no longer bound to this place. It's time for you to set foot into the outside world," the guy continued.

"What did you do to her?" he demanded with fury.

A smile spread across his illuminating lips. "Nothing, yet. I do suggest, though, you encourage her to command fire. She is unbalanced without it. She may be your only hope when the storm comes." He fades away.

The room filled with instant worried chatter.

"Who was that?"

"What does he want?"

"How did he do that?"

The questions fired off in rapid succession.

"Magic," Cameron answered.

Even more questions fired away.

He handed Melia to Darius before taking command of the room. "I know that you are all disturbed and have a lot of questions. The truth is, we don't have many answers. We know Melia was created for a purpose. Somehow, she's the key in bringing back magic. Magic that created Vladimir. Magic that created Gabriel. They were both the first of their kind and given the ability to create more of their own at a time when magic thrived."

He held their complete attention, but heard whispers from the wolves about what he revealed.

"My mother, Immilla, was a witch. She wrote the prophecy of Vladimir's downfall. She was also the one who removed magic from the world."

"How do we remove it again?" someone shouted from the back.

He looked at Melia, seemingly lifeless in Darius arms. "I don't know. What I do know is, Melia may be the only solution."

Part 3
The Dance

Chapter 40
Vince

He sat on a bench outside in the recreational field for several hours in the dark, waiting for the sun to rise. He had her cradled in his arms. She had murmured weakly about needing the sun. He didn't know what the sun would do for her, but he didn't know what else to do. She was too weak to even drink any blood.

He tucked strands of her short honey-blonde hair out of her face. So much shorter, her hair was. A bit choppy, but it suited her. Enhanced her features in a way better than the makeup Niles had applied to her face. She slept angelically even though vampires don't need sleep unless spent.

He had no idea how much time they had before the hooded guy returned. Didn't know what he wanted or what type of storm he had brewing. Obviously, he needed Melia. Needed her to command fire for a purpose. He just wasn't sure if that purpose was a trick in order for him to get what he wanted or a way for her to be able to overpower him.

"Why would you try to stop her?" Camille asked, staring into the bleak dark nothingness with her hands tucked into the pockets of her jacket.

"I didn't do it for you. I did it for her."

He watched Camille nod with acceptance.

He stared at her with conflict. He still found it hard to trust her. She disobeyed an order to stay behind and could have made a run for it like the other vampires, but she stayed. Was even willing to defend Melia against the wolves even though she wouldn't have stood a chance against them with her diet.

"Why are you drinking animal blood? Where did you even get it from?" his eyes narrowed.

"Leo was bringing me some kills," Camille shrugged.

"How long has it been since you've consumed human blood?"

Camille remained silent dodging the question.

Animal blood did not provide the same sustaining benefits as human blood. Wounds healed slower and the body was not as vigorous. Too much over time could cripple a vampire to a human's tendencies.

He studied Camille. She was not the same girl he knew. She was barely even a shell of herself. Once was loud and outgoing. The life of the party. Had big dreams. He took her out on a date for the wrong reason. She liked talking, plus he knew it would infuriate Nadine at the time. He never quite understood how Nadine ended up being friends with her. They were complete opposites. Yet they had a strong bond. One Nadine would have fought tooth and nail, risking her own life. She had defended those not strong enough to stand up for themselves and even harder for the ones she deeply cared about, including him.

"How did Jomar get to you?"

"Didn't take much. He knew my deep, dark desire. Knew what card to play. Gave me his phone that I could turn on so they could track us whenever I gave into temptation," she whispered out into the frosty night.

"Marc?"

She nodded.

"I despised him too."

She rotated her head. "I know you did, but for a different reason."

"I let it blind me."

"Don't. The fault is mine," she looked back into the night sky.

This was a completely different Camille. One gripped with a torture of her own doing. He could see it now. She was haunted by her actions. It hollowed her out inside. Awaited one fate she knew she was destined for.

"I want nothing more than to let you carry the full weight on your shoulders, but the load is not all yours. I had a responsibility too. One I was ineffective with," he admitted as beams of light began to pierce the dark.

"It doesn't matter. The past can't be changed."

"It does matter. It matters now. I don't know what the future holds, but I know it's not something that can be walked into alone. I can't be everything she may need," he glanced at Melia. "She needs you as well. This could be your chance at redemption. I just don't know how to trust you won't betray her too."

She turned and looked him squarely in the eyes. "I don't want redemption. I brought this horror into her life. The least I can do is help her overcome it."

That had to be good enough. They still had a long road ahead before he could ever forgive Camille, but the journey had begun. Even though there was still anger beneath the surface, he could move forward and tolerate her presence. Something he never would have been able to do without Melia.

He looked down at her pale face as faint sunbeams brushed upon it. Sitting here holding her had a way of depleting his own energy. A different kind. As if it flowed from him into her. The rays of sun felt invigorating as it kissed his skin as well.

"How is she doing?" Cameron sauntered over to them.

"No change yet," he sighed.

"Everyone's on edge. We saved all that we could. My kind deserves a proper burial. A burial that's not here. It's up to you what you want to do with your kind."

The image flashed through his mind, letting all the vampire bodies burn inside the asylum after the war. Most of the vampires he couldn't care less about, but there were some that were his men. He never thought they would get here again. Would they ever be able to move on with their lives without tragedies?

"Camille, tell Darius to collect the ashes of my men and let them be carried by the breeze. The rest can be buried underground with the suit," he watched her dismiss herself with a nod.

"What about the ones that escaped?"

"We can compile a team to leave here and have Parker track what he can find, as long as he doesn't get knocked unconscious again."

Cameron nodded in agreement. "I'm going to go locate Noir."

He watched the backside of Cameron walk away. He had forgotten about Noir. She was going to be devastated. She was loyal to Lamont. What would she do now that he was gone? He never saw her loyal to anyone else except Nadine. Her respect was earned, not given. She only tolerated everyone else.

He hadn't even been able to mourn Lamont. So much had happened in the aftermath. So much for him to be able to wrap his mind around. Now he found himself alone with his own thoughts. Didn't know how much more loss he could endure. No one told him what the price of freedom meant. Had to step into a role he never wanted to begin with. If only he could step down and disappear. A luxury he could never have.

He felt Melia stir in his arm. He looked down and was overwhelmed with a sudden feeling of trepidation.

Chapter 41
Melia

She opened her eyes. Was drained, but a warmth pooled into her body. Rejuvenating her along with the solar energy from the sun baring down on her. Her eyes found his laced with extreme worry behind them. With every ounce of strength that she could summon, she lifted her arm, reached out with her hand, and cupped the side of his face. He turned away from her touch, gently pushing down her arm.

"Save your strength," he voiced as he guided her down onto the bench beside him, keeping an arm around her to keep her upright.

There was an ache of discomfort in his motion. She couldn't grasp what it meant or why it hurt her. Something had shifted.

She looked out across the landscape. They were inside the area she had seen the vampires contained to. Only they were the only ones in the area. No vampires or wolves patrolled.

She picked up on a piercing call, followed by a bunch of wailing. A crow took to the sky, passing over head. The rush of memories flooded her mind with everything she had done and the consequences after. "Everything's all my fault."

"You were hypnotized."

She looked into his blue eyes. She had no words. Her mind had not been her own. She had been tricked. Had been fooled. The power she felt hadn't been real after all. She had played a part of herself that wasn't true.

"What do you remember?" he probed.

"I've done terrible things," she bowed her head in shame.

"Do you know why he wants you to command fire?"

"Fire?" She shuddered uncontrollably at just the word.

"What's wrong?" his grip tightened.

"I, I don't want to. Please don't make me," her eyes went wide as her voice shook.

"What's wrong? You can tell me anything," he pulled her closer.

"I'm afraid," she whispered hoarsely into his shoulder.

"Of fire?"

She nodded her head in a jerky motion.

"It's okay," he patted the back of her head.

She heard his soft sigh. He lied to her. He wanted her to think it was okay, but his sigh of disappointment said otherwise. She didn't want to disappoint him. She didn't want to disappoint anyone. Even Max had not been fond of her voicing her fear of fire. Had scolded her deeming it was the truest and deepest part of her that she only allowed to hold herself back from blossoming into one without fear.

Becoming fearless was to be desired. Yet, fire had an iron grip on her. It had control. She did not control it. She did not want to control it. There was something about fire that plagued her.

Out of her peripheral, she saw Camille heading towards them. Camille, who she had every intention of draining dry. She wasn't supposed to stop. He told her she was hypnotized, but that wasn't mind control. Some part of her wanted to do the same thing to Camille that Camille did to her. Just as she had wanted her mother to feel the same scarred pain as her. The same with Pastor Samael with humility. She had done those things and felt superior, but now she felt ashamed. Just because she could didn't mean she should. She had been no better than them. Had no right to make the justified judgement.

"Camille, I'm so sorry," she pushed up to her feet. She was unsteady and fell against Vince, who was quick to catch her.

"Easy," he steadied her.

She noticed the distance he inserted.

"You don't have to be sorry. It was only fair, but if it's any consolation, I forgive you," Camille nodded once knowingly.

Her heart warmed. Not from the sun. Not from Vince's touch, but by her words. She had never done anything wrong that she regretted to feel the need for those words to make things better. It was uplifting. She did not have to be held down by that guilt. She could have closure and move on. At least with Camille.

Only there were mistakes she made she could not change. She had to live with that and what it might have cost her. There was only one thing she could do. She just didn't know if she had what it might take.

"She's awake."

She turned her attention to an unfamiliar guy heading their direction. He had clean cut dirty-blonde hair that was finger-combed back, thick eyebrows, green eyes, and a square jaw. He reminded her of someone. Was young, but carried himself in a way that appeared older.

"Melia, this is Cameron," Vince took the liberty to introduce.

She nodded her head and smiled politely.

"You have the same look she had." Cameron's eyes flicked from Vince to hers.

She frowned with quizzable eyes, exchanging a look with Camille.

"Confused. Lost. Depleted," he continued.

He was right. She felt all those things. Was he talking about Camille? "Who are you talking about?"

"Nadia."

She shouldn't have had to ask. Nadine left her mark on everyone. She had that effect. Should be here not her. She'd probably know what to do.

"I was the closest thing she had to a friend when she turned. There's one thing you have more than what she did," he paused.

"What's that?"

"Support," his eyes flicked to Vince.

She sneaked a glance at Vince. He nodded in agreement. She liked Cameron, instantly. Why hadn't she met him until now? He made her feel the same way Lamont had. Accepted for who she was despite what she had become. "I don't want to hurt anyone else. Please don't let him manipulate my mind again," she pierced Vince's eyes.

"It's the last thing either one of us wants. We just need to know who we are facing."

"He said I could call him Max."

"Max?" she saw the lines on Vince's forehead crease.

"He taught me how to tap into magic. I was able to master it with emotions I had been feeling. The more I used, the more strained I became. I couldn't use too much at one time."

"Like a muscle," Vince uttered, staring out into the distance.

"Yeah," the similarity of it was accurate. "He said it was heavy to the inexperienced."

"How does the sun fit into this?" Camille questioned.

"It restores my energy."

"You weren't using magic when you collapsed," Cameron pointed out.

She didn't know what to say as she transported back in time. She had used up some of her energy, but had not been as diminished as the first night. Somehow, his use of magic drained her completely when he attacked the imprisoned vampires. Was she linked to him or was he linked to her magic?

"When you utilized magic, are you commanding it with your mind or is the object there for you to be able to control?" Vince asked abruptly.

"I was at the river when I reached out and was able to grab an orb of water suspending it above the air," she recalled the details.

"Light magic," Vince stated.

"There's different types of magic?" Camille verbalized.

"What do you know?" Cameron pressed.

"There are two types of magic. Light magic and dark magic," Vince continued.

"Lovely," Camille commented.

"My mother wrote about it in her journal," Vince supplied.

"Mother?" it was obvious she was missing some details.

"She was a witch." Vince's eyes shifted towards hers. "She destroyed magic. Now it's back. At least light magic is. He must need you somehow to be able to bring back dark magic as well in order to finish what he couldn't."

"What's dark magic?" she was afraid to ask.

"My mother described it as cognitive."

"What do you mean by finish what he couldn't?" Camille interjected. "Did your mother write about him too?"

"She mentioned him briefly, Maximilian. Strict rules were put into place after his downfall."

"Well, that sounds just great. How exactly are we supposed to put magic back in the box when it's already out?" Camille stated the obvious.

"I don't think magic was ever put into a box to begin with," Cameron asserted.

Chapter 42
Vince

He had stood there stupefied at Cameron's omission. Had no idea what to say. Apparently, no one did as they had all stood there in dead silence.

Cameron had not elaborated. Claimed he was not the one who could explain. It was a journey they would have to take. One he would only allow the four of them. A risk he knew, but also needed time to allow the pack to mourn back at their old home.

Cameron left a reluctant Caden in charge while he left Darius in charge. After burying the fallen vampires, he gave orders to assist the wolves in taking back the fallen wolves to be buried at their home turf, where they would meet up with them.

He stared out his window as Cameron drove. Another astonishment. He had no idea Cameron had learned how to drive or when he learned it. He had been surprised Lamont had even known how to drive. As far as he knew, none of the other wolves had the expertise. He was becoming more and more aware that he didn't know a lot of things. Had not paid attention to details. Had been focused on only one thing.

Leo purred loudly from his lap as he continuously stroked the back of his head. When he stopped, Leo bumped his head into his hand. There was so much on his mind. Leo had persistently followed them. His soothing vibration of purring was therapeutic. He always seemed to know when he was needed.

He avoided looking at Melia in the passenger side mirror. He had no idea how he could help her. Protect her. Keep her safe from this new threat. He was no match against magic. How could he fight against something he couldn't touch?

He saw the coordinates Parker uploaded upon Cameron's request. They were heading south. Some place in Tennessee. He wondered what could be there. What magic had Cameron come across?

"Why do you wear both halves meant for two necklaces?" Melia asked from behind him.

His eyes instantly dropped to the passenger side mirror and saw her looking over at Camille. He couldn't resist sneaking a glance over his shoulder. He saw she had the pendants between her fingers looking down at them. She let them fall against her chest. One half was white and the other half was black. They were each a curved half that formed a circle when placed together along with two number six charms.

"One belonged to my…" Camille hesitated. "A friend."

"Nadine?"

Camille's eyes lifted to his before nodding. He turned his head away and stared back out the window. He knew she considered Nadine more than just a friend. They had been best friends. He didn't know all the circumstances the necklaces represented, but they had been meaningful to them. They had both wore them every day.

"Is she the friend you killed?" Melia whispered the last word.

His eyes went wide as he sat as still as a statue. Why was Melia bringing this up? What was she trying to get at? He felt uncomfortable just listening. Wasn't sure why he allowed Camille to come with them in the first place.

"Yes," Camille replied in a monotone voice before adding. "Which is why I told you I'm not someone you want to become friends with."

"What made you do it?" Melia persisted.

"What does it matter?" he heard annoyance in Camille's voice. Leo perked his head.

"What made you capable of doing it?" Melia rephrased the question.

"Jealousy," Camille snapped. "Is that what you wanted to hear?"

"Did you know about the prophecy?"

"Yeah," Camille's temper deflated as confusion filled the gap.

He felt as puzzled as Camille in where this was going. Why was Melia grilling her? Did she know something?

"The two of you were close, weren't you?"

Camille didn't respond. He quickly peeked over his shoulder and saw she was staring out the window, chewing on her bottom lip before looking straight ahead at the road.

"I don't think anyone could be capable when you truly care about someone," Melia claimed.

"You're wrong. I was capable of it," Camille uttered robotically.

He felt the tension radiating from Camille. Looked over at Cameron who remained focused on the road, however, he glanced between his rearview mirror and side mirrors. He didn't think it was just the traffic Cameron was viewing in the mirrors.

"You didn't know me. I meant nothing to you."

"What are you getting at?" Camille huffed with annoyance.

He was wondering the same thing.

"You whispered that you were sorry before the darkness. You were sorry even though you knew I'd come back. So, how did you know she wouldn't be completely gone?"

He sat up straighter in his seat as he slowly rotated his head and met Camille's eyes.

She maintained eye contact with him when she answered. "I knew the tea was spiked with my blood and venom."

He tore his eyes away, revolted. She knew Nadine hadn't wanted to become a vampire. He would have never gone against her wishes, but he knew Camille must have known that in order to fulfill the prophecy Nadine would have to turn. He didn't know which betrayal was worse. Camille killing Nadine out of jealously or killing her knowing she would turn into something she never wanted to become.

"I spiked the tea when you left to get blood. Saw an opportunity, but she snuck out the window to find Marc. Was able to confirm that she did indeed have feelings for him after your quarrel, but it was more than just feelings," Camille's voice projected away. "My hatred of Marc festered, turning me against my best friend. She suffered because of me. Ignored her pleas. Ignored her anguish so I could watch him suffer. It turns out he wasn't the monster. I was. When I realized what I had done, the agony I brought to her, the only thing I could do in that moment was end her pain."

He refused to look at Camille. Didn't speak to her. Just stared out the window with a solemn countenance. He didn't want to empathize with her at all. He just wanted to hate her. Hate her actions, but he did understand them. The place your mind went, closing yourself off so you could focus on one thing.

"I deserved everything I endured after for what I did to her."

"Not everything," Melia asserted.

181

His forehead creased with lines. He wondered briefly what Melia meant by that. She was perceptive. Something he clearly lacked. How could she have known there was more to Camille's side of the story? At least he knew for certain Melia was back to her normal self.

Chapter 43
Melia

She was sad Camille pulled away from her touch. Knew Camille had a long journey ahead of her. Carried so much guilt. What Camille did to Nadine tore her up inside. Wore that guilt over every inch of her figure.

The cat, Leo, picked up on Camille's somber mood as he launched onto Camille's lap. Camille was startled before sighing as she stared down at him. He was a good cat. He knew when he was needed. Persistent and stubborn. He didn't take no for an answer. He was bold, something she lacked. Although, she had had that fifteen minutes of boldness. Something Max had activated from the back of her mind. It had been nice to be the one in control without fear. However, she had hurt people in the process. It didn't matter if they deserved it or not. She had been responsible for their pain. The weight of it was heavy upon her chest. Nothing compared to Camille's weight. Talking about it, though, helped to lighten the load. She could at least help Camille in that sense.

She watched Vince in the passenger side mirror. He kept quiet, processing what he had learned. She couldn't be certain if Camille's revelation mattered, but it was important to have all the facts. How one proceeded after all facts were collected was up to them.

The tires crunched upon the hard-crusted snow down a secluded narrow lane. They had been on the road for hours among civilization. Now they had left it behind as they went deeper into isolation. A place of her heart's desire.

A run-down cabin with green shutters, a metal roof, and a front porch came into view. A magical place tucked in rugged land and one she thought only existed in her dreams.

An older woman appeared on the front porch at the top of the stairs. She had long raven black hair, a green, blue, and orange shawl wrapped around her caramel arms, and wore amber loose flowing pants. Beside her stood a ginger-brown husky. The husky stood tall with its ears pointed straight up. Her keen hearing could pick up on a low growl from the husky's throat.

"Stay in the car," Cameron spoke for the first time in several hours.

She watched as he walked behind the SUV and headed towards the woman and the husky. The husky paid him no attention as its gorgeous parti-colored light brown and blue eyes stayed locked on the SUV. Specifically, the occupants inside. Not only were they strangers, but also more than just strangers.

Cameron exchanged some words with the human before she reached out and stroked the husky. The husky's tense body eased some as Cameron stepped up on the bottom step. He spoke to the husky, maintaining eye contact before breaking away and heading back towards them while the husky cautiously followed.

He stopped five-feet away and nodded his head. Vince opened his door first as she followed. He briefly acknowledged her before turning his attention onto Cameron as Camille paused at the back of the SUV, keeping her distance.

"It's best if Melia and Camille be acquainted with Aurora first," Cameron instructed.

"Okay." Vince met her eyes and nodded.

She breathed in the cold air before stepping forward as Camille fell in line behind her. Cameron's eyes fell down to Aurora as he emitted a chuffing-like sound in the back of his throat. Aurora snorted before she stepped past him.

Dogs were different. She knew that making direct eye contact could be perceived as a threat. This was Aurora's domain. She was in control here.

"No sudden movements or direct eye contact," Cameron stated.

Aurora slowly closed the gap as she eyed her suspiciously. She focused on her lower body, away from her eyes. Her legs were long and her paws were huge. They seemed like James and Wyatt's legs, wolf-like.

Aurora sniffed her intently before moving onto Camille and then lastly Vince. She snorted as she marched away and sat down beside Cameron, leaning into him. Her body language was much calmer.

"Welcome," the older woman cheerfully moved in without their awareness.

"Cecily, I'd like you to meet Melia, Camille, and Vince," Cameron introduced.

"Hello, Melia," Cecily approached and embraced her. She had not expected the gesture. She didn't know how to respond. Her hug was tight. She stood stiff unknowing what to do. Before she had a chance to do anything, Cecily moved onto Camille.

She greeted Camille the same way. Saw Camille had the same rigid respond, but there was also a hint of something else in her expression as she lightly patted Cecily on the back.

Finally, Cecily greeted Vince. Only he leaned away from the hug. If Cecily was offended, she didn't show it as she stood back from them all to take them in.

"Everyone, this is Cecily White," Cameron introduced.

Her eyes raised. She recognized the name. "You wrote a book about Wicca? *Wicca: A Guide to Nature.*"

A soft smile spread upon her lips. "Indeed, I did. I assume that you have read it?" her ginger voice inquired.

"I'm afraid I haven't read it in entirely," she bowed her head.

"There is nothing disgraceful about your omission. It's not meant to be read in a single sitting, nor does one master the skills in one day."

"Forgive me for being brash, but what do you know about magic?" Vince interposed.

"I understand you've traveled a bit of a distance, come inside."

"We don't want to impose," Vince vetoed.

"It's not an imposition. And I wasn't asking," Cecily stated with a firmness.

"It's best not to argue the matter when her mind is made up," Cameron interjected.

Cecily's smile was wide as she nodded once in agreement.

Vince sighed, defeated.

"Very well, then," she turned on her heels and took the lead to the front porch.

She was trying to understand something she wasn't quite certain about. Something about Cecily's almond-shaped russet eyes. They were seeing, but she couldn't help think something was off.

"I sense there is a question lingering upon your mind," Cecily slightly shifted her head.

"How did you know?"

"A feeling," Cecily stepped up the first step.

"I'm not sure exactly what to ask."

"I suspect your question will arise soon."

Cecily opened the door and entered. As she stepped through the threshold, she was transported into a completely different environment. The interior, updated. Wood shined from every corner. The walls, the floor, the stairs, even the ceiling. The space was open with minimal objects. Two lively plants positioned beside the door. There dark green leaves with stripes of yellow were sword-shape growing upright. Her eyes raised to the paintings on the walls. They were different. Portraits of nature, however the colorations were unique. One in particular caught her eye. An eggplant purple sky with spiral stars with a light pink hue around them.

"Who painted all of these?" she asked in wonder.

"I did," Cecily answered.

"They're beautiful."

"It's how I see the world."

Chapter 44
Vince

He was captivated by the interior. He hadn't expected it to look so lavish. All-natural wood with hardwood floors. To the left of the open interior was a long sofa and a coffee table. A small red wood stove sandwiched between two built-in length cream-colored shelves the length of the wall with hardly anything placed upon them. There were also some candles, a plant, some crystals, and a few books.

"You see the world in different colors?" Melia asked.

"What I see is energy projected, auras, from outlines of people, animals, plants, and objects," Cecily unwrapped her colorful shawl and placed it on a hook by the door. She wore a loose burgundy u-shaped neck shirt with three-quarter sleeves.

"How is that possible?"

"It was the way I was born."

He was growing more and more impatient. "Listen, we don't have much time before the sun fades. We need to know everything you know about magic before it gets dark."

"Magic is not something that can be learned in just an hour," Cecily scolded.

"It's not exactly safe for you with our presences here."

"Whatever darkness that follows you, it will come to find that it is not welcomed within these walls."

"How can you be so sure when you don't even know what we are dealing with."

"Why don't you all relax and have a seat while I make me some tea? I'd offer you some, but I see that is not part of your diet."

He stiffened, eyeing her wearily. What was that supposed to mean? He glanced over his shoulder, confusion in his stare. Had Cameron mentioned something?

"She knows what I am," Cameron stated in a calm manner.

"You told her?" his eyebrows raised, stunned.

He didn't understand why Cameron would tell a human about his kind. An outsider. Could she even be trusted?

"He did not. I can see the outline of his true form, just as I can see your life force resides within your stomach and not your heart."

He looked down. Beneath the fabric of his shirt was flesh and bone. He wasn't sure how to respond. He was in disbelief. She saw more about them then he liked. It unnerved him.

"Don't worry, your secrets are safe with me," she exited the room, seeming to know what was on his mind.

Cameron sat down in a chair across from the couch. Aurora positioned herself beside the chair keeping a watchful eye. Melia and Camille sat on the couch. Melia in the middle and Camille on the end with her leg crossed leaning into the arm.

He didn't want to sit. He just sat for several hours in a car. Was restless and just wanted answers. They shouldn't be here so far away from the others.

Cecily returned with a cup of tea secured in her hands. She politely took a sip before she sat on the open end of the brown leather couch and sat crossing her legs Indian-style. "I see there is a great deal of conflict within you."

He stopped pacing the floor and saw her studying him. He hadn't realized he started pacing to begin with. She made him more agitated. They didn't have time to waste. "I don't need to be analyzed. Long story short, my mother was a witch who had eliminated magic from the world…"

"What makes you think magic was ever gone?" Cecily cut him off.

"There are no witches?" he hesitated.

"Just because you don't see something doesn't mean it's gone. Magic is still very much present. It's all around you. It's all around this room. If it was truly gone, you would cease to exist."

He was speechless. He was unnatural. Magic is what created his father. Created him. Created the werewolves. "But I can't do magic."

"Because you have a closed mind."

"Are you saying I could be capable of magic? That we all are capable of magic?" he gestured with his hand around the room.

"With a great deal of practice, eventually yes. Anything is possible," she set her cup down on the table.

"Impossible."

Without a word, he watched Cecily rub her palms together in a vast motion before slowly pulling her hands apart cupping them as if she was holding something between them "What do you see?" her eyes opened.

"Nothing."

"I see it! A light-gold sphere," Melia sat up straighter.

His eyes darted to Melia and back to an empty space between Cecily's hands.

"Close your eyes, what do you hear?" Cecily's attention was on him.

He sighed before complying. His mind was all over the place, listening to any and everything except for what he was apparently supposed to hear. "I don't know what I'm supposed to be hearing," he snapped his eyes open.

"Without a focused mind, you cannot fathom magic."

"What we need to understand is how magic can be defeated and how we can protect ourselves from it," he huffed.

"I can teach you how to conjure up an energy shield, but I cannot teach you how to defeat magic. Magic cannot be eradicated. There is positive energy and there is negative energy. Combined, they balance each other out."

He was getting more and more frustrated. "How do we stop someone powerful from taking what he wants by force? Someone that shouldn't even be alive? Someone who can drain the life force from another?"

"You will have to explain it in more detail."

"My mother's journal mentioned the downfall of a witch named Maximilian which was centuries ago. I assumed he had died or at least striped of his magic. Now, he has returned. He took out hundreds of our own and Melia became nearly lifeless afterwards. He wants her to command fire. I need to know why."

"He did die," Melia interjected. "He's a spirit."

"Why didn't you tell me sooner?" he grumbled.

"You didn't ask."

He threw up his hands. "Everything you know about him is important for me to know."

"I'm sorry," Melia shrank into herself.

"I cannot help you in the current pessimistic state you are in," Cecily stood. "You all have traveled a great distance, each carrying a different weight upon your shoulders. You may not require sleep, but each of you need to close your eyes and calm your mind."

"We don't have time for that," he shouted.

"Then you have wasted your time coming here," Cecily walked out of the room.

Chapter 45
Melia

She sensed Vince's tension as he started pacing, again. Knew she was the cause of it. Didn't know how to talk to him. Didn't want to make matters worse. Everything was her fault to begin with.

She looked over at Camille, who sat there as quiet as can be, closed off. Had she seen the sphere? She hadn't spoken a word since they stepped inside. What was on her mind?

"I'm going to keep watch outside," Cameron rose, dismissing himself. Aurora followed him to the front door as they both slipped out. She wondered where Leo had run off. He took off from Camille's lap when she opened the door, not wanting any parts on meeting a new canine.

She missed Rosa. Didn't want to stress her out taking her to an unfamiliar place. She had wanted Niles to look after her, but he had been recruited to lead the team that was sent to locate the escaped vampires, so she left Darius in charge of Rosa.

She pushed up to her feet. Vince noticed the movement right away and paused, but said nothing as he dropped his head and continued to pace. She swallowed the lump in her throat and walked with purpose, following Cecily's trail.

She walked into a small dining room with a wooden table and four chairs. There were green place mats along with a potted plant with glossy dark-green oval leaves in the center of the table surrounded by two tall white candles incased in glass. The room was small, but it radiated with peacefulness.

She continued on her way to the kitchen where she found Cecily standing by a back door staring out into the woods as the light faded. The shiny wood still covered the kitchen with wood cabinets. The only thing not made from wood were the white appliances. Above the stove hung a small succulent that boosted the liveliness of the place.

191

"I suspected that you would be the first to come find me," Cecily commented with her back still towards her.

"Why was I the only one who could see it?"

"Your mind has always been open," Cecily turned to face her.

"Always?"

Cecily nodded.

"Until only just a couple of days ago, I've never been able to use magic."

"You observe and sense things differently than others, correct?"

She hesitated as she processed the words. All her life, she felt like she was always outside looking in. She had a way of reading people. Leant them an ear even when they didn't ask for it and gave advice. Some got angry. It always terrified her. When people got so full of rage, she wanted to crawl under a rock and hide. She never knew what they were capable of.

"Magic isn't something always meant to be forcefully seen. It's felt within," Cecily placed a hand upon her chest. "Being different is nothing to be ashamed of."

"Why do you live here alone, away from the world?"

"I'm not alone," Cecily beamed. "I feel his spirit always."

"Who?"

"Robert. My departed husband. My soulmate."

"Soulmate?" she whispered.

"When we got this place, it was rundown without hope," Cecily looked around. "Everyone warned us it was a lost cause, but he loved a challenge. Loved working with his hands. Loved building shiny character."

"Do you still see him?"

"No. I feel he's at peace."

"How did you know he was your soulmate and it was not just a mind trick?"

Cecily closed her eyes and slightly raised her chin. "A deep, strong warm sense. One that can't be ignored. However, how you connect to a soulmate differs from your twin flame."

"Twin flame?"

"The other half of your soul."

Her mind was swimming with information overload. There was meaning behind Cecily's words. She sensed it. She just couldn't grasp it yet.

"The most powerful thing in the world is united twin flames, but first you need to discover who you are."

"How do I do that?"

"With the right questions asked and the right questions answered."

"Where do I even begin?" she massaged her temple.

"It's all a part of your journey."

She thought she knew who she was already. Was there more to her that she had yet to learn?

Cecily pulled out the top drawer closest to her near the back door and removed a tea light candle, setting it on the counter above. "Would you like to practice by lighting a candle?"

She stiffened. Just the thought of a single flame filled her with dread. She took strained breaths through her mouth. She was surrounded by peaceful energy, however she found it difficult to embrace it now.

Cecily pulled the drawer back out and placed the tea light candle back in. "Why don't you go upstairs, pick a room, lie down for a bit, and clear your mind?"

She didn't argue as she obediently backed away, entered into the dining room and climbed the sleek wood stairs.

Chapter 46
Vince

He paused mid-step when Melia rose, briefly locked eyes with her before tearing his away. Continued his steady rhythm of putting one step in front of another before turning and repeating the motion. He was out of his league. Was never going to become strong enough in magic to overpower Maximilian. Trying not to feel so hopeless. He was supposed to be the strongest creature upon this earth, but right now he felt so powerless. Lost in the dark. There was no light to show him the way. He was blind. All he could do was keep moving forward and hope to find a way out. There were so many of them relying on him. What if he failed them?

"She's right about one thing," Camille stated in a soft tone.

He halted and looked at her. He had forgotten all about her. How long had she been watching him? The memory resurfaced of the truth she admitted in the car. It had only been a few hours ago, but it seemed much longer. He hadn't fully processed it or how he should feel about it. Was just so mentally exhausted by everything.

"You do carry the weight of the world on your shoulders," she continued.

"Someone has to," he griped.

"Didn't work out so well with Nadine, did it?"

"How dare you!" he charged forward.

Camille didn't bat an eye. "Why are you pushing her away?"

"What are you talking about?" he lurched back, puzzled.

"Melia's not like Nadine. She's sensitive."

"I don't have to listen to you," he turned with annoyance.

"You couldn't fix everything with Nadine on your own and you can't do it now with Melia."

The right half of his face twitched, but he refused to acknowledge Camille's words. He shouldn't have let her come. It was a mistake.

Of course, he felt entitled to fix everything with Nadine. It was his fault to begin with. She would still be alive if he had just stayed away from her. Never befriended her. Never fell in love with her.

Melia was different. He didn't blame himself for her state, but he felt compelled to protect her just the same. She didn't deserve to live the miserable life she lived. Didn't deserve to continue to live in misery. She deserved happiness. This shouldn't be her fight to begin with. It was his.

His pacing came to a standstill when Melia reappeared. She paused at the bottom of the stairway that separated her from the room. The face she wore troubled him. He resisted the urge to go to her before she climbed the steps.

He resumed pacing. Suppressed the pang of guilt. Had to remain focused and stay strong. The only thing that mattered was finding a way to get rid of Maximilian before it was too late.

He heard the leather creaking as Camille moved. Refused to avert his attention as he kept his back to her. Listened to her footsteps as she headed towards the stairs. There was a part of him that wanted to stop her, but another part that prevented him. He couldn't be there for Melia like he should be anymore, so Camille was all she had left right now. That had to be good enough.

Cecily said he was supposed to clear his mind. That was easier said than done. His mind was all over the place. How was he supposed to quiet his thoughts? He had to think of a plan. One that was solid enough, as everyone's life could be on the line. He still didn't know what Maximilian wanted or why Melia was supposed to command fire. How could she control something she was afraid of? If Nadine was here, she would face fire head on. Walk through it even. She was fearless. Melia was fearful.

"You're a stubborn one, aren't you?" Cecily stood just inside the room from the base of the stairs.

"I think of it as logical."

Cecily slipped between the couch and coffee table, walking the pathway to a single shelf squeezed between the two wall length shelves. What little wall remained was covered in smooth gray rocks. A cathedral tabletop player sat in the middle. She turned the dial as static screeched out of the speaker before an audible soft and relaxing melody began to hum to life. She proceeded to the end of the couch and sat, folding her legs once more onto the huge cushion.

"Please sit, I insist," she patted beside her.

Reluctantly, he sighed before advancing over and sat on the edge at the opposite end from her.

"Your soul is fractured from an emotional dependency to someone from the past," she studied him with an intensity. Or rather, she was reading whatever he was projecting that she could see.

"I don't want to talk about it," he shot up to his feet.

"Dwelling on what you cannot change only feeds your crippling fear."

He didn't utter a word as he picked up pacing.

"You expel more energy with what you might lose instead of realizing what you already have."

"I have to protect her. I have to protect them all," he cried out.

"Your harrowing only holds you back. Your mind is in control, whereas your heart and soul are unbalanced. There's a reason why there are more skeptics than believers."

"I don't know how to open up again."

She stood and patted the cushion. "You can start by lying down, closing your eyes, and closing off your mind."

He hesitated.

"What else is there for you to do all night until the morning?" she walked back to the player, adjusted the sound, and lit a lilac candle.

He watched as she slipped past him and advanced up the stairs. She reminded him of Lamont, only she had an advanced level of perception. She didn't hold back from pushing any buttons.

He stared at the couch for a long time. Listened to the relaxing melody protruding. It did have a calming and settling effect. He just wasn't certain if he should give in.

He heaved a long sigh before he walked over and stretched out on the couch. Stared at the hardwood ceiling that mirrored the floor.

Slowly, he let his eyelids close. The first image that flashed across his mind was Lamont's lifeless body. His eyes snapped open. He should have been there. If he had gotten there sooner, maybe he could have prevented it. He should have foreseen a distraction in the first place. They should have been more prepared.

Close your mind.

Cecily's words echoed. How was he supposed to balance a heart with no beat? How was he supposed to balance his soul when he wasn't even sure he had one? Wasn't his soul encased in darkness with only one direction to go? One of the main reasons he held back. He didn't want his soul to burn. Had Nadine known what her fate entailed? Why his father feared death knowing he faced consequences.

He shook the overwhelming thoughts from his mind and tried closing his eyes once more. Tried focusing on just the tune playing as he tried eradicating evading thoughts. Inhaled the calming floral scent from the candle. Only the image of Nadine piercing herself with the other half of the wand surfaced as she faded away into ashes. The loneliness swallowed him whole.

It was going to be a long night.

Chapter 47
Melia

S he entered a small bedroom to her right where beige carpet lined the floor. The bed covered in eucalyptus green. A framed canvas hung above the wall. A single dark aqua plant with its stem and leaves outlined in a marigold.

She climbed into the queen-sized bed laying in the core center. Inhaled through her mouth and exhaled. She repeated before closing her eyes.

She heard the stairs creaking. Footsteps approached, but silence before fading away. She toned down her hearing, blocking any other sounds.

There was a knock on the door. She unfolded her legs and set down her homework on the small coffee table. She walked over to the front door and opened it revealing Pastor Samael.

"Good evening, my child."

"Good evening Pastor. Sorry to inform you, but my mother is not home currently."

"Oh," he pushed his glasses up the bridge of his nose. "It wouldn't trouble you if I asked for a glass of water?"

"No trouble, come in," she opened the door wide, permitted him entry.

He stepped into the house and followed her into the kitchen as she opened a cupboard, removed a cheap hard plastic cup, and filled it with water from the sink.

"Thank you," he accepted the water and drank a quarter of it.

She wore a soft smile and watched him wearily. He visited their house often, but this was the first time she was ever alone in his presences. She always let her mother do the talking and answered politely whenever she was asked a question.

"What did you think of my Sunday sermon?"

"It was insightful," she smiled through her teeth.

"You are aware that 'Lying lips are an abomination to the Lord'. *"*

She sighed. "Spencer did ask for help. No one helped. Not even I."

"His action is still a blaspheme against the Holy Spirt and an unforgivable sin."

She lowered her head with a sigh and nodded.

"To doubt me is to doubt Him. I only speak His words."

"Forgive me Father," she raised her eyes.

"You are forgiven, my child," he set his cup on the counter. "May I use the restroom?"

She nodded and pointed. "Through the living room, first door on the right."

She grabbed the cup from the counter and dumped the rest of the water into the sink. It gurgled on the way down as she placed the cup in the left side among other dirty dishes.

She walked back into the living room, pausing at the coffee table as she picked up on a faint smokey odor. She followed the smell down the hall as it grew stronger. It was coming from her bedroom.

She rushed forward, wondering what was on fire before halting in her tracks. Pastor Samael sat on the edge of her bed smoking a cigarette. What was he doing in her room? Why was he smoking?

"Come here, my child," he patted the bed beside him.

"My mother should be home any minute."

He took a deep pull as orange embers glowed at the end before exhaling the smoke. "I asked you to come here, not when your mother is expected to come home," he stood.

Something wasn't right. She knew something was all wrong about the situation, but she didn't know what to do. So, she just stood there frozen in place.

With impatience, he marched over and grabbed her arm, yanking her forward before pushing her down on the bed. He flipped her over, immobilized her with his body, and pushed up her shirt before she felt the burn of the end of the cigarette sizzle out against her flesh. She cried out in agony.

He cupped a hand over her mouth, "I do not take pleasure in this but affliction and suffering are your consequence for your disobedience."

She lied there paralyzed as he hiked up her skirt and pulled down her underwear. Heard the sound of a zipper before he thrust himself into her. She screamed. The pain he was inflicting was forceful. He covered her mouth as he drove into her again and again and again.

"Need I remind you; I am a man of God. No one will ever believe your word over mine," he left her and let himself out.

Tears pulled before spilling bucket loads. She forgot how to breathe before she was gasping for air. Shook uncontrollably as she slid off the bed and collapsed on the floor. Brought up her knees and sobbed. Her stomach began to churn before she shakily pushed up to her feet and crashed into everything before reaching the bathroom and vomited into the toilet. When she had nothing left in her stomach, she flushed the toilet and turned on the shower. She let the hot water turn her skin red as she scrubbed and scrubbed and scrubbed. Nothing she did could wash away the sully.

Her eyes snapped open. Her breaths, hot and heavy. She jumped away from the bed. She hugged herself. He couldn't hurt her anymore, but it didn't matter. She would be forever scarred. The image so vivid, like it just happened. She never felt clean afterwards. Only felt more tainted each time after.

She left the room and walked down the hall to the other bedroom, where she found Camille sitting on the beige carpet with her back against the wooden wall and knees drawn up. The room mimicked the bedroom she left. The only difference was a different portrait of a plant.

She quietly sat down beside her. "Are you able to close your eyes without seeing nightmares?"

"I don't close my eyes," Camille stared straight ahead.

"You didn't deserve it. No one deserves it."

"I'm here for you. I don't need you to be here for me."

She looked over at Camille. She sat solemnly. Camille was taking the sole blame. A punishment dished out to her as a price for her betrayal.

"I'm grateful you picked me."

"Why?" Camille's eyes narrowed.

"It was a blessing in disguise. You gave me a new life."

Camille scoffed. "If only it were a better one."

She slumped down as they sat in silence for countless minutes. Camille was a hard shell to splinter. The small pieces she was able to peel away only caused Camille to clamp up tighter.

"Here you two are," Cecily appeared with a smile. "Such a beautiful halo of deep red. Survivors."

She perked up. Survivor. She never thought of herself as that before. She only ever strived to make it through another day.

She shifted her head over to Camille, who chewed on the bottom of her lip. A creak redirected her attention as Cecily slipped back out of the room.

Chapter 48
Melia

She stared at nothing in particular after Cecily left, absorbing the single word she spoke.

Survivor.

Even though a part of her had died inside, she was still capable of standing. She wasn't strong. She wasn't brave. She was often afraid. Yet, somehow, she had still carried on. Somehow, even in her darkest hour, she could still see a light.

Hope.

Hope that one day she would understand why she had had to suffer such a brutality. Hope that one day she could overcome it and not be alone.

She looked back at Camille. She had seen the look in her eyes. She was without hope. She had been swallowed by the darkness, drowning in her own despair. Allowing herself to be pulled under.

Tenderly, she rested her hand on top of Camille's left hand. She wasn't unhinged when Camille snatched hers away. With persistence, she lowered her hand to Camille's right arm.

Camille's eyes fell upon her hand and inhaled sharply before raising her eyes. In one fluid motion, Camille shook off her hand and rose to her feet.

She stood facing Camille's back, looked down at her palm, and rubbed it with her thumb. "The first time, I was alone when he came to the house. He asked for a glass of water. Questioned me why I questioned him about his sermon. Asked to use the bathroom, but instead waited in my room. Burned me with the end of his cigarette before he forced himself onto me. Told me not to tell anyone because no one would believe me. I told my mother anyway, but she called me a liar and burned my hand."

Her voice trembled while streaks of red streamed down her face. Releasing the trauma felt a bit freeing. A weight lifted off her shoulders. She could talk to someone who knew what she was going through. Someone who would believe her. She didn't have to carry the burden alone.

"I was fastened into a straightjacket before shoved into a cell with the same face of the vampire that killed me. I thought he was dead. He played the part well. Pretended he was distraught over Nadine's death until I caved and told him what I did to the tea. When I confessed, he tore off his own straightjacket and attacked me. Ironic, the same face that killed me was also the same face to," Camille paused before choking on a whisper, "rape me."

She watched Camille fall to her knees. She rushed over and fell down beside her grazing her shoulder. Red tears stained the beige carpet in front of Camille. Camille tilted her head and met her eyes. She pulled Camille into an embrace. Camille gripped her firmly as they both cried harder.

She didn't know if Camille felt the same feeling she did, but there was an empowerment blossoming within. A strength she didn't have before. She finally had the comfort she always needed. Held her father tight several days after, but she couldn't tell him. Even when he asked, she just couldn't find the words. Had such shame. Believed it was her fault somehow.

"What was your life like before you became a vampire?" she asked over Camille's shoulder.

Camille didn't say anything for a long time before a soft chuckle emitted. "Less complicated."

She pushed back and scanned Camille's face. Smudges of red were all over her checks. She looked down at her stained, disheveled hair before back at Camille as they started to chuckle at how ridiculous they looked. "I could use a nice hot shower. How about you?" she stood.

"It's been such a long time since I've had one of those," Camille rose to her feet as well.

"I think there was a bathroom in the other bedroom," she reached out for Camille's hand.

Camille nodded with a cracked smile. She smiled weakly before she walked out of the room, across the hall, into the other bedroom, and stopped at the mirror in the bathroom.

Her cheeks mirrored Camille's face. Caked in clay red bands. Something out of a horror movie. She turned on the faucet and scrubbed her face watching streams of red wash down the drain. The makeup she once wore was long gone. At the time, she had enjoyed it on her face. Only she didn't need it to be who she was. It wouldn't tell her anyway.

She looked like a completely different person with her short choppy hair. At the time, it made her feel light and free, but now she didn't recognize the girl in the mirror.

She stripped off her clothing, leaving it in a heap, and hopped into the shower, letting the water cascade all around her. The water did not burn her skin except for her hand. It pulsated, reacting to the heat. That pain, that agony, she had condemned her mother to. Anger. Such a strong emotion. Had learned how to restrain it. Held it back. Ruled it from ruling her. Resisted its desire to lead her down a dark path. Fire was evil.

She stepped out of the shower. Opened the cabinet behind the mirror and found different herbal medicines. She also saw a small silver shear.

She finger-combed through her damp shoulder-length hair before gathering a section of it in the front and cut it. She couldn't remember a time when she ever had bangs. Her face appeared more oval as she trimmed her tattered ends more evenly.

She still didn't know who she was or who she was becoming, but she was no longer that girl from the past. That girl only shaped her into who she was today.

She grabbed a hand towel and dampened it before walking out of the bathroom and stopped in her tracks. Laying on the bed was an elegant olive-green jumpsuit. She peaked out into the hall, but there was no sign of Cecily or Camille.

She picked up the jumpsuit. It was sleeveless, with a round neck. A silver belt around the waist. Loose ankle-length legging. It even had a train in the back.

She walked back into the bathroom and slipped the garment on. She admired herself in the mirror. The green in her eyes popped against the brown. Her neck appeared longer. She never had this sense of confidence before.

"I won't accept it," she heard Camille shout.

She ducked out of the bathroom and paused at the doorway as Camille hurried down the stairs. Cecily appeared in the doorway of the other bedroom.

"What happened?"

"She's not quite ready," Cecily sighed before smiling. "You look radiate. It suits you. You like it?"

"Yes. Thank you"

"It's yours now."

"Really? Thank you so much."

"It was nothing. Now, how about you help me remove this stain from the carpet?"

"I'm so sorry about that," she hastened forward. "I was…"

Cecily put up her hand, silencing her. "No apology required."

She nodded her head.

"Let's see what you're made of," Cecily beckoned.

Chapter 49
Vince

He couldn't take it anymore. He was drowning in the recess of his own mind. Nothing but gloom. The music did not relax him when his eyes closed. It dissolved away when all the torment invaded.

He couldn't stand the atmosphere. It was too bright. To calm when he was nothing but inside. He swung his legs to the floor and stood. Everyone was upstairs. No one would notice if he slipped out.

He slowly opened the door and stepped onto the porch, taking in the landscape before him. Woods surrounded them in every direction. The night had descended.

There was only one way he knew how to clear his mind. He stepped off the porch and ran into the woods. He let himself run free. The ground was hard with dirty, crushed snow. He navigated around the long thin trees. Ran towards the mountain in the distance, closing in. He could scarcely remember a time when it was hard to catch his breath. An image of him running on the sandy shores of Tenerife scratched the surface of his mind. The waves lapped against the edge. Birds called to one another flying overhead. The turquoise water was tranquil and vibrant.

Peaceful.

A time of his innocence. A time with no worries. A time when he was balanced.

"Hey there, little man with an abundance of energy. Want to watch me try to catch a fish today?" Kumal stabbed the ground with his spear.

His whole body filled with excitement as he yelled in agreement.

"Follow me," Kumal beckoned.

He skipping with jubilation as he followed to the rocky shoreline. They travelled further from home that he had ever gone before. He was adventurous. What treasures could be found?

He ran up near the water and scanned the tide edge as shells tumbled forth as a gift from the ocean before receding back with the chance of never being seen again.

"Vinson, you're falling behind," Kumal called out from a distance.

He looked up and saw that Kumal was roughly fifteen meters away. He quickly covered the distance, in seconds, blazing past him before stopping momentarily looking for unique shells. This time he kept his eye on Kumal. When he got five meters away, he dashed after him and put a bit of distance before resuming his treasure hunt.

"Look what I found, look what I found," he rushed towards him with a whole shell half the size of his palm.

"That's a mighty fine moon shell you got there." Kumal picked it up and admired it before returning it to his hand. "I'm sure your mother will be delighted to see it."

He followed behind Kumal the rest of the way as he admired the smooth round spiral shell with swirls of cream and dusted autumn gold. The singular dark center resembled an eye.

"Why don't you put your shell some place safe for now?" Kumal pointed at a pile of rocks out of reach from the low tide.

He scrambled over and placed his shell in the groove of a jagged rock, the furthest away from the water, before making his way back.

Kumal scooped him up and placed him on his shoulders before walking out into the water, waist deep. The water was crystal clear. Could see the bottom floor. "I need you to be very quiet and very still, Vinson."

"Okay," he whispered.

He watched, memorized. They stood in the clear turquoise water, but just beyond faded to a morning sky blue into a deep night.

His eyes scanned the immediate area, but he saw no fish. He waited for what seemed like forever, but no fish appeared. "Where are the fish?"

"Shh," Kumal hushed not breaking stride.

He watched patiently for a few minutes more, but his patience was growing thin. He never understood why Kumal spent hours fishing, only to bring home a few small fish. Some days he caught a bigger fish that lasted them for more than one meal. How did he watch with tolerance? He fidgeted on his shoulders.

"You're scaring off the fish," Kumal whispered.

"I don't see any fish," he complained.

"They can feel vibrations in the water."

"I'm not in the water," he whined.

"But I am," Kumal turned and headed for shore.

He was disappointed he didn't get to see Kumal catch a fish as Kumal pierced the rocky ground with his spear. He hefted him off his shoulders and placed his feet into the water.

"I want you to close your eyes, place your hand against the water, and focus on what you feel?"

He did what Kumal instructed. After a moment, he peeked one eye open. "I just feel wet."

"You're not feeling with your mind, body, and soul. Without balance, there cannot be harmony. Without harmony, you'll only graze the surface."

"I don't understand," he grumbled.

"One day you will understand, today is not that day."

They headed home to the small stone hut concealed among tall pines. It was just the three of them however that was soon to change.

"Mommy, mommy, look what I found," he raced into his mother's small workshop. A place she handcrafted tools and furniture for the islanders.

She stopped the lathe and greeted him with a warm smile as she admired the shell in his hand. Her long, wavy brown hair was pinned back. She smelled of pine and sawdust. "It's beautiful."

The warmth of her love shined as bright as the sun from her almond-shaped brown eyes with specks of green surrounding the pupil. His smile faltered as his eyes fell upon her large, swollen belly.

"What's wrong, my love?"

"Will there still be enough love left for me when my sister comes?"

"Of course. My love for you will never go away. Come with me," she reached out her hand and stood.

He took it as he bounced alongside her outside. She sat on one of the rocking chairs she crafted and set him on the end of her knees.

"You are the light of my life. The sun in my night sky. My love for you is infinite. Whenever you feel lost and alone, all you have to do is

close your eyes and I'll be there to guide you with the warmth of my love. Nothing will ever separate my eternal love for you."

He felt the warm sunrays on his innocent face, soaking him with warmth from the outside in.

He stopped hard in the snow-covered woods and leaned against a tree. The memory had been vivid. Heard his mother's sweet, gentle voice. Felt the sunshine warm him to the core he hadn't felt in a long time.

He tossed his head back and looked between the branches into the night sky. It was cloud covered. No stars to be seen. With disappointment he dropped his head. He stared at nothing in particular before taking in a deep breath and closing his eyes.

He heard night creatures prowling. Trees creaking as they swayed in the night breeze. Snow crunching from shifting footsteps.

He reached deeper inside himself, tuning out all the noise and focused on projecting what he felt. It was hard for him to concentrate. It had been a hair of a second feeling his mother's love, but it was gone before he could fully absorb it.

He fixated on feeling the sunshine on his face. Longed to feel that warmth within. Imagined the sun in the sky raining down rays of light.

A warm stream reached out and tickled his face before flowing up against his confined stone heart. He turned towards the current and stepped forward. Slowly, he followed. With each step, the stream strengthened. Part of him wanted to run the opposite direction, but another part wanted to know where it would lead.

He walked for a long time until he emerged from the woods and faced the cabin. Swallowed hard. He wanted to plant his feet into the ground, but they did not listen. Before he knew it, he was climbing the porch steps and faced the door hesitating at the doorknob. He knew for certain where it was leading him.

A groan from the wood alerted him that he wasn't alone. He whipped his head to the right and saw Camille standing at the end of the porch with her arms stuffed into the pockets of her jacket while Leo sat on the railing ledge, tail flicking with annoyance.

"What are you doing outside? It's not safe in the dark," he snapped.

"I could ask you the same thing," Camille raised an eyebrow after tossing her head over her shoulder.

"If anything happened to you, she would be upset."

"Well, then, you'd have to convince her that I'm not worth saving."

Chapter 50
Vince

He heaved a long sigh before turning away from the front door and walked over to the bench positioned at the front of the porch and dropped down. "She'd be highly mad you said that."

"Melia, mad?" Camille scoffed.

"Not Melia. Nadine."

Camille inhaled sharply as she turned away. "Tomorrow's December 17th. She should be here to turn another year older."

"Did she ever tell you how she found out what I was?"

"No," Camille shook her head.

"It was at Greg Pierce's party, remember that night?"

Greg Pierce. A typical bully. One he had enjoyed messing with when compelling Tommy from doing Greg's homework or putting down the wrong answers. Only he should have been helping Tommy to stand up to Greg of his own accord, not made him against his will. He was the cause of the crossfire Nadine nearly found herself in when Greg got livid enough to start getting physical.

"Vaguely," Camille answered. "I was kind of drunk that night."

"Well, I remember. Your father called her looking for you. Told her not to worry, but she was determined to find you. Called several classmates until she found out about the party. Stormed in with her fiery attitude." He smiled to himself. He had followed her and heard the commotion. She had been called the party crasher. Only she wasn't the one who stopped the party.

"Sounds like her," Camille commented.

"Greg's father came home early. She was going to leave with you. Should have left, but she didn't. Greg's father got physical and she went back to talk him down. Defused his anger. Then Greg came at his father with a knife. Even though she was defenseless, she put herself between them, waiting for the inevitable. I took the hit for her."

Camille slowly turned to face him.

"They didn't deserve her empathy, but even in their darkest moments, she refused to stand by and watch them tear each other apart."

"She would have made the world a better place if she was still here, even if she was a vampire," Camille whispered.

"She went through the tunnels. Passed by all the cells. She would have had to intercept you at some point. She could have done anything she wanted to you after what you did to her, but she let you go, didn't she?"

Camille shifted uncomfortably.

He had thought about it often when he discovered Camille was still alive. Couldn't fathom why Nadine would just let her walk away. He knew he wouldn't have been strong enough to do that. "Even when she lost her way, there was still a part of her that remained true."

Camille reached up and gripped her necklace. "She still had my back, even when I didn't have hers."

"I think some part of you did."

Her eyes lifted to his.

"At least, in the end."

"I should have stopped Jomar, not break her neck," the necklace dropped from her hold as she looked out into the distance.

"I've spent a lot of time wondering, what if? The problem is, it doesn't matter. Neither one of us can change it. She's gone and she's not coming back," his glaze traveled to the woods beyond her.

Camille sighed. "I wish I had a chance to apologize."

"And I'd like to know why she choose to end her life."

"Wait. What? What, what do you mean by that?" Camille's voice rose an octave.

He hesitated. Should he tell her? She already held onto so much guilt. However, he knew firsthand keeping the truth only messed with one's mind. "She could have survived after she took down Vladimir. I begged her to take my blood, but she ended her life instead."

"That doesn't, that doesn't make sense. The Nadine I knew would have never done that," she shook her head.

"You of all people know what you are capable of when you let the darkness in."

Camille stood quietly for a minute. Without a word, she sauntered over and sat down on the opposite end of the bench. "I never told you that I was in a mentally abusive relationship."

He studied her while waiting for her to continue.

"There was a time I used to be popular. Had a sizeable group of so-called friends. An athlete boyfriend. I thought I found my high school sweetheart. Thought I was heading down the same path as my parents. I had no idea I was being manipulated, but Nadine did. She saw right through him."

Leo hopped up on the bench between them and curled up in a ball. He stroked the back of his head.

"I didn't believe her at first. Didn't want to, but she got inside my head. The more I started questioning, resisting, the angrier he became. She gave me the courage to break it off with him. To take back control," she paused. "I lied to you."

His hand paused above Leo's head. "About what?"

"I wasn't hypnotized."

He didn't know what to say.

"I have Nadine to thank for that. She once told me, 'Never let anyone have the power to control you. You control your own mind and your actions. You are not to be used as a tool for someone else's means.'"

"Then why?"

"He would have found someone else. I was sending a message to alert you."

He stared at her, dumbfounded.

"That's beside the point. My abusive ex-boyfriend found someone else to manipulate. Nadine tried to warn her. She didn't want to listen. Got in deep, in over her head. Replaced me in the popular circle. Nadine kept a close watch on her. I remember Nadine telling her once 'If you feel uncomfortable around them, then they are not the right friends for you.' She tried so hard to help her like she helped me, but it wasn't enough. She ended up committing suicide."

He wasn't sure what exactly the purpose of Camille's reminiscence of her past was all about until she uttered that last word.

"She expressed to me," Camille brought up her hands making air quotes. "'When it's not your time to go, death does not solve your problems, it just creates new ones. Pushes the pain you carried onto the people you leave behind who truly care about you.'"

He pushed up to his feet. He had more questions now than ever. If Nadine was against suicide, why did she take her own life? What reason did she have? He looked back at Camille. "I didn't treat you any better than that guy did. Never gave you a fair chance. In that respect, I'm sorry."

"You don't need to feel entitled," Camille shrugged as she petted Leo, who was now in her lap.

He sat back down on the bench and stared at the worn floorboards of the porch. "I never thought I would ever be able to reach this point. I think, however, it's not just important for me, but it's also imperative for you." He paused and inhaled deeply before turning to face her. "I forgive you."

Camille turned her head, breaking eye contact. He heard an emitted sniffle. She carried enough of a burden for her actions. She didn't need any more weight on top of it. He could see clearly that it tortured her. The road ahead would be much longer for her to be able to forgive herself.

Somewhere along the way, he realized, he had acknowledged to himself that he forgave her, but saying it out loud was freeing and with it came a peaceful energy within.

"You should know, I ship the two of you," Camille whispered as she quickly swiped at her cheek.

"Ship?" he frowned in confusion.

"You and Melia," Camille slid over and bumped her shoulder into his with a small smile.

His eyes diverted to the door. The warm trail he had been following was leading him to her. He didn't know if he could go through it again. "I'm afraid," he admitted.

Camille sat there quietly, gazing out into the woods. "'Do not let the whispers of fear limit you from progression.'" The words rolled off her tongue. "Another thing Nadine told me."

Chapter 51
Melia

She held her left hand with her fingers clawed downward as she focused on that pulsating force before beads of red rose from the carpet towards her hand. Held them suspended in the air as she walked them over to the bathroom sink. Let them fall in as she washed the blood down the drain. She walked back over to the spot. No evidence remained. The threads were without any stain.

She turned to face Cecily with a wide smile, proud of her accomplishment. Her smile faltered. Cecily's golden-brown eyes were with concern. Her mouth slightly parted.

"Did I do something wrong?" she asked.

Cecily walked over to the bed and sat on the edge. "Sit with me."

She complied as she closed the gap and sat beside her.

"When did you start practicing magic?" Cecily inquired.

"Just a few days ago," she shifted her feet uncomfortably.

"The magic you used, it's on a level far greater than your skill."

"I don't understand."

"It's very advanced. You could say ancient even. You were not one with the magic. You commanded it. Forced it to do your bidding."

"Is that bad?" anxiety squeezed a hold of her. She didn't really have to ask to know the answer.

"Over time, you could lose sight of yourself to it."

"Then I won't use it anymore."

"You have not been properly shown. I can teach you a more mindful technique."

She was uncertain if she should agree. What if, by default, she reverted back to using magic in a negative way? Being able to use magic made her feel invincible. Boosted up her confidence. No one had the power to hurt her anymore without her being able to defend herself. Yet, at the same time, that power could hurt others, including the ones she cared about that she didn't want to hurt. It had consequences. Repercussions.

"Just like a spiral, small ripples help develop our growth and expand our journeys."

She looked down at her necklace. Picked it up between her thumb and index finger. Rubbed its smooth surface. "How do I trust myself?" she let the spiral drop.

"Close your eyes, calm your mind, and feel the energy surrounding you," Cecily urged.

"It didn't work so well the first time."

"Don't listen to your mind, listen to your heart. Feel the energy around you and where it may lead."

She inhaled and exhaled a few sharp breaths before slowing them down. Slowly, reluctantly, she let her eyelids fall. She focused on the darkness behind her lids before flicking them open.

"Sometimes it helps to sit up tall on a level surface," Cecily advised.

She slipped off the bed and sat cross-legged on the floor as she focused on a positive, happy memory. One where she was with her father fishing. They didn't always need to speak to feel the positive vibe around them.

Calmness.

Peacefulness.

A warm feeling of happiness.

She could hear the water trickle as if she was with him on the side of the banks. Hear the birds sing with glory. Feel that moment in time where she was transported to a place with no uncertainties. Had the impression that everything was going to be okay because she was with that one person who gave her strength instead of extracting it.

She felt that warmth reaching out, stroking her face as it flowed down to her core. It called to her. Beckoned her to follow to the source.

Her eyes slowly flicked open as she rose to her feet. She moved in a trance-like state trusting her impulse. One step at a time, she leisurely descended the stairs. When she reached the front door, the energy intensified. She heard the wood creak under the gentle footsteps approaching. She hesitated. A groan shortly followed before she heard his voice from the other side of the door.

She backed away quietly and approached the living room. A relaxing sound drifted from a speaker on a shelf above the red wood-burning stove.

"Why did you resist?" Cecily tilted her head from the bottom of the stairs.

"He mourns for another," she shrugged. "Besides, I've only ever disrupted his life with mayhem."

"I see," Cecily approached the couch and sat before patting the cushion beside her. "Why don't we work on an energy orb?"

She was glad for the distraction. Glad Cecily didn't push her to reconsider her looming thoughts. She had an unexplained connection with Vince. Felt it the first moment they met. It terrified her then and it terrified her now. When this was all over, he'd probably want nothing to do with her. His heart was with someone else. Someone she could never be a replacement for.

"Follow my lead," Cecily rubbed her hands together vastly before changing into a circular motion pulling her hands slowly apart. The light-gold sphere appeared, expanding as Cecily pulled her hands apart.

With a deep exhale, she mimicked Cecily. She felt friction between her hands. Wasn't certain when to start the circular motion. Just followed her instinct as she changed the pattern. She felt a tingling magnetize from her palms as she pulled them apart.

"Your energy is a reflection of you."

She heard Cecily speak, but kept her mind focus at the energy she was forming in her hand. She spun her hands slowly around her own sphere, memorized. At some point, she had stopped rotating her hands around it. Just as quickly as it formed, it withdrew back into her. "What does clear mean?" she turned to Cecily.

"Purity."

She looked away. Was she pure? At one time she would have believed it, but certain circumstances made her question it.

"Can I ask you something?"

"Sure," she tilted her head in Cecily's direction.

"What are some words you would describe fire?"

Her eyes grew as images flashed. "Damaging, Destructive," she paused. "Harmful."

Cecily hummed. "I see."

She sensed there was something more on her mind. She waited for Cecily to go on. All her life all she saw was the dark side of fire.

"Yes, fire can be all those," Cecily paused, "but doesn't fire also bring warmth on a cold night? Light in the night sky? A necessity for life itself?"

She said nothing as she looked at her palm. Knew there was truth in the words. She just didn't know how to embrace that truth.

"Some words I tend to describe fire are; Manifestation. Regeneration. Purification."

She tried to view the scar on her palm as something good that resulted from it. None of those words represented the scar on her palm or on her stomach.

"Just like energy, a positive charge will only attract a negative one, but repels one that is alike."

Her mind was spinning, trying to make sense of it all.

"You've already conquered your fear."

"What?" she aspirated.

"Energy is fire from your soul."

A single word whispered from the depth of her mind.

Survivor.

Chapter 52
Vince

Fear had a grip on him with an ironclad. He wanted nothing more than to open that door and go to Melia. The fear of possibly losing her, though, held him at bay. Losing Nadine nearly destroyed him. He couldn't risk total devastation. The feelings he suppressed for Melia were somehow different from the feelings he had for Nadine.

Lamont once told him, "Someday you'll remember all the good instead of the sorrow." He never thought he'd see that day, but talking about Nadine with Camille was less painful. Nadine wasn't present anymore, but she had affected all of their lives, in a good way. There was no doubt in his mind she would want him to move on and be happy.

Subconsciously, he had approached the door. His mind visualized his hand reaching down and twisting the knob to open it, but his hand disobeyed.

A yelp pierced the night. He whirled away from the door and took two strides forward on the porch, focusing out into the distance.

"What was that?" Camille joined him.

The door behind them creaked open. He redirected his attention as Melia appeared in the doorway. "What's going on?"

He found no words to answer her. He was momentarily breathless. She had transformed herself again. Every change she made only made her appear more confident. Stronger. Boundless.

Doubts entered his mind there would be any room left for him. Nadine had been independent. She hadn't needed him or wanted him. Something she had made clear that he had ignored.

A howl rang out, snapping him back into reality. His insecurities didn't matter. What mattered now was defending and protecting Melia at all costs.

"Stay inside," he spoke with authority before stepping off the porch and heading in the direction of the commotion.

He raced through the crystalized snow-covered woods, veering around trees like he was in a maze. He picked up on Cameron's scent and stayed the course.

He slid to a stop when he came upon the scene. Aurora was on her side, injured, while Cameron licked her wounds. His wolf head whipped into his direction before he shifted.

"Where's Melia?" Cameron eyed the area behind him with alarm.

"She's still inside. What happened?"

"He's here. He was watching you. Aurora and I picked up on a faint scent from him. Before we had a chance to close in, he lured us away. Aurora attacked him, but he cut her with some sort of stick he had."

"Where did he go?"

"Disappeared into thin air."

"I should get back. She going to be okay?" his eyes shifted to Aurora, who was meekly rising to her paws.

"Nothing I can't heal."

He spun on his heel before tossing over his shoulder, "I'm sorry I got you involved in all of this."

"I'm not."

He craned his neck further, meeting Cameron's eyes before he shifted back to wolf form. With a nod, he took back off through the woods. He pushed through them as fast as he could manage, but it still wasn't fast enough. Not when this evil spirit could disappear and reappear anywhere at any time.

He came to an abrupt halt at the edge of the trees. Ice coursed through his veins to his spine. Max was there, on the porch, with a firm grip around Camille's neck, facing Melia still standing in the doorway.

"No," he shouted as he charged forward.

He didn't have a plan. Didn't know what it would take to fight against him, but he had to try. Even if he died trying, it wouldn't be because he didn't give it his all.

"Let her go," he demanded from the bottom steps.

"I think I'll hold on to her for a little while. As an incentive," he paused before whispering in Camille's ear. "This might be an uncomfortable experience for you." He disappeared before Camille was sucked into some unseen vortex following behind him.

219

He was discouraged. Melia was safe, for now, but Camille was simply gone. He was overwhelmed with mixed feelings. There would have been a time when he could have cared less what happened to her, but time had shifted. He cared now.

"Camille!" Melia shrieked as she stepped out onto the porch, staring at the last place Camille had stood.

He didn't overthink it as he closed the gap and grasped her by the shoulders. "I'm going to get her back," he promised, even though he didn't know if he could keep it. He would be the support she needed until she didn't need him anymore.

"Not just you," she shook her head. "We."

He stared down into her brown-green eyes. She wasn't that same scared, innocent girl anymore. She had grown. Grown right before his eyes. She had always been much stronger than he gave her credit for. She didn't choose this life. Instead, she was embracing it. She was beautiful not just on the outside, but on the inside as well. It blossomed from within. Someone would be lucky to be chosen by her.

He heard padded-paws pounce off the hard snow as they closed in to the cabin. He automatically redirected his attention as Cameron shifted.

"What's going on?" Cameron asked.

"He took Camille," he released his hold on Melia, dropping his head.

"Aurora and I will search for them," Cameron turned away.

"You won't find them here," Melia voiced.

"Do you know where he went?" he searched her eyes.

She nodded. "A place with a lot of negative energy."

He frowned, uncertain what she meant. Wasn't good with all this sorcery. He was lost in the dark.

"A place with a lot of death."

He stiffened. He didn't need to know much about magic to know what she meant. He had felt it. The way the charred earth drained him just by standing next to it. Not due to just who he had lost, but the fight in itself. A vicious one with no mercy when darkness was the only path.

"There's nothing any of you can do at the moment. Come inside we must converse," Cecily motioned with her hand.

Chapter 53
Vince

He trailed behind Melia. Cameron followed behind him, with Aurora close to his heels. It was clear to him they shared a fondness for each other. Cameron had left and found a way to move on. Possibly happiness. Only now he got sucked into a new battle. One he wasn't sure they stood a chance at winning. There was no prophecy foretold about this. They were on their own.

They entered the living room. Cecily sat on the end while Melia sat next to her in the middle. He didn't feel like sitting, so he remained standing.

"Sit," Cecily urged.

"I'd prefer to stand," he dismissed.

"I insist on you sitting," Cecily pushed back.

His eyes narrowed before darting to Melia, who patted the cushion beside her. He sighed before dropping on the edge.

Cecily turned at an angle to face him. "Do you know what he wants?"

"For Melia to command fire."

"Why does he want it?"

He hesitated, shifting his eyes from Melia back to Cecily before confessing. "I don't know."

"Would you like to know what I saw?"

He nodded once.

"Darkness."

He wasn't amused. He had gathered that much already when knowing who they were dealing with. Maximilian was someone bad enough to be exterminated in the past and he didn't believe the threat had changed in the present.

"Complete darkness," Cecily reiterated. "He is nothing but a void incapable of his own conjuring."

"We saw him though, kill hundreds of vampires with power."

"Power he siphoned."

His eyes dropped to the hard-wood floor as he recalled the event. He lifted his head and met Melia's eyes.

"That's why you collapsed. He siphoned from you," his eyes diverted back to Cecily. "How?"

"He would need some kind of link."

"The broken stick," Melia answered.

"What broken stick?" Cameron stood tall, on alert.

"My mother's wand," he whispered. "It's protected. It can't be destroyed. The only way to destroy it…"

He stopped before abruptly lurching to his feet and began to pace. Nadine had destroyed the other half. Destroyed it when she implanted herself with it. He longingly looked at Melia. This couldn't be happening again.

"What happens if Melia would command fire?" he pierced Cecily's dark brown eyes.

"He is not whole. He is powerless. To ascend, he would need to take a host."

"No," he clenched his hands into fists as he yelled. "I won't let him."

A deep-throated growl began to emit from Aurora.

"Vince," Melia rose walking towards him gently placing her hands over his fists. "It's okay."

"No, it's not," he grumbled, pulling back. The feel of her skin unnerved him. Like a hot coal to the touch.

"He won't get inside my head again," Melia asserted.

"If we get the broken wand from him, he would remain powerless and unable to siphon from Melia?" Cameron inquired.

"I believe so, yes," Cecily answered.

"Let's go," he turned in the direction of the front door.

"You can't go to battle without a shield," Cecily spoke calmly.

"I'll find a way," he tossed over his shoulder with determination.

Cameron cut into his path. "Vince, we can't charge in there without a plan."

He sighed in surrender at the irony of the words he once told Nadine. Cameron was right. So was Cecily. He was letting his emotions get the best of him. A mistake. He knew better then to charge in without a level head. Besides, by the time they drove to the burned down asylum, daylight would be arriving. There would be no time to get it done.

"In the meantime, you have the rest of the night to practice in opening your eyes and seeing," Cecily's low voice urged.

"They're open. I see clearly."

"Your mind is still closed. You see nothing but empty space," Cecily redirected her attention and nodded, "Melia."

He stood there watching her rub her hands together before pulling them apart shaping an invisible object in her hand.

"Come over and touch it," Cecily beckoned.

He was tentative as he rubbed the back of his neck and rolled his shoulders. With a puff of impatience, he walked over to the couch, stood before Melia, and passed his hand through the empty space between hers. He saw nothing, but he felt warm air between Melia's hands. It could only be a coincidence.

"Good. Very good. Now, I want you to practice creating your own energy orb. Melia can help you," Cecily rose.

"Where are you going?" he asked with a frown.

"Unlike you, I require rest to recharge. I will see you in the morning," Cecily retreated towards the stairs before climbing them.

Chapter 54
Melia

Her energy orb had magnified in brightness when Vince's hand touched it. She swallowed the lump in her throat when Cecily was quick to retreat. She wanted to ask her about it. Wanted to know what it could mean.

Max had been angry. Angry she wouldn't step outside. Angry he couldn't get inside to her. Threw spiteful words in her direction. Told her Camille was her enemy. That she was naïve to think she could ever be friends with her. Camille had betrayed her in the worse way possible. With death. She was supposed to embrace how that made her feel.

Angry.

Vengeful.

She was neither of them. Rather, she was empathetic. The feelings she was supposed to have were what was supposed to fuel the fire. She didn't have that fire. That fire was hurtful and cruel. Something she didn't believe in.

She formed her energy orb. Cecily said it was fire from her soul. He had been displeased. Claimed that was not commanding fire. Threatened to hurt Camille. Had tossed Leo off the side of the porch into the trees.

Cecily reassured her not to listen to him. That he wasn't capable of hurting Camille. That he was just trying to get inside her head. She stood there at a standstill with uncertainty when Vince appeared.

That's when realization dawned. He had backed away from her energy orb. A flash of fear had momentarily crossed his face. He was the negative energy. She was the positive. He fed on her darkness for strength.

"I'm going to head back to the pack and your clan," Cameron's voice refocused her mind.

"Clan?" Vince expressed with perplex.

"Is there something else you'd like me to call your vampires?"

Vince sighed. "Clan is fine. We only brought one vehicle."

"I can take Cecily's truck."

"Cecily drives?" Vince's eyebrows pinched up.

"She sees differently. She's not blind."

"Oh."

"We'll meet there at sundown."

Cameron stroked the top of Aurora's head, who sat perched next to him, before heading for the front door. Aurora followed with her nails clicking on the wood. She hadn't left his side the moment they arrived.

She smiled to herself. Taking Cecily's truck meant he would have to return it. Would have to cross paths with Aurora at least one more time. She wondered how he handled it now that he was in charge of the pack. Two different lives separate from one another. When this was all over, he would have to leave one behind. He couldn't live both.

Aurora sulked back into the room. She raised her head, alternating her eyes between Vince and her. With a slight snort, Aurora continued on her way to the stairs and flew up them.

She was left alone with Vince. The first time in what seemed like a very long time. She was uncertain what to say. How to break the silence.

She saw Vince glance her way from her peripheral. He seemed in a frozen state of mind too. The quiet was awkward. There was so much she wanted to say, but now was not the time. "Cecily said to help you practice, so..." she patted the cushion beside her.

Slowly he eased to an upright position, leaving space between them on the couch.

"Deep breath."

She watched his chest rise and fall as he complied.

"Now, emulate me." She rubbed her hands together as Vince mimicked. She didn't need to chafe so much anymore for the energy to gather to her hands, but she continued for Vince's sake. "Do you feel friction between your hands?"

"I guess," he responded, but there was a hint of doubt.

"Focus on that heat. Pull your hands slightly apart. Shape it in a circular motion."

She demonstrated as Vince watched from the corner of his eye. He followed her lead. She saw a small, dark blue orb with black streaks sparking with resistance.

Vince dropped his hands and lurched to his feet. "This is pointless. I can't do magic."

She studied him before she let her eyes fall. She reached out to him. Felt what was beneath the surface. He was scared. Carried a heavy load on his shoulders. Surrounded by chaos of his own making.

She couldn't deny what was standing before her. She sensed it the first moment they met. Was able to read his feelings like an open book. Even though she could read people well, Vince had always been different. She was deeply sensitive to his emotions. He was her soulmate. Someone she thought she'd never have a chance to find. Only she dreamed one day he'd come riding in on a white horse, sweep her off her feet, and protect her from a life that tried to crush her spirit. If her life of hardship taught her anything, it was that if she could be strong enough to stand on her own, her strength would only flourish when others stood by her. Her belief became their belief. A force unstoppable.

"Don't be afraid," she rose, brushing her hand against his. He yanked it back. "You're not alone."

"I know I'm not, it's just..." he let his words hang.

"Darkness does not drive out darkness. Only light can."

His eyebrows pinched together. He didn't speak. Didn't move. Just stood as still as a statue.

She didn't overthink it. She shifted closer to him. Rose on her tiptoes, closed her eyes, and lightly pressed her lips against the side of his cheek.

There was no doubt in her mind that she was in love with him. He made her feel worthy. Safe. She could do anything she set her mind on. The only unconditional love she knew was from her father. Being just herself was enough. Vince made her feel that way, too. She was enough as she was.

It didn't matter if he couldn't love her back. Maybe one day he could. He gave her new strength. A desire to not run anymore. To stand up and fight. She found in herself what was worth fighting for. As long as he was by her side, that was all that mattered. He didn't need to be able to use magic. She could be enough for them both.

226

Chapter 55
Vince

He exhaled a heavy stream of air. He had not expected Melia to kiss him on the cheek. So soft. So delicate. The ice that had grown inside his core, started to melt. Time stood still. Everything faded to background white noise. The only thing on his mind was Melia. He wanted to pull her close and kiss her on the mouth. His body screamed like steam from a tea kettle, but he couldn't bring himself to do it. He couldn't allow himself to be selfish, again.

He wasn't sure what the hidden meaning was behind her words of darkness and light. They both could drive each other out. It was which one was strongest. He feared darkness would prevail this time. It never stopped. There was always something dark that emerged. He was so tired of fighting it. It was always there to drain him.

He was at war with himself. If he surrendered now, it would be detrimental. He wouldn't have Lamont to lean on who knew the truth. He had a dark side. It wanted freedom. One more broken straw would crumble his reserve.

He hated himself for hurting Melia. Rejecting her. Had no choice. He had to. He couldn't bear to stick around and see her wounded face.

He found himself on the front porch, standing where Camille had stood staring out into the darkened woods. He thought he masked it well, but she saw. Camille was once oblivious. At least he thought she was. Only she had seen his conflict with Nadine. He didn't think he was one to wear his heart on his sleeve. Thought he was good at masking it. He had been wrong.

Camille had given him her stamp of approval. Not like it mattered what she thought, but in some way, it was reassuring to know. What scared him the most was moving on. Nadine had deserved happiness she never got a chance to relish in. He was partially to blame for that. Did he deserve a chance at happiness?

Leo leapt up onto the railing. He rubbed against his arm as his motor ran. He patted the top of Leo's head. Somehow, Leo always made him feel slightly better than the state Leo found him in. Almost like Leo knew he needed comfort. His affection was contagious. He never questioned adoring the cat. It was easy with Leo. Unconditional. He didn't expect anything in return. Pushed away the darkness just by being there.

And yet, when Leo had looked into his eyes, into his soul, he didn't find darkness there. Darkness wasn't who he was. Deep inside himself, he was good. He just needed a light to help guide him during this dark time.

He was getting dangerously close to surrendering. He was at a crossroads, with only one direction he wanted to go. Instead, he ran the opposite way. Ran through the snow-covered woods once more. He was in disarray. The pull was strong. He couldn't ignore it. It tormented him. Veering onto the path without realizing it and quickly jumping back off of it.

He stopped in the clearing facing the cabin. The door still left open letting the cold seep in as the warm air traveled in his direction. All he had to do was follow it and let it melt the rest of the ice encased around his heart.

He tilted his head and looked up into the night sky. Saw the stars flicker bright against the dark contrast. Even in darkness, there was still some kind of light to look for. "Please don't take her too," he begged to whoever listened.

He didn't know if he even had a right to ask. He just needed a sign. Hope that everything would turn out okay this time. He needed to believe this time wouldn't end in tragedy.

He closed his eyes and let down his defenses. Focused on the energy around him. Harnessed what surrounded him. With eyes still closed, he rubbed his hands together. Embraced the traction of heat between his palms. Slowly, he pulled his hands apart. Felt a magnetic pull to his hands as he continued to spread them further apart.

He opened his eyes. A blue glow blinded him. Energy pulled from his palms, shaping into a small orb that was suspended. He was in disbelief, but he couldn't deny what he was seeing. It was right there in front of him. Nothing had changed. He felt the friction before. Felt the magnetic pull. The orb had been there all along in his hand, but he couldn't see it until now. As bright as the stars in the sky. As the moon. As the sun.

How many times had he talked about his mother being a witch? What had caused him to be doubtful he couldn't possess magic too? Why had he been blinded to it?

The universe had given him a sign. His eyes returned to the open door. The light within called to him. He couldn't turn away from it anymore. He was drained from surviving in the dark. Tired of being alone.

In a trance, he crept forward. Climbed the steps. Entered the cabin. He took a second to absorb the energy inside. Followed the strong source, like a compass. Paused to catch his breath.

Melia sat back on the couch, tossing a clear orb shining bright between her hands. He watched memorized. His eyes were wide open now. He saw perfectly.

"Vince?" Melia sat up, analyzing him. "Are you okay?"

He strode forward without a sound. Stepped over the coffee table and sat on it across from her. "I can see now."

A bright smile lit up her face. He reached out and cupped the side of her face. Her hand slipped over his as he traced her bottom lip to the top with his thumb. If his heart still had a beat, it would be pounding on overtime right now.

He took two quick breaths before he leaned forward, closed his eyes, and placed his lips upon hers. His soul was on fire as he devoured her lips passionately with hunger. He was drunk for them. Something he never felt before. On sensory overload. There was nothing he had to worry about. No questions to hold him back. He had his strength renewed. His mind for the first time quiet. He was dizzy as the world around him faded away. Sparks flew in this moment of desire.

He could only comprehend deprivation when Melia suddenly pushed him back. His vision blurred before he could focus. Her eyes were fully blown. Her teeth extended.

He grazed his tongue over his upper canines. They too had lengthened. They had brought out the primal in each other.

"It's okay," he saw a worried look cross her face as he tucked a wisp of her sunshine hair behind her ear.

"What if…"

He placed two fingers on her lips. "I trust you."

She flung into him, wrapping her arms around his neck, as he slid across the coffee table and they both crashed onto the floor. She was just as hungry for him as he was for her. He never felt so grateful that he didn't have to stop to catch his breath.

Chapter 56
Melia

She never craved someone so much in her life. He craved her, too. She could tell by the way he kissed her. Like it was a necessity. It did something to both of them. Lost in the ecstasy of the moment. She wanted him in a way she had never wanted before. It thrilled her and terrified her.

He said he trusted her. There was no apprehension in his eyes. His trust in her allowed her to trust herself. She loved him without a doubt. Wondered if it was too soon to say the words out loud. The only thing she knew for certain was she would never willingly want to hurt him.

She giggled when they crashed onto the floor. Giggled again when their teeth scraped against each other. These feelings they shared were charged. Her mind was not her own. This time, it was different. She didn't have to fight it. She could let herself go wild.

The sound of a zipper slowly opening made her pull back and freeze.

"What's wrong?" he sensed her anxiety.

"I, I don't want to go too fast," she stuttered before rolling off of him and stared at the ceiling.

"Okay," he propped himself up on one elbow, leaning towards her.

She met his blue, sparkling eyes. He was willing to wait for when she was ready. She didn't have to give him a reason why. She loved him even more. "What color was your hair?" she reached up and grazed over his bald head.

"Light brown."

"Will it ever grow back?"

"No."

She was both happy and a little sad. She would never have to worry about her hair growing out again, but she would never see Vince with his natural locks.

"Where did you get this?" he picked up her spiral and twirled it around in his fingers.

"I found it at my father's place. I think maybe it's a family heirloom. It was in an old wooden box. The name Synklar was inscribed on the top."

He studied it. Traced the smooth curved wood. She wondered if it meant something to him as he let it fall back onto her chest and perched to his feet. She watched him begin to pace, deep in thought. There was definitely something on his mind.

"What is it?" she asked coming up behind him.

"I was very young, but I remember my mother carving a spiral on her lathe. The same style as the one you have. It was a darker colored wood, though, and the name isn't familiar."

"You think your mother carved this one too?" she grasped it in her hand.

"I don't know," he shrugged.

She could sense there was more. "What else is on your mind?"

"I had a sister."

She stood quietly waiting for him to continue.

"It's a vague memory. One I just recently remembered. I don't know what happened to her, but I think maybe my mother made the spiral for her."

She wove her fingers with his. He automatically curled his around hers, joining them tight.

"There could be someone out there that I'm related to," he implied.

"We can search for them."

"It's not going to be easy. The only record I had from my mother was burned and there's no one left to question. They are all gone."

"The answers are somewhere. We just have to ask the right questions in the right place."

"I never got to know her," he half laughed. "Remember being unhappy when my mother told me. I wanted a baby brother. All I had was my mentor, Kumal, growing up, but he couldn't be there like a sibling would have."

She knew what he meant as they stood there in silence.

"I could have a sibling out there somewhere too. My father cheated on my mother, which is why they divorced. Why she became bitter," he squeezed her hand. "I often daydreamed I had a sister that my father would bring with us on our fishing trips. I always wanted to ask about the past, but I never worked up the nerve. I longed for female companionship. My mother never gave me that."

"Your mother is a cruel woman. You deserved better. I don't know how you survived, but I'm glad you did," he pulled her close and kissed the top of her head.

"I'm glad you found me," she tilted her head.

He pressed his lips upon hers, gently. They soaked into each other. Savoring. Cherishing. She never wanted this moment to end. He was hers and she was his. There was no denying it anymore. A sweet surrender.

She didn't really know if having a sibling would have changed anything though. All she ever wanted was to have someone love her for who she was and not have to wait every other weekend to get a dose of that love. Her mother wouldn't even allow her to have any pets. Her mother believed all pets were too much of a burden. She declared she would take responsibility, but her mother refused. She had her own responsibilities. There was no room to add a pet. Not even a goldfish.

"We should practice some more," she took his hand and led him back over to the couch. They dropped down beside each other with little distance between them.

In union, they created their energy orbs. She noticed this time that his was fully blue. No streaks of black blended in. She had gotten more skilled mastering her orb, but she didn't know what all she could do with it. They would have to wait for Cecily to ask questions. For now, at least his mind was open. She wasn't as alone in this. With him by her side she could do anything. She had the support she needed. They were going to get Camille back and stop Max from bringing darkness into the world. All they had to do was get the wand back from him. Once it was in safe hands, they could go back to normal. Although, living in a facility wasn't normal. It was confinement.

She exchanged a glance with him. He made her feel safe. She didn't have that grasp of fear holding onto her. The one that caused her to hold back from speaking her mind. Vince never once criticized her. He listened. He wanted to hear her. She could tell him anything. She felt like the luckiest girl in the world.

Chapter 57
Vince

Light was starting to filter in through the window by the front door. Melia was tucked into his side with his arm draped around her. They practiced conjuring up their orbs while they talked about any and everything.

He lived a long time of unhappiness. He forgot what it was like before darkness overcame his life. Vladimir had been a plague that sucked out all of his blissful memories. Melia returned them.

He was still concerned, though. He knew in his heart what he felt for her. Would die for her. If things didn't go according to plan, he wanted to spare her that heartbreak. He couldn't tell her how he truly felt. He already took it too far. There was a reason why he resisted. He should have listened to that voice of reason inside his head.

"Good morning," Cecily descended the stairs with Aurora following her heels.

Melia jumped, quickly pushing away from him like they were caught doing something wrong. "Good morning," Melia fiddled with her hair with a guilty complex.

He smirked to himself. She was terrible at acting. She wouldn't be able to lie, even to save her life. Her honest heart was beautiful.

"It's about time you two came to your senses," Cecily commented as she passed them, heading to the front door. Aurora darted out as soon as the door opened.

He sensed hesitation from Melia as she kept her eyes trained on Cecily. She briefly flicked her eyes his way before back to Cecily, who reached for her shawl before stepping out.

"You two coming?" Cecily's voice called back to them.

Melia popped to her feet. He followed behind her. They stepped out onto the porch and found Cecily standing out in the open, her head tilted back, soaking up the sun.

"Are you two going to join me or just stand there all day?"

Melia grabbed his hand and jogged down the steps, releasing her hold when they approached Cecily. He watched Melia mimic Cecily, closing her eyes and bathing in sunlight.

He wasn't entirely sure what the purpose was. Cecily wasn't exactly forthcoming with explanations. It was a bit frustrating, just like Lamont's riddles.

He inhaled deeply as he shimmied his shoulders. Allowed himself a moment to relax, closing his eyes, and stepping into the sunray. He could see light seep in through his eyelids. Never really took a moment to pause and just appreciate something he took for granted.

Sunlight.

Energy beams.

Positive rays.

His mind wanted to wander, but he resisted. Focused on the present instead of the future. The future would come soon enough. He wanted to enjoy this moment of peace. Of calm. Of clarity.

"I want you to focus your mind on the image of your energy orb," Cecily uttered in a soft voice.

He kept his eyes closed and listened as he brought up the image of his blue orb.

"Now expand it."

The sphere grew larger in his mind. He wasn't sure how much he was supposed to expand it. He visualized it as a large medicine ball.

"Step inside it."

He widened his orb further before complying. Stepped forward, feeling a tangible current surrounding him. He inhaled sharply as his eyes cracked open. He looked down and saw a blue glow emitting around his arms and legs. He was inside his own orb. A shield.

"Project it," Cecily continued.

He magnified it further. Pushed it out towards the trees, encompassing them partially from the ground up to his height. He was still in disbelief, but he couldn't deny what he was seeing.

"Very good," Cecily praised.

His concentration broke as he looked over. Cecily and Melia were both watching him. How long had they been staring? Had Melia even attempted to create her own shield?

"You are ready."

"What? That's it?" he asked, perplexed. He expected more. He didn't think this prepared them enough for what they faced.

"Everything you need, you already have."

He wasn't so certain that was true. Even though they knew what they needed to do, he doubted it was going to be that easy. The plan was simple; get the other half of the wand. The task simple, but also problematic.

"And you're not alone," Cecily added.

He followed Cecily's gaze towards Melia. Beyond her he spotted Leo in the open, acting as if he was rubbing up against something that was invisible to his eye. He expanded his hearing and heard him purring.

"What if he weakens me again?" there was apprehension in Melia's voice.

"A double shield is more effective."

He could shield her. He would shield her. Protect her with everything he had. Keep her safe. He was ready. Ready to end this.

"Thank you," he uttered.

"The gratification was all mine," Cecily nodded. "You are welcomed here anytime."

"Thank you for everything," Melia flung against her and hugged her tight.

"You are a spirited warrior. Never forget that," Cecily whispered.

He reached out his hand to Melia. She took it while she waved goodbye to Cecily. He walked her to the SUV and opened the passenger door, waiting for her to climb in. He closed the door and walked around the back. Leo was still content standing in the same open area. He strode over and scooped him up before scaling into the driver's seat.

Leo jumped from his arm into Melia's lap, kneading, before curling up in a ball. He slipped on his seatbelt with a curious look. He had never saw Leo interact with Melia before. Wondered if he ever looked into her soul through her eyes. Leo wasn't the type to just walk right up and look for himself.

He pushed the topic from his mind as he drove down the lane and back into civilization. They had been at Cecily's place for a little over twelve hours, but he suddenly realized it had been a much-needed refreshment for his mind, body, and soul. He was starting to feel deprived as the distance widened. Fears and anxiety started to creep back into his mind.

A light touch grazed his arm. He looked down and saw Melia's small hand. Looked up and met her seeing eyes. Smiled softly as he removed his right hand from the wheel and turned it up. She immediately slipped her hand into his and all the concerning thoughts ebbed away.

Chapter 58
Melia

She stared at the orange tabby on her lap, lying serenely. Leo never bothered with her before. He always stuck around Camille or Vince. She was trying to fathom Leo's sudden interest in her when she heard Vince start drumming on the steering wheel. An anxiety antic. Something she had learned about him along the way. He fidgeted when worry was on his mind.

Her light touch brought his mind out of his current state as he relaxed. He griped her hand with dependency. She understood why he was restless. He was quick to carry all the burden on his shoulders. This wasn't just his fight, it was theirs.

The ride was different this time. One not meant to be silent. She pulled her hand back out of his. He peered her way as she fiddled with the radio. "What type of music do you like?"

"You can put on whatever you like," she saw him shrug his shoulders from the corner of her eye.

That was a loaded response. She wasn't sure what she actually liked. She never really had a choice in the matter. Her father liked rock. Her mother liked gospel.

She shuffled through the stations with indecision. She was quick to change the channel when advertisements played or when there was a bunch of chatter. The few stations that had music playing she just didn't connect with. It was either loud or had too much obscenities. It was a fruitless task.

"Music isn't like it used to be," Vince commented. "Too altered and biased."

"What was music like when you were growing up?" she paused on a station with a decent beat and softer tone. She read the display broadcasting as soft rock. The artist showed as Fleetwood Mac and the song titled *Dreams*.

"Lullabies from my mother."

She smiled before it wavered. Her mother never sang her lullabies. She never realized to what extent she missed out in her childhood.

Vince placed his hand on top of hers, curling his fingers around them while gently massaging the back of her hand with his thumb. Her smile returned instantly. How easy it was between them to lift each other up when one started to feel down.

She closed her eyes and relished in the moment. When Vince's thumb stopped moving over the back of her hand, she opened her eyes to study him.

Without warning, he quickly turned off the radio. As the display dimmed, she caught the artist's name before it faded away completely.

Richard Marx.

Leo perked his head in Vince's direction. Something about the song had sentimental meaning. "You know you can talk to me about anything, right?"

He jerked his head over before back to the road. After a long pause, he sighed. "It's not fair to you to always bring up someone from the past."

"Nadine?"

He solemnly nodded.

"It's okay," she touched his leg.

"I'm sorry. I thought those wounds were healed."

"You don't have to be sorry. Some wounds leave a permanent mark," she paused and looked at her hand. She recalled her conversation with Lamont about scars. He wasn't ashamed of his. Told her it has a story of character. She hadn't full comprehended the meaning behind his words. Only grasped half of the implication. Had gone through a traumatic experience, yet she lived through it. Survived it. It was nothing to be ashamed of.

She glanced back over at Vince. "She was a significant impact in your life. It's nothing to be regretful about."

His eyes stared at the road straight ahead. He was quiet for a moment. "We danced to that song at her prom. Maybe if I hadn't asked her for a dance, things wouldn't have gone all wrong."

She blinked her eyes. "She was destined to take down your father, right?"

"Yeah."

"So, if nothing happened that night, destiny would have just found another way."

He spied her a glance before flicking his eyes back to the road. He was silent for another moment, in reflection, before he reached out and turned the radio back on.

The song came back to life. There was only an instrumental playing. She read the title of the song, *Right Here Waiting*. The male vocalist began to sing. She listened to the lyrics. It was a lovely song filled with emotion.

"It was also one of the happiest moments of my life," Vince declared as the song faded.

"I'm sure you made her happy, too."

She saw Vince purse his lips, but close them just as quickly. Without a sound, he reached for her hand, turned it upright and kissed the back of it. "You make me happy now."

She smiled brightly and stroked his arm with her other hand. "You make me happy too."

They continued to listen to the soft rock station as they fed off of each other's energy. Happy. Such a warm feeling. A moment of pure bliss. Everything in the past seemed so far away. It didn't have a hold on her anymore. The future was just something to take away from the moment they were sharing right now. As long as he was by her side, she could do anything she set her mind on. She didn't dwell on the unknown.

He turned off the main road onto a long single lane. A wide expansion of green landscape covered both sides. Her mind turned to Camille with a bit of guilt. She had spent the last several hours content while Camille must be in dread. She suddenly felt selfish.

Leo stretched out on her lap before butting his head into her arm. She grinned as she scratched the side of his cheek. He purred with glee.

The SUV screeched to a halt on the grass. She shot Vince a look as he shifted into park and turned to her with his full attention. "Before we get any closer, we both need to be at our strongest."

She gawked at his outstretched arm with his wrist upright. His intent was clear. She shuddered.

He slipped a finger under her chin and lifted it, meeting her square in the eyes. "You are in control. I trust you."

He dropped her chin, leaving his wrist just inches away. She stared at it once more. He was right. She needed to power up to be the strongest she could be, physically and mentally.

Slowly, she placed her left hand on the back side of his and gently raised it to her lips. She met his beautiful blue eyes, sucked in a sharp inhale before exhaling at a gradual pace.

She let her eyelids fall as her teeth lengthened. She sank into his flesh, tore into a vein, and tapped his sweet elixir. She sucked a mouthful of his blood and swallowed it into her half full tank. She drank some more, a little more greedily. Her mind phased out, focusing only on hunger.

Chapter 59
Vince

He moaned with both pleasure and discomfort. He trembled with desire at her touch while the back of his mind screamed with alarm to pull away. With the additional blood that was pulled from his vein, the more drained he became.

He fought against his instinct. Knew he could trust her to resist temptation. Was betting his life on it. Even if she couldn't find the will to stop, he couldn't think of any other way to die peacefully.

His love for Melia was much stronger than his love for Nadine. He realized it when Melia talked about destiny. He had wanted a future with Nadine, but it was not their fate.

He recollected on all the hurt, but he hadn't made room for all the enjoyment. Nadine had been something good to come into his life when he had been spiraling with desolation.

Melia tore herself away. She was beautiful even when she was savage. He traced the side of her face before he leaned over and pressed his lips against hers with tender. She gasped, responding accordingly. Their kiss grew feverishly. He was on cloud nine. He never wanted this moment to end.

"What about you?" Melia broke away.

He rested his forehead upon hers with a pant. "There's a stash in the back."

"Time for you to replenish."

He sealed her lips with a kiss once more before he opened his door and stepped out. He reached the back, opened the hatchback, and grabbed the cooler stocked with blood. As soon as he finished the first bag of blood, the puncture marks left from Melia sealed shut. He indulged himself to two more bags before closing up the back.

He walked over to the other side of the SUV where he found Melia standing, soaking up the last bit of sunrays before it lowered below the horizon. He took a moment to stand with her as the sun continued to fade.

"We should continue on," he urged. They needed to meet up with the others before complete darkness descended.

When they gathered into the SUV, he noticed Leo was nowhere to be seen. He wondered for a brief moment where he would have taken off to, but there was no time delay.

He sped down the rest of the lane and pulled into the parking lot where the others milled around, waiting. This was it. They were back here again. The circumstances were different, but he still had that sick feeling in his stomach.

He noticed right away the wolves were clustered in their own group away from his vampires. There was still a rift among them he would have to address later. The only thing that mattered right now was that they needed to all worked together once more for the greater good.

"Thank you all for coming," he paused to assemble his thoughts.

Melia joined his side, reaching down and squeezing his hand, providing him the support he needed.

"Once again, we are faced with something sinister. This place represents a bleak time for us all. We fought and prevailed, but not without tragedy. A new evil has arisen to threaten our coexistence. We will not allow that. We will not allow this vice to tear us apart. To tear this world down. We are here for a reason. We have the power to defend," he paused and swept the group.

His inspiration stimulated from Nadine's speech, right before they marched into war. She spoke about freedom and what was worth fighting for. He didn't fully understand what she had meant then. His only concern was to make it another day forward. He had no vision. Had no direction. Now he had a guiding light to show him the way.

"Evil will not prevail," he swung up his arm, still joined with Melia's hand.

His vampires threw a fist in the air and hooted. Cameron took a knee and bowed his head as his pack mimicked. He saw looks of disgust cross some of the pack's face, but they did not object.

He once viewed leadership as a role he wasn't meant for. He had only gained it by default. During challenging times, someone had to step up to the plate and be the voice of reason. Not everyone agreed with decisions made, but during trying times they could set aside their differences and come together. That was what mattered most.

He released Melia's hand and strode over to Cameron. "So, the plan is simple. A diversion. Once we get Camille safe out of his hands, we throw everything we got to expel his energy. The wand is on him somewhere. Once it's out of his hands, it's end game."

"There's a cluster of trees to the right. I'll have the pack linger in the shadows until I give the signal."

He surveyed the area. It was mostly open, with the exception of the small patch of trees. "I'll tell my clan to do the same."

He turned and saw Melia engaged in a conversation with Darius. He closed the gap and informed them of the plan before they all headed for the trees.

"I'm staying with you for added protection," Cameron disclosed.

"I'm capable of projecting a shield now," he dismissed.

"It was not a request," Cameron stood firm.

"I'm staying too," Caden stepped into line with Cameron.

"What makes you think I can trust you?" he narrowed his eyes.

"I remember everything now. Nadine sensed this looming darkness. Sensed it after I bit her. She thought the only way to stop it from coming was to cease to exist."

He sucked in a sharp inhale. Why would she not tell him? To go through that on her own. He could have helped her find another way.

Melia slipped her hand in his and squeezed tight. He breathed her in, renewing his strength. He had more than one reason to fight.

"We're going to take him out, in Nadine's honor. We won't stop until he goes back to where he belongs," he looked at Melia. "And he's not going to use you as a host."

"I'm ready," Melia answered.

He took off walking with purpose. They stopped at the edge of the green grass where charred ground began, facing where once the front of the asylum stood.

A sliver of sunlight remained. He closed his eyes and focused on his shield. Once he had it locked in his mind, he opened his eyes and expanded his shield to cover over the four of them. The only thing left to do was wait.

Chapter 60
Melia

It wasn't long before darkness swallowed them whole. They stood at the edge of the singed ground. They remained on what was full of life. A light snow started to fall. It was the calm before the impending storm.

Vince already had his shield up. He encased all four of them. She thought it was too soon for him to project it. He should conserve his energy.

She was happy to see Darius. A familiar face. The rest of the vampires were a little reserved to see her. She couldn't blame them after what she put them through. There had been one, Ryker, someone mentioned, who had made a rude comment that she overheard. That she wasn't worth protecting. She knew she was going to have to earn their respect in time.

She spied a glance towards Caden's dark brown wolf form next to Vince. She was a bit deterred at what he said about Nadine sensing darkness when he bit her. She sensed something too, but it wasn't darkness. It was a whispering light. That whisper led her here to find the other half of the wand.

Swirling particles, like dust, formed before Max apparated in the center of the burnt grounds. She was discouraged to see that he was alone.

"Where's Camille?" Vince demanded.

"Where she belongs, reliving her nightmares. Where's my fire?"

She gasped. Camille was somewhere, alone, with only her mind to keep her company. She had to get to her. As fast as she could.

A snap redirected her attention. It reverberated from beside her. She dropped her eyes as Vince lowered his hand back to his side. He had snapped his finger. It was the signal. He knew where Camille was.

Chaos ensued. Vampires and werewolves bolted out from hiding. A mass swarm heading in Max's direction. She heard an ominous laugh echo as he disappeared and reappeared in different locations, disrupting the falling snow.

No one got within an inch of Max. They were all in disarray as they crashed into each other, trying to change course at the last second only for Max to disappear again and reappear further away.

The ground beneath their feet began to tremble. They staggered, trying to stay upright. Debris rose from the ground and began slamming against the adversary.

Vince stepped forward and projected his shield out to encase all the vampires and werewolves. Only he soon found out it did not protect them from hurling inanimate objects.

"Fall back," she cried out.

Confused looks were exchanged. She was not the one they were accustomed to take orders from.

Out of her peripheral, a large tree rose into the air, ripped from the ground with roots hanging, before it sailed towards a cluster of vampires and werewolves.

"No," she shouted. With everything she had inside herself, she stopped the tree in midair.

Her arms shook with violence at the weight of the tree pushing down. She heard Max chuckle before an iron bar impaled a vampire through the stomach. The tree faltered when she took her eye off.

"Fall back," Vince ordered.

This time, the vampires and wolves listened and started to retreat.

"I can do this all night," Max declared.

She angled her head towards the sound of Max's voice. He also had his hands suspended in the air aimed at the tree.

"We won't let you," Vince growled.

A blue orb blasted towards Max. It impacted him, but he didn't falter. It made little headway. Max grinned.

The longer she continued a tug and war battle with Max over the tree, the strength seeped from her.

Her eyes caught sight of his outlined luminous hand. There was a red prominent mark protruding. A burn. A memory of him touching her resurfaced her mind. He had been quick to pull back when he had touched her shoulder.

She mustered every last bit of energy she had and severed the thick tree in two, throwing both halves as far away as she could from the vampires and wolves.

Before Max had a chance to react, she encircled her own energy orb and flung it in his direction. It hit him on the shoulder as he grunted.

She glanced towards Vince. His shield was diminishing. He could only project it barely around himself.

She closed her eyes tight and projected her own shield outwards. When she reopened them, she was encased and expanded it to Vince.

She heard a yelp. She turned and saw Caden knocked to the ground as Cameron raced forward. He leapt into the air, only to be hit by a large block of stone. Cameron's wolf form smashed to the ground and rolled several times. He remained motionless.

"Stop, please stop. I'll do it. I'll command fire," she declared, stepping forward.

"Melia, no," Vince voiced, cutting her off as he blasted a blue orb towards Max. Max didn't step out of the way. He let it hit him before he blasted his own dark orb towards Vince. It did not penetrate her shield, but she felt slight draining.

Back and forth Vince and Max hurled energy orbs while her energy continued to drain. Her shield around Vince was waning at a steady pace.

"You're in over your head, my dear. I don't need you anymore."

He absorbed another blue orb. It was then she saw it only gave him more vigor. He couldn't use her as a host. He couldn't even touch her. She had her own strength, but it was Vince who gave her the dark power.

Max shaped a different type of black orb. This one spiked with white-hot charges of lightning. A smug grin crossed his features. At that moment, she realized Vince was standing there without her shield. He had drained her until it had completely deteriorated. She barely had anything left around herself.

With the last remains of her shield, she gathered her energy, stepped out from behind Vince, and aimed it at the black orb of lightning Max sent hurling. Hers connected with his and exploded in midair, like a firework. Only he was quick to gather another one. She had nothing left. Her energy depleted. It's what he had planned all along. There was only one thing left she could do.

She put herself in the path. The velocity of the strike sent her flying backwards. A white flash clouded her vision. She couldn't see anything. Her mind muddled.

"Melia," a gut-wrenching scream penetrated her mind.

The white canvas began to ebb away as color returned, however it was distorted. More like a watermark.

Her eyes continued to focus from small pixels into a whole picture, watching the shapes of snow fall down upon her. Only something was off she couldn't quite grasp.

"Melia, wake up, please wake up," she heard Vince's broken voice plead. She lifted her head and saw Vince clutching a motionless body. Her body.

She rose to a stand as she tried to make sense of it.

"Come back to me, please, come back to me," his voice was filled with such a grievous sorrow.

"Vince, I'm right here. Look at me," she reached out to touch him, only her hand went right through him.

"He can't hear you."

Chapter 61
Melia

S he whipped her head towards the sound of a different voice. A feminine one. Saw a girl her age standing there. She had long, wavy brown hair, prominent hues of green in her hazel eyes, and stood an inch taller. She wore a forest green vest over a long-sleeve black shirt, jeans, and dark brown boots. Something about her seemed familiar. A deep magnetic connection. A divine awareness.

"Do, do I know you?" she asked, mystified.

"We meet, once upon a time, however I was a different version of myself and took your memory away."

"Nadia?"

"Call me, Nadine."

She stared at her, dumbfounded. The image she had shaped in her mind by the ones she left an impact on did not measure up. She saw her as someone highly. A class of her own. Only she was just another ordinary girl like her.

"Am I dead?" she glanced over at Vince, who clutched her lifeless body in his arms sobbing. "Why can't he see me?"

"You're in the in-between."

"In-between?"

"Life and death."

She shuddered even though warmth swirled all around her. It was odd. Suspended in limbo she felt peaceful.

"I pushed your spirit outside of your body before impact and took the hit instead."

"You can do that?"

Nadine semi-laughed. "Apparently, I can."

"So, I can go back?" She redirected to her listless body, with hope. She wasn't ready to die. Had only barely begun to live.

"If that's what you desire."

"Why haven't you?" she frowned.

"I have no body to return to. It combusted and turned to ash."

"So, you've been stuck here in the in-between?"

"Yes, as a condition of self-discovery to redemption."

"So, we don't automatically get condemned?" She read a book from the school library about vampires and their myths. That they were evil and their souls were condemned to Hell.

"Who you were as a human is our Maker's ultimate decision."

She perked up. "Have you met Him?"

"No," Nadine shook her head.

She was disappointed. Had so many questions and not enough answers. She looked back at Vince. Her heart swelled seeing him in so much pain. His pain was her pain, even if she didn't feel it right now. There was no doubt in her mind that she was going to go back to him. Fear was not going to stop her.

Her eyes moved away and narrowed at Max. He was slowly approaching. Vince was lost in his despair to even notice. "How? I didn't have much left in me. He's much stronger," she turned back to Nadine.

"Darkness does not drive out darkness. Only light can," her voice softened.

She perked up. "I said that. You've been with us the whole time?"

"From a distance, until a cry for help allowed me entry."

She studied Nadine. She hadn't prayed. Had had faith that they would succeed. That in the end, good always won against evil. "Did you love him?" she cast her eyes down and asked in a whisper.

"Yes, but not the same way you do."

"Because of Marc?" She met Nadine's eyes. Nadine wore a soft smile. It was clear to her that Vince loved Nadine. Only Nadine had no body to return to, but she did. If Vince had a chance to get Nadine back, would he want her instead?

"No," Nadine shook her head.

Her eyebrows pinched together, surprised, "Were you ever able to reunite with him?"

"Not in the in-between," Nadine looked off to the side.

"You've been alone all this time?" her eyebrows pinched.

"It's complicated."

"I'm so sorry."

Nadine's eyes flicked back to hers. "You don't have to be sorry. I know Marc is at peace. That's all that matters."

The same thing Cecily had said about her husband. Her soulmate. Marc must have been Nadine's soulmate, which was why she couldn't love Vince with her whole heart.

She sighed. "I don't know how to command fire."

"The fire he wants you to command, you are incapable of."

She narrowed her eyes and tilted her head. "Were you able to harness magic, too?"

"Yes, and I already commanded fire."

"You did?"

"I'm the reason he reemerged. A breath of life that freed him. He already has all he needs from you. He wants you to command fire so that you are no longer a threat to him."

"How am I a threat?"

"You have not taken a life. Therefore, your heart remains pure."

That was why she burned him. Was why her energy orb could impact him the way it did that Vince's orb could not. "How do I get close enough to him to get the wand? I don't even know where it is."

"You know, I have a spiral just like that. Inherited from my lineage. The wood is darker, though. I think it was made from blackthorn. The name that was inscribed, Drehseler"

She looked down and automatically grasped her spiral. She was puzzled at the change of topic.

"One thing I've come to realize. Darkness doesn't always mean dark. You cannot have dark without light. Light without the dark. They are meant to complement each other," Nadine rambled on.

She still wasn't quite following. There was a key piece of knowledge she was missing that Nadine clearly knew.

Movement caught her eye. Vince had released her and rose with a mask of fury. Red streaks were pasted to his face from the tears he cried. He had totally shut down. There was only one thing left on his mind.

"Vince, no," she panicked, racing over to him. She reached out and tried to touch him, but her hand went through him. She was powerless. He couldn't see or hear her.

He had little energy left, yet Vince started firing off energy orb after energy orb to no veil as Max laughed with mockery.

"Nadine, help. I have to stop him. Have to stop Max from taking over Vince as a host."

A wide smile spread across Nadine's face as she extended her hand. She shifted forward and placed hers into it. A fiery glow heated up from their joint hands.

A twin flame.

"I can help you now, but it does not come without a sacrifice."

She glanced over her shoulder at Vince. Whatever the cost, the sacrifice would be worth it to save Vince. "Let's do it," she turned back and nodded in agreement.

In union, they turned to face her still body.

"Ready?" Nadine asked.

"Ready."

"Good because no one messes with my sister."

Nadine stepped forward. She followed. They both merged together as one.

Chapter 62
Vince

A bright light temporarily blinded him. He looked away, blinking his eyes before his vision returned. When he looked back, he saw Melia flying through the air before slamming onto the ground.

"Melia!"

Everything around him faded. The only thing he cared about was Melia and the fact that she wasn't getting up. He rushed over to her and fell to his knees, begging her to wake up. Begging her to come back to him. He felt nothing as he picked her up in his arms. No warmth. Just emptiness. It was like someone stabbed him in the heart and kept twisting the blade.

"You gave me a sign," he shouted angrily to the sky.

He felt so betrayed. Felt like such a fool for believing for one second that everything was going to work out all right this time. That his heart wouldn't be broken again. Only this time, it wasn't broken. It was shattered.

"Why?" he sobbed as he held her close to him.

Why had he surrendered to his feelings? Why had he let her in? She made him a better person. Made him want to be better. He could see a future with her. One he wanted so badly. One they both deserved. Now it was bleak. Death was a better sentence than living in eternal misery.

In a trance, his eyes snapped open. He laid her down gently before he found the strength to push up to his feet. He turned towards Maximilian, who stealthily crept in. There was only twenty feet between them.

With fury, he powered up what energy he had left and fired orb after orb. Max's laugh was contemptuous. It only angered him more. He had recognized his energy did not cause damage the way Melia's energy had, but he continued the assault anyway. He had nothing left to lose.

A strong gale stirred up the larger flakes of snow that fell harder. He ignored it as he threw another orb of energy. It hit Max square in the chest and did nothing. Only then did he realize Max had stopped laughing. His eyes narrowed. For the first time, he saw fear in Max's eyes. Something behind him had his full attention.

He turned and saw Melia's lifeless body suspended above the ground, shifting from lateral to vertical. Facing in their direction. Her eyes opened. Dancing flames inside them.

The numbness when she fell rekindled with an overwhelming sensation. His soul fired off like bolts of lightning. He was overcome.

"You want fire?" Melia's sweet voice was tinged with attitude as rings of blue flame ignited from the right palm of her hand.

He watched the flame launched towards Max. It hit him in the chest and knocked him off his feet as he screamed in agony.

"I'll give you fire," she continued with zealous.

He never saw Melia angry before. He watched incredulity as blue flames engulfed around Max encircling him inside. The flames danced up to the sky with intensity.

"No," Max cried in a panic.

Slowly, Melia lowered back down to the ground.

"Melia?" he spoke in a hoarse voice. He wasn't sure if this was real. If she was still alive. Or if he had died.

"Guess again, Vinson."

He stiffened. This wasn't real. He was dead. What kind of Hell was he in?

"Nadine?" he whispered so faintly he barely heard it himself.

"Go get Camille. We've got this taken care of."

He looked over at the blue ring of fire. Max was still inside. He stood frozen in the center. Fear still etched on his face.

"Don't worry, he's not going anywhere."

"Where's Melia?" he looked back. She was all that mattered to him now.

"I'm here," her voice softened as her hand reached out to his. The contact of skin intensified. "Nadine is keeping my soul safe. Now go get Camille."

He slowly backed away, afraid to take his eyes off of Melia's form, which apparently was possessed also with Nadine. He just couldn't wrap his mind around it. It was impossible.

She turned her attention away from him and walked over to Caden first. Her hand emitted a light orange glow as she placed it down on him. When she removed her hand, the glow disappeared and Caden rose to his paws without pain. She had healed his injury. She was going to go heal them all. *They* were going to heal them all.

He turned and took off to the tunnel underground. The only thing not burned in the fire. The place Camille had been subjugated to when she was at the mercy of the vampires. She was in the furthest cell at the very end. She held Leo clutched to her chest, shaking uncontrollably. He should have known Leo had taken off after her.

"Camille."

"Vince?" she looked up with a red-tear soaked face.

He pulled the cell door off its hinges and tossed it to the side. Walked over and placed a hand on her shoulder. "You're safe now."

At least he thought the danger was over. He didn't know for sure, but the one thing he did know was that Nadine was a force to be reckoned with. Her anger was greater than fear itself.

"Where's Melia?" she asked in a state of panic.

He scooped her off the floor into his arms. "You wouldn't believe me if I told you. You'll have to see for yourself. Let's get out of here, shall we?"

"Thank you," she whispered.

"That's what friends are for," he flashed a smile.

A tear brimmed over from Camille's eye. It was then that it hit him there was ill-history in this place. What had she had to endure here after she snapped Nadine's neck? He had spent a year trying to plan his father's demise before they brought the war to his doorstep. It had not crossed his mind what she might have faced here. She must have gone through a year of Hell.

He ran back out into the open. The blue flame still burned in a circle around Max, who hadn't moved from the center. Hadn't aberrated either. Seemed to be stuck there with no control.

His fallen vampires and the fallen wolves were now restored, including Cameron who had his paws draped over a kneeling Melia's shoulders licking her face like a young pup.

"He's still alive?" Camille noticed Max.

"I don't think for long."

She looked at him, mystified. He did not elaborate as he closed the gap. His clan and Cameron's pack stood at a distance, ready for orders.

Leo jumped from Camille's arms as he set her down and looped an arm around her waist to steady her. It was strange to see Melia, but know it was also Nadine he was facing. He would think he was dreaming if he slept. Leo rubbed up against her legs before she scooped him up, kissed the top of his head, and hugged him tight. Did he know Nadine was in there?

"Melia," Camille called out.

"Cam."

He felt Camille go rigid beside him.

"Why, why, did you call me that? You've never called me by that name before."

"Maybe I'm not who I appear to be," Nadine released Leo.

Camille stood there silently. "Who are you?"

"Truth or dare?" Nadine took a step forward.

"What?" Camille jerked back.

"I'll make it easy for you, dare." Nadine stared pointedly at Camille. "I dare you to forgive yourself."

"Nadine?" Camille's voice cracked.

"In the flesh, well, sort of."

"But what I did to you, it's, it's unforgivable."

"It would only be unforgivable if you did not regret your action and what you've endured after, not even my worst enemy deserves."

Something cruel had happened to Camille. He felt a pang of guilt. Had treated her so poorly. He knew how his father was. He couldn't even fathom what torture she had had to endure.

"I'm so sorry," Camille rushed over and embraced Nadine in Melia form.

"Even in your darkest hour, through thick and thin, you still had my six. It's time you stop holding onto the guilt because I forgive you."

Camille sobbed into her shoulder.

"Being a vampire does not have to be a curse. It can be a gift. There has always been potential. I choose not to see it, but I trust you can find it with Melia's help."

"What's going to happen now?" Camille pushed back.

He was wondering the same thing. There was a time when he wanted nothing more than to have Nadine back. He had that chance now, but all he wanted was Melia instead.

Chapter 63
Melia

I t was the strangest sensation. She was inside her own body, but she was not in full control of it. Nadine currently was. She could see and hear everything going on, but it was like she was in the backseat far away from it all. No one could see her. No one could hear her. She saw so many images that were not her own. Nadine's memories. Was this what it felt like to be possessed? To feel like all your screaming would go unheard. To have recollections that confused your mind if they were yours or someone else?

She had a moment when she took center stage. She could tell Vince was in shock. He didn't know how to react. Just minutes ago, he had been grieving over her. Thought she was gone for good, just like Nadine. He had been at a loss. She sparked some life into him when she touched him. Her senses were on overload. She wondered if Nadine could sense her blushing.

Together, they healed all the wounded. They were one and yet retained two minds. When they came across Cameron, he had broken ribs and collapsed lungs. He strained to breathe, but he fought to hang on. Together, they pressed both hands down upon his side. Her fingertips tingled with life as the broken ribs mended and the air stopped leaking from his lungs.

Nadine took over as she was sent to the backseat once more. Even so, she felt her hand stroke Cameron's pelt. "My dear friend," she heard Nadine utter through her voice.

Cameron tilted his head. A soft whine emitted before he pushed up onto her shoulders and began licking her face. He knew it was Nadine.

When she heard the pain and sorrow in Camille's voice, she wanted to reach out and comfort her, as herself, but she let Nadine have the moment. She was glad to see Camille safe. Nadine had known exactly where she was. Had seen Nadine's thoughts.

"What's going to happen now?" she heard Camille ask.

She was eager to know as well. The longer Nadine's soul remained with hers, the further she felt away. They had become one, but their minds still remained separate. Yet, there was still a dominant presence fighting for control.

She felt darkness within Nadine. A darkness she wasn't afraid of. A darkness that was powerful, but not evil. She also felt light. She had called her sister. Had the same spiral, but made from dark wood. Vince had told her he had a sister. He didn't know what happened to her, though. His mother made a spiral. Made from dark wood. What if she also made another spiral? One that was made from a light-colored wood. Who would she have given it to?

"Immilla had a sister, Serene, who also had a child," Nadine's voice reverberated loud in her mind. Answering her as if she had asked the question out loud.

"You know what I was thinking?"

"I can see your mind as you can see mine. However, knowledge that came from the divine is something you cannot see."

She was a little more connected now to her body. As if there was more room made for her.

"Are you ready?"

"Ready for what?" she asked, bewildered.

"To reclaim your body."

"What about you?"

"I don't belong here."

"Yes, you do. They need you."

"They don't need me. They need you. I was the darkness hanging over their lives. You were the one who provided them a light at the end of the tunnel."

She took a moment to process. *"Okay."*

Nadine took control again. She walked up to the blue flames licking up to the sky. A different kind of fire. One that imprisoned Max. Together, they walked through the fire. It did not burn them. She should be afraid of it, but she wasn't.

There was a rage within Nadine. Rage that fueled her with great power. Power she was in control. It was only a means to protect herself with. She used anger as a shield. A defense mechanism against fear.

Images of Nadine's childhood flashed through her mind with rapid fire. Nadine was tormented and teased in school like she was growing up. Until one day, Nadine found the courage to stand up for someone else. That day changed Nadine's perspective. She no longer allowed herself to be influenced by others.

Another imaged flashed by. Nadine fishing at a stream. She was upset when she caught one. Took it off the hook and stormed away. A man's voice tried to reassure her that the hook did not hurt the fish. Nadine refused to believe him. Demanded to go home. Got even more upset when he called her Nadia.

"We have the same father?" she gasped.

"Synklar is Serene's bloodline."

"Don't touch me," Max demanded.

She hadn't realized they stood right before him. She had never been this close to him. Her eyes caught a name etched on the left side of his hood, chest level.

Drehseler

"Immilla was his daughter. When he was defeated, the Synklar family took her in."

Drexel. Her name was Nadine Drexel.

The final piece of the puzzle. Nadine was a descendant of Drehseler and a descendant of Synklar. Vince was also a descendant of Drehseler.

"Maximilian can only possess someone from his bloodline."

Nadine raised her hand. An energy surged from their minds before the wand appeared from beneath Max's cloak. He grabbed for it at the same time as Nadine and yelled as his hand burned at the touch.

With the wand in her, the feeling was exceptional. It was full of life. Of wonder. Magic was extraordinary. So much good could come from it along with so much bad in the wrong hands.

"Immilla closed everyone's minds from this type of magic. It's too influential. It's time to close it off again."

Nadine impaled Max's chest with the jagged end. He screamed in anguish as fire consumed him from the inside out. An inferno right before her eyes. Caught up in the flames was the wand which caught fire too. In a blink of an eye, Max was gone along with the wand and the ring of blue fire.

A force threw her back from her feet. She was dizzy as the dark night mixed with snow blurred together. There was also a lulling. Her mind was calm. Her mind was her own. Her soul splintered again. Yet there was a force calling to her like a magnetic.

"Nadine? Melia?"

Her eyes refocused as Vince came into view. She lay in his arms. Smiled up at him and cupped the side of his face. Sensed his uncertainty.

"Nadine?" Camille inhaled sharply.

She tore her eyes from Vince and looked out into the open landscape. Standing before them, with an illuminated crystal glow surrounding her, was Nadine.

"Nadine," Vince whispered.

"Take care of her," Nadine said as the illuminating glow started to dim.

"Nadine, wait," Vince reached towards her. "I have so many questions."

"Melia can answer them," Nadine smiled at her.

"Nadine, you're fading," Camille cried out.

Nadine didn't respond, as something caught her attention off to the right. "Marc."

She watched Nadine wander over, spellbound. She reached out a hand to nothing but snow filled air. At least, to them, that is what they saw. However, what she reached for made her hand disappear.

"We can touch." Nadine gasped before looking over her shoulder and swept her eyes over them all. "Until we meet again, know that I am forever with you. All of you. Even if you can't see me, I'm still with you always."

She watched as Nadine stepped through some invisible portal and vanish through the veil of snow. At the same time, she felt a warmth within her soul.

"She's at peace."

Chapter 64
Vince

He watched hypnotized as Melia's frame walked through the blue fire. The flames were dark and bright blue. He couldn't see anything pass the ring of fire. Had no idea what Melia or Nadine was doing to Max. No idea if he should help.

Orange flames erupted from the core of the blue ring. Then right before his eyes, the flames extinguished into themselves until nothing remained. Not even a trace.

Melia's frame forcefully flew back. He ran towards her, dropped to his knees, and caught her in his arms. Her pupils rolled far back with only her whites showing. When they returned to a normal state, she blinked several times.

"Nadine? Melia?"

He wasn't sure what had just happened. If they were both present or not. He wanted to believe Melia was the one in his arms, but he was on overload with so much ambivalence.

She smiled at him. That smile of hers that just melted his heart. When she touched the side of his face, every insecurity faded away. He had his Melia back.

He heard a voice in the background, but didn't process. He was spent on Melia until she tore her gaze from his. Followed her line of sight and saw Nadine dressed as Nadine and not as Nadia. She still carried that spitfire presence of hers. Saw the halo light fading from around her. She was fading from sight.

"Nadine, wait," he reached a hand towards her, "I have so many questions."

"Melia can answer them," she reassured.

He looked back down at Melia's face. She shared a smile with Nadine. Seeing her full of life, he was able to crack his own smile.

"Marc," Nadine's voice uttered.

He lifted his head back to Nadine. She looked off into the distance. He followed, but saw nothing but snow still falling from the sky. Yet Nadine was compelled to walk over, reach out, and touch air. It made her hand disappear. She paused to take one last look with some final words before she completely faded away. There was a sense of contentment. He was finally able to fully let go.

"She's at peace," Melia confirmed as his eyes met hers.

He pulled her in close and held her tight. He never wanted to let go. He inhaled her scent. Her lively scent. He had been so scared. "I thought I lost you," he choked back a sob.

"I know. Your call for help allowed Nadine to save my soul."

He looked up to the snow filled sky. He had been heard. Didn't think someone like him even had a right. Nadine had not been at peace, but now she was and she was with Marc. She was at peace and happy.

"Camille," Melia lurched to her feet and rushed over to Camille, embracing her. "Are you okay?"

"I'm okay, now," Camille spoke in a feather whisper as she stood stiffly before surrendering and hugging Melia back in a tight embrace.

"Miss. Melia, it's an honor to have you by our side," Darius took a knee and bowed his head respectfully. One by one, the clan followed suit.

Cameron strolled out front from the pack and bowed as well as the other wolves followed.

Melia surveyed her eyes over each and every one of them, unsettled. When Camille took a knee beside her, Melia glanced over at him with questioning eyes.

"They respect you, and so do I," he kneeled as well.

Melia was the only one left standing. "Am I supposed to give a speech?" she whispered to him.

He looked up at her with a small smile. "No, just relish in it."

She was so innocent. So pure-hearted. There was no mistake that she was one of them. She belonged with them. This was her world now. She would be their guiding light into the future. He had nothing holding him back now. It was time for them to find their place in the world.

He rose to a stand. The others followed and looked to him for direction.

"Together, we have overcome another dark force. Evil did not prevail. We have earned the liberty to be unchained from what we view as a curse. The time has come to find our place in this world and use our abilities for the greater good."

He heard Nadine through Melia. Heard what she said to Camille. That had been what she meant all along. To stand up for those who were not strong enough to stand up for themselves. To help those get back up on their feet when they got knocked down.

"Let us go home and emerge into a new dawn." He held back a cringe.

Home.

Their home was a prison. A prison was not a home. A prison is what they had been subjugated to their whole life. He had taken them from one prison to another. Surely Lamont recognized that. Why had he never said anything?

Only a handful of Vladimir's vampires remained. He would take it upon himself to deal with them. As for his vampires, they deserved a life of their choosing. So did the wolves. If they could come up with a governed truce.

"Cameron, a word, please." He kept his voice low after they walked a short distance. "You should take the pack to the cave and figure out what direction you want to take them. There isn't much for them at the facility."

"What about the vampires that escaped?"

"With the help of my clan, I will track them all down."

"You want to part ways?"

He glanced over at his vampires before shifting his eyes to the wolves. They stood divided from each other. They only worked together for a purpose. That purpose was no more. He had heard the chatter from the wolves. They had been unhappy. Didn't have the room to roam like they should. Stuck inside a prison when they were meant to be free. Lamont always provided some excuse that kept them partially satisfied, but it was not their way of life. They were wolves first.

"This was never a content life for them. You and I both know it. Which is why Lamont allowed some of them to stay back."

"The life my kind lives, is a life torn. We are wolves and yet we are capable of turning into men. We can live in the wild or we can live a tamed life. That's not something I can decide for them. They have to decide for themselves."

"Then I think that time has come."

"I agree," Cameron nodded. "What will you do?"

"I'm not sure yet. It will have to be one day at a time. To be free to decide the fate of my future is a daunting task. I never thought I'd live to see that day." His eyes drifted over to Melia. His future had always been bleak. Now it was staring him in the face.

"I can't speak for the rest of the pack, but I will always be available to you whenever the need arises."

"Thank you," he extended his hand.

"Time for us both to start a new foundation." Cameron shook his hand.

He watched Cameron walk away. It was the end of an era as a new one was beginning. He recalled Lamont's words. "Maybe a new generation is meant to carry us into the future."

He didn't know what the future held, but he had faith Melia would show them all the way.

Chapter 65
Melia

*H*ome.

 The word was grim. A prison was not meant to be a home. It was, in fact, the opposite. Confinement. None of them belonged in a structure like that. All it was, was a gloomy place. Nadine's words rang true. They should embrace vampirism as a gift. Though they required blood to survive, they could do so much good with this power as long as they maintained in control. There were so many people in this world that suffered. That needed help, but didn't know where to start looking. They could make a difference in the world. Be protectors of the day and night.

She watched Vince and Cameron stride off a distance. She was tempted to eavesdrop, but respected that the conversation was one meant to be private.

"What do you think they are talking about?" Camille inquired.

"I'm not sure. Maybe possibilities of what comes next," she shrugged.

Vince sought her out. She smiled hearteningly. No matter how brief the eye contact was, it always made her warm inside. She didn't know what cards the future held. It was an odd feeling to have so many possibilities. There was nothing lingering over them anymore.

She watched as Cameron parted ways with Vince. Cameron announced to the pack that there was much to deliberate on as they return to their old home. He asked Caden to lead the charge until he was able to join them. One by one, the pack followed in Caden's footprints until all that remained was Cameron. He turned and headed towards the parking lot.

"Where are you going?" she asked Camille, who stepped after Cameron.

"I think I should go with him," Camille tossed over her shoulder.

"You'll come back, right?"

Camille paused. "When I'm ready."

"You know that whenever you need a friend, I'm always here for you, right?"

"I know," Camille sought her eyes with a small smile.

She nodded her head with a sad smile knowingly. Camille needed some time to self-reflect. Time away from them all. To find herself again. A journey of self-discovery in a peaceful place.

She watched Leo trail after her. Nadine's cat. Nadine's faithful cat that had adored her. It all made sense now. He recognized that she was connected to Nadine. Only she did not need his affection. His love. Camille did.

Her eyes traveled over to Vince. He stepped towards her. There was so much she had to talk to him about, but she suddenly didn't have the nerve. Things were different now.

"I'd going to ride back with Darius," she dismissed herself before taking off after him.

She didn't look back. She felt Vince's perplexity. Was confused herself. She just didn't know how to be alone with him after everything that had just happened.

"Darius," she called out.

"Hey, Chica."

"I'm going to ride back with you."

"It will be an honor to have you accompany us," he grinned brightly with his large lips. "You know Tony here, but have you formally met Michael?"

She skimmed her eyes briefly over Tony before landing them on the other vampire, Michael. He had dirty blonde hair with buzzed cut sides, light brown eyes, thin eyebrows, and a prominent Adam's apple.

"Nice to make your acquaintance, ma'am," Michael dipped into a slight bow with an arm around his abdominal.

"The pleasure is all mine," she remarked with a bit of self-conscious.

"You can ride up front with me," Darius opened the passenger door of one of the many SUVs parked in the parking lot for her.

"Thank you," she slipped into the seat as the others climbed into the back.

Her eyes wandered until they found Vince. He stared at her longingly. Had a pang of guilt stir for leaving him behind as the SUV rumbled to life. She tore her eyes away as Darius drove forward after backing out of the spot.

The wipers could hardly keep up with the snow as they drove into the storm. The snow was accumulating faster now and sticking onto the road. She felt the wheels slip a little, but Darius kept the vehicle on the road like a pro.

"Is driving difficult to learn?" she asked while studying Darius.

"No one taught you how to drive, Chica?"

"No," she shook her head.

"Well, we are going to have to change that. Just not in a snowstorm," Darius smirked, keeping his eyes trained on the road.

"You guys want to listen to some music?" she stretched her neck back and swiveled her eyes between Tony and Michael.

"Whatever you like, ma'am," Michael responded.

She glanced over at Darius with questioning eyes. Would he prefer silence over music that could potentially distract him?

"I don't mind listening to some music," Darius professed.

She turned on the radio and spent some time fidgeting with the channels until she found a soft rock station. She let it play and kept the volume low.

She gazed out the side of her window, watching in the awe the symmetrical shapes of the snow. She may not possess strong sorcery magic anymore, but magic was still all around them. One just had to open their eyes to it and see. They did not have to control it to their bidding in order to appreciate it. Just like them, it was meant to be free.

"What were your lives like before you became vampires?" she looked over at Darius.

"I was at the lowest point of my life when Vince found me and offered me a new outlook on life. One with purpose," Darius answered first.

She craned her neck back to the others.

"I had the same experience," Tony agreed.

"Taking orders is all I know. When I got medically discharged after my right leg was removed above the knee, because of a freak accident, I didn't know how to cope. My life felt meaningless," Michael responded.

266

"You have an amputation?" her eyebrows pinched together in astonishment.

"Yes, ma'am."

"Wow," her eyes drifted down to his camouflaged pant. She never suspected anything altered. He carried himself with grace.

She sat back in her seat, pondering. Vince's vampires understood the gift of vampirism. They were broken soldiers out in the world that needed direction. Vince provided them with meaning. Now it was time for them to find their own path.

"Have you ever thought about what potential impacts you could provide in the world?" She was met with silence.

Life dealt many roads one traveled in a lifetime. Nothing remained stable forever. The stretch always came to an end, making way for a new journey. A new crossing started out with many bumps that derailed. Those bumps were there to strengthen them and make them grow. Alone, the trek was more difficult, but not impossible if they set their mind to it. Together, in numbers, the undertaking was not as daunting. She looked forward to the task at hand.

Chapter 66
Vince

There was a void as he watched Melia walk away and leave him alone. He couldn't understand why she choose to ride with Darius and the others. Had he done something wrong? He was itching to spend some time alone with her. Eager to drive back with just her. Now he was left feeling cold and standing on his own in the snow.

The wind whipped up, swirling the snow into his face. He blinked the snow from his eyes. The snow reminded him of the night he confessed to Nadine he was a vampire. He smiled to himself. She had not taken it too well. Thought she had the strength to fight him. Going down without a fight was not her style.

Lamont was right again. The day had come when memories of Nadine no longer brought pain. She was at peace. He was as well. He never thought he would get to this point. In getting here, he was free from so many burdens. A heavy lift off of his chest. There was only room for one thing. Yet, it was another unknown.

He climbed into the last SUV. Turned on the radio and let the soft rock channel play as he drove through the snow, keeping his mind focus on the road ahead. The roads were slick. He fishtailed a bit around the turns before he advanced to the main road.

It was a strange feeling as he flicked his eyes to the rearview mirror and watched the burnt down asylum fade away. It had been nothing but bad memories before. Now the vibe shifted. A positive vibe had risen from the ground like new life does after a forest fire. Darkness and despair did not have an iron grip anymore. Something good had come from all the bad.

He resisted the urge to step down on the gas. He just couldn't wait to see her again. Talk to her. He didn't know why she suddenly had the need to avoid him. It didn't matter. There was only one thing he knew for certain.

A new song began to play. He listened to the words to keep his mind calm. They instantly spoke to him. Had a way to say everything he was feeling inside. Like it knew how he wanted to express himself.

He committed the song and the artist to memory as he continued onward. The snow was coming down fine now. The roads were only wet. He had traveled outside of the storm. The further north he went the less snow.

When the facility came into view, it looked exactly how he had come to realize. A prison. There was nothing homey about the place. It was just a structure that had little value. There was no reason to remain here any longer.

He parked the SUV and headed inside. He found them all milling in the lobby, waiting for him. All except Melia. When all eyes were directed at him, he spoke. "When you were lost and down on your knees in life, you were given a choice. To find your way out on your own or to aid me in something that was worth fighting for. You have all aided me well, but the fight is now over."

He paused, allowing them to process his words as he scanned each one of their faces. Exchanges of bewilderment upon them. He had had the time during his drive to think things through blocking out everything else.

He continued on. "I never thought we would reach this day so soon, but we have. This place is not a home. There was a time when you had expectations of what the future held for each and every one of you. We may be different, but that should not stop us from our potentials. Together, we will find our place in this world. We are, first and foremost, a family. One that will always support one another. It is time to reflect on the next step of our individual paths."

He heard whispers immediately. The start of denial and shock had commenced.

Darius stood out front, the tallest among the group. He closed the gap to him. "Where's Melia?" he asked.

"The two of you think alike," Darius commented.

He tilted his head, stumped.

"She's with Niles and the others at the holding cells."

The other vampires. The ones that had been on the run. He forgot about them. He didn't know how many were captured and how many were still at large. Nothing that couldn't be dealt with. So much had happened, that was the least of his problems.

He maneuvered around the crowd. When they started to bombard him with questions, he didn't feel as uneasy as he once did. He muttered answers along the way enough to satisfy them for now. He knew it was a process. It was going to take time, but he was going to be with them every step of the way like he was when they first turned. Setting them up to fail was not his intent.

He heard her voice. It was refreshing and infectious. He held himself back from rushing in there and sweeping her up off her feet into his arms.

"Vince," Niles exclaimed. "Thank goodness you're back. I am not the type of guy who gives orders, especially to these knuckleheads. Don't ever put me in charge of this crew again."

"Looks like you've done well despite the circumstances," he nodded his approval at the nearly dozen vampires locked up.

"You have no idea the drama I had to go through."

He chuckled at his expense. Niles could always be a bit theatrical.

"Are you laughing at me?" Niles asked, flummoxed.

"Oh, come on, Niles, we make your life more entertaining," Oliver punched him in the arm.

"Ouch," Niles hollered.

He grinned from ear to ear as he swept from Oliver over to James and Wyatt. They were the last of the wolves that remained here. It was time for them to go home as well.

"Niles, I'm afraid I must ask you for one more task."

"Oh no," Niles's face had an ashen expression.

"I need you to take Oliver, James, and Wyatt home."

"Home?" Oliver frowned.

"Your services are no longer needed here."

Oliver exchanged a glance with Niles while James and Wyatt exchanged one as well.

"Can we go with them too?" Dante inquired alongside an eager Graham.

"Of course, if that's what you would like."

"Do I have to?" Oliver dragged his foot on the ground.

He tilted his head as he studied him. He never gave it a second thought that maybe some of the wolves wanted to stay with them. He wasn't sure what to say.

"Come with me, Oliver." Melia looped an arm around Oliver's arm and tugged him along. She paused beside him. "Would you give me a minute with him?"

He nodded. He resisted the urge to reach a hand out to her when she was so close to him. Every fiber in his wellbeing was electrified with the little distance she shared with him.

"What's going to happen to us now?" Graham queried.

He smiled at them. They all exchanged weary glances before he elaborated.

Chapter 67
Melia

T he first thing on her mind when they arrived back was to go find Rosa. It seemed like such a long time since she saw the reddish-tinged bat. She asked Darius about her. He informed her she still slept upside down in the dark corner of the cell near the open window.

With grace, she hastened down the hall. She heard voices coming from the room. She slowed before she was able to identify some of them. With excitement, she rushed through the door and saw familiar faces.

"Niles! Oliver! Dante! Graham!" Her eyes met each one with glee. Also present were James and Wyatt in their normal wolf form.

"Melia! You're okay," Niles exclaimed.

She didn't think anything of it. She launched towards him and hugged him tight.

"You're not going to eat me, are you?" Niles stood stiffly.

"No," she shook her head as he loosened up.

"Maybe just crush you to death," Oliver mocked.

"Oliver," she released Niles and flung over to him. He patted her on the back.

She shared a turn each with Graham and Dante. James and Wyatt declined with a slight shake of their heads. She understood they were just guarded when it came to vampires. She had not had an opportunity to share a bond with them.

When she turned her attention towards the cells, she was stunned to see vampires locked up inside, including the cell with the bent bars. Her eyes maneuvered to the end cell where Rosa hung on the top bar at the far end. She took a step in her direction.

"Let us out," one of the vampires cried.

She paused and looked over at them once more.

"We don't belong locked up like caged animals."

All at once, they began to shout over top of one another.

"Shut up," Oliver yelled over the top of them.

"Blood. We need blood. We're so thirsty. Help us," the incursion continued as they reached towards her weakly through the bars.

"Don't mind them," Niles turned her away, inserting himself between them and her.

"Don't turn your back on them. Remember, that one has a mean right hook," Dante rubbed his jawline.

"What's going to happen to them?" she looked over at Niles as he handed Rosa over. She happily hugged Rosa to her chest and stroked her.

Niles shrugged his shoulders. "Up to boss man."

"They put up a good fight," Graham cracked his neck. "It was exhilarating."

"Exhilarating?" Niles cocked an eyebrow.

"The most action we've had since…" Graham cut himself off.

"A bit dysfunctional at first," Dante admitted.

She heard a snort from James. Neither James nor Wyatt were amused.

"We got the hang of it, after several attempts." Oliver waved a hand like it was no big deal.

She couldn't even imagine what they were implying. She probably didn't want to know. Ignorance was bliss. Sometimes it was best to let it remain that way.

She inhaled deeply through her nose when she saw Vince appear in the doorway. Heard his mesmerizing voice. The desire to fly into his arms was there, but she remained planted in place.

Niles was delighted to see him as well. She listened quietly to their conversation, choking back her own laughter when Niles was offended by Vince's snicker. Vince's laugh melted her heart.

She saw the look of dismay cross Oliver's face while James and Wyatt had ears forward with optimism. So much change had happened over the course of a few days. She also sensed another kind of anxiety from Oliver.

She released Rosa before she made her way over to Oliver and escorted him out of the room. He followed obediently. She was momentarily captivated by Vince's blue eyes. She felt the energy zinging at the close proximity to him. She refocused on her task and left the room.

"Would you like to talk to me about your brother?" she inquired.

"You know Cameron is my brother?" Oliver shot her a stunned look.

She nodded. She had had her suspicions. Their pelts were similar yet also different. Having access to Nadine's mind she was able to confirm. Cameron had been an outcast. The other wolves ridiculed him including Oliver.

"I wasn't fair to him. I should have been a better brother, but I was upset he was the only one who managed to get away from the vampires when he was caught. No one ever made it out alive once captured. Our other brother among them."

When he paused, she stood soundless waiting for him to continue on.

"We were all on guard for days, thinking it was a trap. Then the others started grilling him. Laughed in his face when he said that vampires could be capable of good. He was my baby brother. I should have had his back, but I was scared to be excluded from the pack as well."

She rubbed his upper arm gently.

"What if he doesn't want me there?"

"You're his brother."

"He could banish me."

"Then you can come back here, but I don't think he would do that to you."

"He should. He has every right."

"You want to know what I've learned these past couple of days? It's that fear is always there to hold you back from progression. Fear is the hardest thing you will ever have to stand up to, but once you do, nothing will ever be able to hold you back again."

She took a second to process her own words. They rang true even for her. She was afraid to know how Vince truly felt now that Nadine was gone for good. Feared there would be a shift in their development. She was afraid of the answer, but at the same time it tortured her not being able to talk with him. She also didn't know how he would take the news that he was related to Nadine.

"Thank you, Melia," he flashed a goofy grin before wiping it from his face. "I'm going to miss you."

"You can come visit anytime," she encouraged with a smile.

"I'd like that. Can I have another hug?"

"Of course," she squeezed him tight.

She was going to miss the presences of all the wolves. She had no idea what the future held for them.

They walked back into the room together.

"I'm ready," Oliver nodded.

"Sweet, road trip," Graham exclaimed.

"I call shotgun." Dante raced out of the room first.

She giggled and watched them file out one by one until the only ones remained were the ones locked up, her, and Vince.

Chapter 68
Vince

They were alone at last. He suddenly forgot how to speak words. The environment didn't feel right. The last place he wanted to talk with Melia was in front of a bunch of corrupted vampires.

"Melia," he stepped forward.

"Vince," she mimicked at the same time.

They both lost their train of thought as they snapped their attention to each other.

"Ugh, get another room," one of the vampires uttered, displeased.

He shot an annoyed look in their direction.

"Can we talk outside?" he found the right words.

"I'd like that, yes."

He turned his hand palm up and waited for her to depart first before he trailed after her. Slammed the door on the way out. Followed her as she made her way to the side door and stepped out into the dark night. The snow had not reached the area, however there were remains left from a prior snow. The environment still didn't feel right.

"Follow me."

He put on a burst of speed before he leapt into the air and scaled the electric fence. She smirked before she picked up her train, wrapped it around her waist, and followed his lead.

"Meet me at the creek?" he sought her eyes.

She nodded with a smile.

He took off across the landscape and into the trees without holding back. Stopped near the edge of the water and waited for Melia to appear. Stood momentarily frozen, trying to dismiss the thought that maybe she had reconsidered.

When she emerged, he lit up from ear to ear. He was glad he did not have a beating heart that would give him away. He never felt so terrified in his life.

"You know what I'd like to do?"

"Fish?" an eyebrow rose as her eyes darted between him and the water.

"Dance."

She reeled back her head, confused.

He pulled the phone from the SUV from his pocket and swiped to the song he had left on standby. The volume was up high as he placed it on the ground next to him and moved in towards her.

Another memory he gained about his mother was how she loved to pick him up, hold him in her arms, and sway while she sang lullabies until he fell asleep.

"I don't know how to," her eyes dropped to the ground.

He closed the gap between them, placed his left arm around her waist and reached out for her right hand, extending it outward. He saw her pinch her eyebrows as she took in both sides. "Just do what comes naturally."

She moved taut with her head down low, watching his every foot move. She came to an abrupt standstill.

He paused with a hard swallow.

"This song," her eyes drifted to the phone. "I heard it on the radio on the way back."

"I did too," he couldn't help but smile.

She looked up at him.

"Exactly how I feel, 'When I See You Smile'."

"Vince," she whispered. "I'm sorry about Nadine."

It was his turn to reel back with surprise.

"She didn't give me a choice." She pulled away and folded her arms into herself.

"Choice? About what?" he stared at her back.

"Her spirit could have stayed in my body. You could have had her back."

He was flabbergasted by her admission. Now he understood why she was acting so weird. "But I love you," he could finally release the words he had been holding back. They easily slipped off his tongue. It didn't pain him to say them out of desperation like he did with Nadine.

"I know you loved her too," she whispered.

He strolled over, spun her to face him, and looked her square in the eyes. "It doesn't compare to the love I have for you. She wasn't my

277

Juliet. You are." The last thing Nadine referenced before she took her life. He didn't understand it then, now he understood clearly.

Melia's eyes glistened red as she threw her arms around his neck, rose onto her tip-toes, and pressed her sweet lips upon his. "I love you, too."

Now his eyes were glistening. He had been denied hearing those three words back. Had started to wonder if he was simply unlovable.

He crushed his lips onto hers and deepened the kiss. He was consumed with hunger for her. He never wanted this perfect moment to end. He loved her and in return, she loved him. He wasn't alone anymore. He had someone by his side. Forever and always.

Even though he loved Nadine, he realized with Melia, his love was a different kind. Melia had his whole heart. It just felt right with Melia. Melia gave him back so much more. He never wanted to spend one minute without her.

"She left something that belongs to you in a cave behind a waterfall," Melia pulled back, resting her forehead on his.

"Humm?" he murmured.

"The other spiral," she grasped her own. "Descendant of Drehseler."

He blinked a few times as he processed her words. His eyes opened wide as the dots connected. "That would mean..." he pulled his head apart from hers.

Melia nodded.

He looked away, still wrapping his mind around it all.

"You should know that she loved you too."

The words he once longed to hear Nadine say back to him when he confessed his love for her before she ended her life. He had always believed she'd rather die than to love him. Why she referenced not being his Juliet.

He tilted his head and looked up into the cloud covered sky as light snow began to drift down. He focused beyond the clouds and towards the stars. One seemed to glimmer at that moment from Orion's belt. Nadine's favorite constellation.

"Thank you for telling me," he kissed her forehead.

"There's one more thing I want to talk to you about."

"You can tell me anything."

"This place, I mean this facility, it's not a home."

"I know. We're not going to stay here forever. We're going to find a new place, but it doesn't matter where because you're my home."

Her smile was his ray of light when he thought he would never see beyond the darkness. In his despair, he believed love to not have been enough when love had ended up being everything and more. He pressed his lips upon hers once more and let the light blossom within.

M. C. Ryder

A Dance Between Light and Darkness
Music that Inspired

Part 1
"Unlovable" by Diamante
"Never Surrender" by Live Ash

Part 2
"Bring me to Life" by Evanescence
"Everybody's Fool" by Evanescence
"Refuge" by Skillet
"Destiny" by Skillet

Part 3
"Love is the Answer" by Natalie Taylor
"Lioness" by Daughtry
"When I See You Smile" by Bad English

The End...
Or is it?

Sneak Peek Feature From
A Darker Demise (A Compilation of Dark Shorts)

The Path to Redemption
A Nadine Short

By M. C. Ryder

Chapter 1

You open your eyes to gray. Clouds of light gray overcast the sky between the treetops. Woods are fogged over in gray mist. The ground beneath your feet is dead with withered leaves. There is no sign of life here. No sun to light up the sky. No stars to shine down on a blacken sky. Life here seems hollow.

Your mind is hazy. You can't recall how you got here. You shut your eyes and listen. There is no sound. No birds sing. No paws scurry. No leaves rustle. No air flows.

Gloomy.

That is what this place is. That's the effect it has on you. You have no idea where you are or where you are supposed to be going. How did you even get here?

You reopen your eyes and push yourself up from the ground. You survey the area all around you. Everything looks the same. A mirror image of itself. Nothing stands out as a landmark for you to know where you've been and where you have yet to go.

You dig your heel into the ground and disturb it. Next, you make a line pointing straight ahead before you take off in the direction. You stroll into the mist, dragging your foot every now and then to leave a trail. When you glance over your shoulder, the mist covers over the trail from the position you stand. You only have to kneel down and look past the mist to see the trail you left behind.

You wander the dejected woods, cautiously. Normally, being surrounded by nothing but nature would renew you. It's the one place you can go that's not a toxic environment. A place where you can let your guard down. A place where you can breathe in clean, pure air. A place full of life and harmony you can take time to stop and appreciate.

This place is the opposite. A void. It completely lacks any positive or negative energy. You feel nothing. The mist that touches you leaves no evidence behind. You do not feel cold. You do not feel warm. Like you are detached from all your receptors.

Is this a dream? Do you just have to wait patiently until you wake up? The sensation appears similar. Surely your alarm clock will soon wake you or Leo walking up the length of your body, purring into your ear persistently.

You long for one of the two to soon happen, however a whisper of mis-doubt tells you otherwise. Something about this place is different. That it's not a dream-like state. That it's permanent.

The landscape ahead does not change. You turn back around and retrace your steps back to where you began. You take off in the opposite direction, leaving the same trail of scattered upturned leaves.

You glance at the watch on your left wrist. It's blank. It does not work here. There is no date. No time. It is lifeless. You have no idea how long you have been here or how long you will remain lost in this timeless place. You have so many questions and have no idea where to begin finding answers.

You look up at the gray sky once more. Narrow your eyes, watching intensely. The clouds do not appear to even move. It is like they are a painted illusion.

You reach out and skim your hand upon the mist. Disturbed by how your hand appears to go right through it. Try to grab a handful. Nothing you do disrupts it. You don't even feel moisture on your hand. Even your hand appears colorless and gray. A sheer contrast.

You look right before looking left. Neither direction offers much hope. Everything still remains the same. You are literally in the middle of nowhere. There is no telling which way you went or could be the right path to take. You have yet to explore the other two directions. You are starting to wonder if it even matters. All paths eventually lead you somewhere. You just have to pick a direction and stick with it. It may not lead you where you want to go, but eventually you have to find something that is familiar. You just have to be brave enough to walk into the unknown. Answers are out there if you're not afraid to find them.

You look back over your shoulder one last time to see if you missed anything along the way. When you're satisfied nothing has changed, you continue to walk onward. This time you do not leave a trail. You do not plan on returning to your start point. There is no reason to. There is nothing there for you to return to.

You walk with purpose in your stride. The more ground you can cover, the sooner you might find a scrape of information to stumble upon. The surrounding atmosphere does not change. It is still gloomy and dim. You don't know how much time you will have until darkness sets in and your sight becomes obsolete. You will have to deal with that when the time comes. For now, all you can do is put one foot in front of the other.

A bright, blinding light appears off to your left. You have to look away and shield your eyes. You blink a few times as your eyes adjust to the different cast to the environment. Slowly, inch by inch, you angle your head back into the direction of the light as your eyes adjust to the contrast. It's a laborious task but when your eyes are finally able to adapt to the brightness, you inhale sharply.

"Marc."

Sneak Peek Feature From
A Darker Demise (A Compilation of Dark Shorts)

A Unity of Balance
Immilla's Journal
(A Dark short to *The Darkest Side of the Moon)*

By M. C. Ryder

Entry 1

Mutter often described how the sky was ignited with a vibrant orange glow from the setting sun on the blackest of nights when I was born. She felt that fiery energy within me. I was the last born to three sisters before me. There was no son for my Vater to carry on the family name.

I was the youngest, separated five years from my eldest, Ada. Greta followed a year later. There was a two-year gap before Serene and then I followed.

We shared gossip and fought like all sisters do, but my bond was strongest with Serene even though we were opposites. She was the calm, patient, and reason of voice, whereas I was bold, short-tempered, and daring. Even so, our strengths and weaknesses completed each other.

My Vater was a powerful sorcerer of dark magic, whereas my Matter was a sorceress of light magic. In order to keep balance and peace, there was no in-between. No witch could represent both due to the treaty put into place after the Thirty Years' War. Many witches were put on trial and burned in order to harvest their magic by one of their own. When a witch dies, their magic is released back into the universe.

After the fall of Maximilian, strict laws were put into place. Magic could only be wielded in what was considered a secure location by the council. It was forbidden for magic to be displayed in front of human eyes.

Magic is to be respected. It takes a great deal of discipline to master it. Everyone is born with the ability to harness it. Only the young and innocent are able to practice the feel of both light and dark magic until their twelfth birthday, where, during the witch's Summoning Oath, they decide their pledge.

Magic is like a muscle. The more you use it the stronger it gets. The more you practice, the better control you have. Light magic is reflective. An object must be in place for intuition to take control.

289

Dark magic is cognitive. Words of commandment allow the mind's desire to come to life. However, dark magic does not come without consequences, as a great deal more energy is required.

Until our twelfth year, our Mutter and Vater taught my sisters and I the elemental basics during sunset or sundown. Most of the games Mutter had us play was with water from the creek near our home. Serene was a natural. She loved water.

We would toss bubbles of water back and forth without touch, however, on more than one occasion, the bubble would burst upon my catch. I would absorb the water from my wet clothing and throw the bubble to whichever sister laughed the loudest.

Our Vater had us practice very small spells. Instructed us how to visualize, in our mind, what we wanted to portray, like lighting a candle. Our nights did not last long with him, as our energy would be depleted. A lot of times, my sisters were not successful and became frustrated easily. Absorbing the energy of a flame and moving to light another object is easier than creating a flame from within. You can tell a candle to light, as many times as you want, but if you do not speak the word with commanding energy, the candle will never light.

I was the first one to light a candle. The energy it takes is indescribable. There's a great deal of focus. A pull and tug sensation that drains you. My sisters always slept for many hours after a session. However, I was always able to recover quicker.

When I wasn't practicing magic, I loved watching my Vater woodturning on his lathe. I'd watch for hours as he shaped all different types of wood into beautiful detailed pieces. His primary work was furniture. Magic hadn't crafted this beautiful art. Hard work did. A trade I was eager to learn.

On my seventh birthday, my Vater got me my own lathe. My Mutter had not been happy. She thought it was too dangerous for a girl of my youth. She feared I would harm myself, especially if I work unsupervised. Only I thrived. The pieces I crafted were simple, rings and spoons first, before advancing to bowls.

The time for my Summoning Oath was nearly upon me. I found myself alone for the first time. My sisters had all pledged to light magic and traveled to the Academy of Light Magic where all young witches are taught how to stay in control of their power and the laws of magic.

My pledge should have been easy, but I was conflicted. Ada had returned home, but would soon marry and leave, starting a life of her own. I asked her how she knew which magic felt stronger as well as wrote Greta and Serene. Ada and Greta did not reveal too much. Simply told me to trust myself. However, Serene divulged further. She didn't know what to expect either when she went in the Summoning Oath room, only she felt the light magic call to her. An experience she had never felt before or could ignore.

When Mutter tucked me on the eve of my Summoning, she probed my apprehension. I was her fearless daughter. I wasn't one to overthink things. In that moment, I voiced my greatest worry. What if I pledged wrong? She reassured me that there was no wrong choice. Magic was a gift, not a curse.

The Summoning room was majestic. A five-pointed star was shaped by unlit white candles, which were surrounded by a scorched circle. A pentacle of mass proportion that I was instructed to stand in the center of.

I took my place standing before the council. Five members representing light magic and five members representing dark magic, my Vater among them. Witnesses gathered behind eager for my vow. I could hear their whispers. Most assumed I would pledge myself to light, like my sisters before me, but others hoped I would pledge dark. Dark sorceresses were few. Those who pledged to light magic far outnumbered those who pledged to dark magic.

A council member of light stepped forward with a lit candle and with a blink of an eye, the candles all had a flame. My Vater stepped forward next and with an utter the scorched circle ignited with witch-fire. Orange with a tinge of black.

I felt the heat as light and dark energy surrounded me completely. Listened to the crackles. Felt the heat and the tug of war within. The light did not drain me like the dark. Light magic was like walking a straight path, both safe and predictable. Dark magic was like walking up an inclined path, both rocky and attentive.

My Vater had expressed, one day, when we were in the workshop, that he didn't think I was prepared for the toll dark magic would take on my body, mind, and soul. In the end, it was my decision, but if my Vater didn't think I would flourish who was I to think I would master the magic?

The flames cast shadows in the room. The heat was intense from the scorched circle. My eyes were drawn to the lick of flames that seemed to be reaching towards me from the circle, whereas the flames from the candles seemed to pull away.

I closed my eyes. Listened to the sizzling. Listened to the pops. Smelled the charred smoke. Felt the fiery heat. I closed off my active mind and focused on the chanting of my heart.

My eyes snapped back open.

"I pledge myself, to dark magic."

Sneak Peek Feature From
A Darker Demise (A Compilation of Dark Shorts)

My Salvation
Marc's Story
(A Dark short to *The Darkest Side of the Moon)*
By M. C. Ryder

Chapter 1

From the shadows, I watch Glenn toy with the two girls that are in the woods at the dead of night. We heard them shouting. I hang back, studying, while he's eager to play games.

Jomar had sounded the alarm, the moment he set eyes on the one marked by the Dragon's Eye from a witch's prophecy. As he collected additional information, he kept us informed of the possibilities of places to thoroughly search. The cabin nearby is one of those locations. He gave a vague description of the girl who bared the Dragon's Eye mark. The mark is behind her right ear, has long brown hair, wears a red dress, and has a bold attitude.

Both girls have brown hair, one has slightly longer hair than the other and neither are dressed in red. A pity not to see how it might hug the curvy figure of the girl bold enough to lash back at Glenn. Red would match her fiery attitude. The other girl clings to her with a death grip. I can hear how fast her heart is racing. Smell the fear leaking from her pores.

A hindrance.

As soon as Glenn confirms the trembling girl is of no use, he will slowly have his way with her. Enjoy her scream and pleads for mercy as he tortures her slowly. Pain is to be savored. Pain is to be digested slowly. Pain is power. What Vladimir, our maker, taught us when he bestowed his gift. We learn to live the way he wants or he will just as quickly terminate his gift to us. He is the one in full control. He is the only one who you need to please.

I find it satirical that Vladimir lives in apprehension hiding his identity from humans only for the marked one to be human. Not only human but a female one at that. How insulting to his ego. If only I could laugh at the mockery from the universe.

The girl in front buries her fear behind anger. She knows what Glenn is, yet she still stands up to him and is willing to fight as she whips out a blade. There's no doubt in my mind we found who we're looking for.

Like a speeding bullet, I whisk away the cowering girl. Her shriek is loud to my own ears, even though I've tuned back a couple of notches.

"Let her go," the girl speaks strong-mindedly as she takes a step forward.

I do anything but as I sink my fangs into the side of the girl's neck and tap her vein. I suck greedily. She means nothing to me. Is no one to me. Is just a fuel source. It makes it easy.

"No," the other girl shouts as she rushes forward with blade in hand.

I see in her eyes she will not go down without a fight and intends to use the switchblade. I let the girl drop to the ground and swiftly close the gap, ripping the blade from her hand, and pull her against me. A volt courses through me as if I'm struck by lightning. I tense, surprised by the sensation. I haven't felt much in so many years. I've had to become numb to feeling at all.

"Hey, I found them first, Marc, mind sharing?" Glenn complains.

"Maybe you should learn not to play with your food, Glenn. That way you wouldn't easily lose it," I state back with little amusement.

"It's called having some fun. You shouldn't always take everything so serious."

"I see no point in prolonging the inevitable when we have a job to do."

Glenn narrows his eyes, "You didn't even bother looking for the mark before you fed."

"There's no need. Unfortunately, this is the one we're here for." I was able to confirm that she was indeed the one with the mark during the struggle. It was clear enough when her hair moved and I caught a glimpse of a partial blemish behind her right ear, right where Jomar said it would be.

I fill with fervor the longer I hold her against me. The zest courses through my well-being. I can't risk Glenn noticing. I shove her forward, watching her fall to her hands and knees. The fire from her goes with it but still lingers. It unnerves me.

She doesn't hesitate to make a run for it. There is no way she is able to outrun either one of us, but that doesn't stop her from trying. She's a fighter who doesn't give up easily, even when it seems hopeless.

I let Glenn go after her as I turn back to the other girl. She lays there in shock. As I approach, I hear her whimper. Tears stain her face. I have no idea what is so special about the other human girl who is meant to take down Vladimir, but if she fails; I want to be prepared. I'm going to break the rules.

I kneel, grab a fistful of her hair, slice into my wrist with my teeth, and shove it against her parted lips. "Swallow," I demand.

She cries even harder as she tries to pull away. My blood smeared all over her face. "Please," she begs. "I don't want to die."

"For you to transition, you have to," I swiftly break her neck.

The sound of the bone cracking sickens me. I've learned how to master burying the sympathetic part of myself in order to survive. It's effortless when I know nothing about a person, but I instantly feel regret for what I just did to the innocent girl. I wish I could take it back. I just destroyed her life.

"I'm sorry," I whisper, even though she can't hear my remorse.

A glint of silver catches my eye.

About the Author

M. C. Ryder has been composing stories, poems, and lyrics from the beginning of time when reading became a learned trait. The sky is the limit but enjoys exploring the beaten path both figuratively and literally. Resides in the Keystone State with a clowder of felines who rule the house. Enjoys long trail walks during the cozy tinge of Autumn, appreciates music with deep lyrical meaning, and relishes in reading a variety of genres.

Website: https://www.mcryderauthor.com

 M. C. Ryder (page)

 MCRyder0

mcryder0